_Su..._

Dirty
DEALS

The Complete Sexy Manhattan Fairytale

Michelle A. Valentine

Stay Naughty!

_♡_

Michelle A Valentine

Contents

Dirty Deals

This book is a work of fiction. Names, characters, places, and incidents either are products of the author's imagination

To Contact Michelle:
    Email: *michelleavalentinebooks@gmail.com*
    Website: *www.michelleavalentine.com*
    Facebook: *www.facebook.com/AuthorMichelleAValentine*

Disclaimer:
This book is intended for an adult audience due to strong language and naughty sexual situations.

Books by
Michelle A. Valentine

The Black Falcon Series

ROCK THE BEGINNING
Included in the Complete Series Collection
ROCK THE HEART
ROCK THE BAND
ROCK MY BED
ROCK MY WORLD
ROCK THE BEAT
ROCK MY BODY
<u>Hard Knocks Series</u>
PHENOMENAL X
XAVIER COLD
<u>The Collectors Series</u>
DEMON AT MY DOOR
COMING SOON—DEMON IN MY BED
<u>A Sexy Manhattan Fairytale</u>
NAUGHTY KING
FIESTY PRINCESS
DIRTY ROYALS
DIRTY DEALS (The Complete Sexy Manhattan
Series Box Set)
<u>Wicked White Series</u>
WICKED WHITE
WICKED REUNION
WICKED LOVE
<u>Stand Alone Titles</u>

COMING SOON—LOVE, SEX, MUSIC

Naughty KING

A SEXY MANHATTAN FAIRYTALE: PART ONE

Michelle A. Valentine

Chapter I
THE CURSE

Alexander

I stare down at the woman on her knees in front of me. Her eager hands work quickly to undo my belt then they move on to my zipper.

She tosses her blonde hair back and grins. "I'm gonna suck your cock so good, baby, you'll be begging for more."

I thread my fingers through her mass of curls and fist them, forcing her to look up at me. "Coming in your mouth has a two hundred dollar price tag. You'll do the job I paid for, and then you'll get the fuck out. I'll want nothing more to do with you after that. Understand?"

She narrows her brown eyes at me. At first, I think this one might actually have a little backbone to her, and may just tell me to go to hell like I deserve, but she doesn't. They never do. Instead, she gets right to work rubbing my semi-hard cock through my boxer-briefs.

The only thing women see when they are in my presence is money—I'm surrounded by it. They see the material shit I have and their eyes light up like they've just found their golden fucking goose.

It's been both a curse and a blessing since I was twenty years old and inherited my father's billions. Every single woman I've ever been with has convinced herself that she'd be the one to tame me. That her magical pussy would make me fall madly in love with her—that I'd marry her and sign over half of my fortune.

Not fucking likely.

I know this looks bad. Most people would be both disgusted and curious as to why a devastatingly handsome, shrewd, successful businessman like myself would stoop to hiring a hooker. Truth is? It's fucking convenient. I send a text, and I get whatever I'm in the mood for. No questions asked.

That's why for the past few months I've relied on paying for escorts from a discreet service. It's less hassle than trying to find a slutty socialite to bang. I did that for two years straight, and it created more work for me than the lay was worth because I had to deal with kicking their annoying asses out the next day.

That shit gets exhausting.

The blonde reaches down inside my shorts and then shoves them down, resting the waistband under my ball sack. There's a wicked gleam in her eyes as she licks her lips and then pops my head into her mouth.

Now we're fucking getting somewhere.

The bitch goes to work licking, sucking, and deep-throating my cock. Her saliva coats my shaft, and I lean my head back against the leather couch in my office as I finally start enjoying what I've paid for.

There's nothing like a blowjob to start my day off right.

The handle on my office door moves, and my head snaps up just in time to make direct eye contact with my new secretary, Margo, as she steps into my office, unannounced, closing the door behind her. She's been doing that for the past two days. This girl needs to fucking learn how to knock before she comes waltzing in here. I'm about to teach her that lesson right now.

I fully expect my mousy new employee's cheeks to flush as she rushes from my office, but she surprises me as she stands there, only allowing her mouth to fall open as she takes in the sight of the woman pleasing me.

The blonde attempts to stop, but I'm enjoying making Margo uncomfortable, so I place my hand on the back of her head and order, "Don't you dare fucking stop."

Margo gasps, raising a well-manicured hand to her pouty lips while her blue eyes widen behind her dark-rimmed glasses.

It takes her a minute, but when she turns to leave, I have a different idea in mind. "Margo, if you walk out of that door, you're fired."

She halts mid-step at my domineering command. She needs this job. She and I both know it.

Margo smoothes back her black hair which is still perfectly in place in her uptight bun, and slowly turns back around to face me. "Why do you want me in here?"

I give her my cockiest shit-eatin' grin. "Because I want to stare at you while I come in this bitch's mouth."

She shakes her head. "This is absolutely insane. I'm not going—"

"You *will* stay," I order again. "Because if you don't, I'll make a phone call to Daddy and tell him that our little deal is off. Your call, princess."

She folds her arms over her chest, and I raise my eyebrow in challenge to her. That bitch honestly thinks she's better than I am. She's so uptight and highfalutin. Ever since she walked in here two days ago, I've wanted nothing more than to break her. I've been thinking of creative ways to show Margo that I run shit around here, and that the only reason I've even allowed her to have a job in my office is because her father begged me. Part of the deal to buy out his company included that she'd have a secure job.

Margo needs to know that I'm her new daddy. She's no longer the princess of a million-dollar empire because as soon as I ink this deal to bail her father out, I'll own her, just like I'll own her family's business.

I lick my lips while I wait on Margo to make her move. Her eyes flit down to my mouth and then down to the blonde who is now gagging herself to please me.

I lift my hips off the couch as I hold the blonde's head in place and fuck her mouth while Margo watches me.

Margo's chest heaves and my eyes are drawn to the tops of her tits mounding out of the top of her blouse.

I quickly close my eyes because I don't want to think about Margo's tits, but for some strange reason, I can't stop. Suddenly, it isn't some random prostitute sucking me off. It's uptight Margo in her naughty wannabe schoolteacher outfit.

I slide my teeth along my bottom lip then bite down as I suck in a quick breath. My eyes snap open, making direct eye contact with Margo as I come hard, shooting my load down the blonde's throat as my employee watches with a scowl on her face.

A shudder rips through me as I bask in the afterglow of one fine orgasm. I smile as the blonde unwraps her mouth from my cock and licks the tip of my dick to make sure she swallows down every last bit of come.

Margo continues to shoot daggers at me. This is all kinds of wrong and a fucking sexual harassment lawsuit waiting to happen, but I honestly don't give a shit.

All I care about is making sure my point is crystal clear with my new bitch of an employee—she is here to serve me. Not the other way around.

I sit up, stuffing my cock back inside my underwear before zipping my pants up. "Margo, pay the lady."

Margo's plump lip curls in what I'm sure is an expression of thorough disgust. "Pay for your own fucking whores."

Her words shock me at first, but then I find myself highly amused. I burst out in a deep laugh, which only makes Margo's face even redder before I fish my wallet from my back pocket. I lay two hundred-dollar bills on my knee for the hooker while never taking my eyes from my heated secretary. "You're free to leave now."

Relief floods Margo's face as she turns, but I stop her. "Not you, Margo. I was talking to my . . . *guest* here."

The hooker stuffs the money down in her bra and then winks. "You tasted yummy. Request me anytime."

Margo rolls her eyes behind the woman and shakes her head, but I simply nod at the woman. "What was your name again?"

"Candy." She grins.

"Of course it is," Margo scoffs.

I push myself up from the couch and button my jacket, putting myself back together. "Sorry, Candy. I never request the same girl twice. More than once and you bitches get clingy and forget I hired you just to get me off, not to talk. Matter of fact—" I glance down at my watch. "—it's time for you to get the fuck out. I've got a meeting to prepare for."

Candy's nostrils flare. "You can't treat people like this."

"Of course, I can. I'm Alexander King, and I can do whatever the fuck I please. Now leave before I call security and have you forcibly removed from the property."

"Asshole," Candy calls over her shoulder as she leaves without another word of protest.

You would think being called that would cause me to flinch, but no, I revel in the name. I like that women hate the way I treat them. It ensures they keep their distance.

The door slams and Margo points her gaze in my direction. "I assume you're done with me now that the show's over?"

Since we're alone, I take my time to rake my eyes over Margo. She still appears angry enough to chop my dick off.

Good.

I want her to hate me.

I want to make it clear that we are not friends.

"Margo . . ." I can't help smirking as I adjust the cuff of my jacket. "I'm just getting started with you."

She arches a perfectly manicured eyebrow. "What's that supposed to mean?"

I laugh. "You seem like a bright girl—I mean, not just anyone earns two degrees from Harvard. You know that sooner or later you'll be on your knees before me."

She laughs bitterly. "You can't be serious. I would never be one of your two-dollar whores."

I take a step toward her, reducing the gap between us to mere inches. She's close enough that I can feel her breath coming out in warm little puffs. "Don't pretend like that didn't turn you on. I saw you watching—waiting your turn like a good girl. Don't worry, you'll get your chance someday."

"Fuck you," she spats.

"Not yet, but you will." I trace the exposed flesh on her chest with the tip of my finger. "You'll beg me for it. You'll beg me to fuck you, hoping that it'll be you who changes my asshole ways and makes me fall in love." She opens her mouth to protest, but I press my finger to her lips, cutting her off. "You will. I have that effect on women, but you're smart enough to know that if you do that—if you let me have you—you'll quit when you don't get your way like the spoiled little brat your father has raised. And we both know that you quitting will piss off Daddy, don't we?"

"I needed a secure job that will pay the bills after my family goes bankrupt. You know that. It's part of the deal with my father," she argues, but I'm not stupid enough to buy into that.

"Don't lie to me," I scold her roughly, and she stiffens. "We're both highly intelligent human beings so let's not play dumb. You're here to spy on me—to figure out a way to stop me from buying your father's company for pennies and then sell off everything he's worked for piece by fucking piece, in turn making me an even richer man."

She lifts her chin. "You're a bastard, you know that?"

I shrug. "Maybe so, but I'm honest and just to show you that infiltrating my business doesn't scare me one damn bit, I'm going to allow you to stay. But know this: I'm going to make your life a living hell while you're here. I'll have you dying to fuck my brains out or needing to walk away before you kill me with your own bare hands. Either way—you're fucked."

Margo takes a deep breath and closes her eyes, giving me a chance to study her features. She wears the dark hair on her head pulled back, but I imagine that when she lets it down, it hangs in long loose waves around her shoulders. When she opens her eyes and gazes up at me, I notice the blue of her eyes standing out against the contrast of her dark hair, and it hits me—I bet she'd be an amazing lay.

She licks her lips, not in a way that's meant to be sexy but in the way people do when they're nervous, and my eyes are instantly drawn to her mouth.

Dammit all to hell. This would be so much easier if she was ugly—to humiliate her by playing with her emotions and knowing there'd be no way in hell I would actually fuck her except out of spite. The problem is that's not the case. She's exactly my favorite type of woman to fuck: beautiful and bitchy. When I take her, I can't allow myself to enjoy it. I won't give her that satisfaction.

Margo stares at me for a long moment, and just when I think she's about to lay into me again, she twists her hand around my tie, yanking me closer. Without warning her tongue darts out and touches my top lip, causing a tiny shudder to tear through me before she pulls back with a sly smile on her face. "That's where you're wrong, Mr. King. That prediction implies that I would actually fall for your juvenile antics of seduction." Her hand presses against my chest and then moves down to my stomach, drifting even farther south. "Those boyish tricks would never work on me. I'm a woman who always gets what she wants." I let out a low grunt of half pain and half excitement as she grabs my semi-hard cock through my slacks. Stilling her hand on my cock, she leans into my ear and whispers, "When I want it." The urge to throw her onto my desk and fuck her senseless surges through me. Never has a woman asserted herself with me, and as much as I fucking hate to admit it, I'm totally turned on by it.

Margo kisses my cheek before she pulls back and releases a hearty laugh. "Who's fucked now?"

Angry that I allowed myself to be distracted for one moment, I shove her away a little rougher than I mean to. "Get the fuck out. We're done here."

Margo laughs as she takes a step back toward the door. "Oh, Mr. King, that's where you're wrong again. We both know this little game of ours has only just begun."

"I said we're fucking done with this conversation." I glare at her.

"As you wish." She smirks and actually fucking curtsies before heading out my door, invoking my hatred even more.

The moment the door closes, I plop down in my chair and loosen my tie. How in the holy hell did that just happen?

My nostrils flare and I take a deep breath, trying to maintain my composure and not throw something. The one thing I fucking hate is to be shown up. I'm always the winner—number one at all times. She will not take control of this situation.

No fucking way.

I won't allow that to happen. Ever.

If Margo Buchanan wants a fucking war with me then, a war is what she's going to fucking get.

Chapter II
DIRTY LAUNDRY
Alexander

The door to my office opens and I scowl, fully expecting Margo to waltz back in for round two. I relax when Jack walks through the door instead.

His neatly trimmed dark hair matches his pressed black suit. Jack hasn't looked in my direction yet to see my utter disarray because he's too busy running his hand through his hair and staring at my man-eater secretary.

When the door shuts behind him, Jack's wearing the biggest shit-eatin' grin known to mankind. "Damn. You didn't tell me that you hired a new hot piece of ass. Have you tapped that yet, or do I still have a shot at getting in there before you? You know how I fucking hate your sloppy seconds."

I roll my eyes. "Brother, if I were you, I wouldn't touch that bitch with a double-bagged dick. She's fuckin' trouble."

Jack's face lights up as he glances back at the door before turning back to me, wiggling his eyebrows over his dark eyes. "My favorite kind."

Oh, shit. I've just enticed him even more. Jack has been my wingman for a long time, and I know he's just as smooth with the ladies as I am. If he sets his sights on Margo, he won't give up until he's fucked her seven ways till Sunday.

I've got to correct this situation stat. Throw a little ice water on him, so-to-speak, before he goes getting any crazy ideas like asking her out.

"She's Dan Buchanan's daughter," I quickly inform him before he has a chance to get a full-on chub thinking about how damn hot Margo looks sitting out there on the other side of that door.

Jack's eyes widen. "No fucking way! Buchanan produced that? I don't believe it."

I lean back in my chair and straighten my tie. "Afraid so."

"So what's she doing here? When you said you'd give her a job, I didn't expect it to be as *your* assistant. Doesn't she know that we're about to dismantle her father's business and sell it for parts? She should hate our guts, not be out there working for the enemy."

I nod. "She knows, and it's the very reason she's here. The last time I met with Buchanan, as you know, he only agreed to sell me Buchanan Industries if I promised to give his darling daughter a job, so I figured I'd put her where I'd be able to keep my eye on her."

His brow furrows. "He can get her a job as a secretary anywhere."

"He was afraid that since she's a new grad, she'd have a tough time finding something that paid well in this economy."

He shakes his head. "I still don't understand why make it part of the deal that she has to work here for you?"

I drum my fingers on the desk. "Think about it, Jack. Buchanan is a crafty old son-of-a-bitch. He's going to fight tooth and nail to figure out a way to save his business. By getting his daughter in here, he figures he'll be able to get info about the buyers we have lined up and cut us off at the pass. Then he'll try to make a deal with them first to sell off pieces of his company that are easily discarded, leaving him with less overhead and keeping him afloat until he can figure out his next move."

"And you agreed to let her come here knowing that? Shit, Alexander. She could ruin everything." I hear the edge in Jack's voice. He's never been one to keep a cool head when he stresses. "We've got billions riding on this deal. You have to become the activist shareholder in Buchanan Industries."

I hold up my hand, stopping him before he even gets started. "Relax, Jack. I have this under control. Do you honestly think that Margo Buchanan is a match for me? Come on, man. You've known me for how long now?"

He shakes his head. "You're right. I do know you, which means I know that women are your fucking kryptonite. Face it; you've been in a rut for a couple of years now. Hell, you've not been the same since Jess fucked you over. You haven't been with a woman longer than one night since her. If Margo wags her hot ass in front of you, you'll leap, my friend, and your self-control will be flushed down the fucking toilet. She'll get in your head, and this whole deal will be fucked."

I know Jack thinks that I've hit a dry spell since Jess Fontaine left me for another man two years ago—that she crushed me—but he couldn't be more wrong. Jess taking off with some tennis pro she met at the country club only hardened me more. It made me stronger—made me realize that love really doesn't exist. It's just this thing people created to comfort themselves within stories—a mythical thing like Santa Claus and the Easter Bunny. I learned a long time ago that fairy tales don't exist. People need to stop wasting their time searching for something that isn't real.

Paying for pussy is definitely the way to go.

So Jack needs to stop worrying about me. Margo Buchanan will not get to me no matter how tempting she may be.

I chuckle. "Trust me. That's not going to happen."

"Make sure it doesn't. We need Buchanan to sell you his shares. Our Japanese connections want pieces of his company, and the only way we can make that happen is if you're the main shareholder. We can't afford for anything to go wrong."

"You've got to stop worrying. You're going to make yourself old and gray far too soon." I push myself away from the desk and walk over to the small bar that's in my office. The crystal decanter holding my favorite thirty-year-old scotch clinks against the glass as I pour the amber liquid. "Come have a drink with me. Let's celebrate our victory before we close this deal over lunch."

Jack walks over and lays a couple of papers on the wooden bar. "I've got the latest numbers on the Buchanan stock. It's down thirty points. Everything is lining up for us perfectly. We're on the road to making our biggest deal yet. Your father would've been proud."

I hand Jack his glass as I smile at the thought of my father. It pleases me immensely to know that if he were here, Father would be partaking in this celebratory drink. Fucking cancer. It took him away from me much too soon, forcing me to grow up way too fast.

I tip the glass back and down my drink before pouring myself another. I need a fucking subject change. "I heard a rumor about you."

Jack's eyebrow arches. "Me? From whom?"

I smirk. "One guess."

"Fucking Diem." Jack rubs the back of his neck. "What did your darling sister tell you about me now?"

I laugh. "Rachel Winslet, Jack? Really? How fucking desperate were you to take that home?"

"Dammit," Jack mutters. "I was at a benefit at the Waldorf, and I had one too many to drink. I spent most of the night talking to your sister. When it was time to find someone to share in the pleasure of my company for the evening, all the good women were taken. Rachel was my only willing body."

"Her body's always willing," I say, and then laugh, unable to hold it back.

Jack shrugs, like it's there's nothing else he can say. It's a well-known fact that the woman is working her way through our social circles on her back.

I hold up my hands. "Hey, no judgment. A lay is a lay as long as you don't plan on taking it any further than that."

Jack tips back his glass and then sets it down on the bar. "Did Diem say anything else?"

I shake my head. "No, but what in the hell were you doing talking to my sister all night? You're not fucking her, are you? You know that's the one thing that would cause me to murder my best friend."

His face contorts, and his top lip curls. "It's not like that. You know we've always been friends. She's your little sister for Christ's sake."

"Well, what were the two of you doing together?"

"Diem and I were *just* talking."

"About what?" I ask a little agitated.

"Mainly . . . we were talking about you."

This causes my brow to furrow. "What the hell could possibly be so interesting about me that would cause the two of you to chat all evening?"

He shrugs. "She worries about you a lot. It's not healthy for you to work all the time and then spend your evenings alone."

I roll my eyes. "So you and Diem are experts on what's best for me now?"

"No. We just want to see you happy."

I level my stare on him. "Is anyone ever truly happy with their lives, Jack? The best someone can hope for is to have enough money not to be miserable in their existence until they die."

Jack sighs. "That's a pretty depressing outlook on life, man."

"Yeah, maybe, but it's an honest one. Seriously, you and Diem need to find more interesting topics of conversations."

He laughs. "What can I say? The King is a hot topic of conversation these days. It's hard to avoid talking about you when I'm out in public. I think you've pissed off over half of the females on the Upper East Side. They all say your name with such disdain that it's comical, and unfortunately, your sister and I are assholes by association. We've bonded through our pariah status. I would stop being your friend, but I like getting laid for being the nice guy out of our duo."

I chuckle. "Ah, so being the best friend of Manhattan's biggest prick has its perks?"

Jack fills his glass again and has a twinkle in his eye. "Sometimes."

A quick knock on my door catches my attention just as it swings open. Margo steps into my office and makes a big show of checking out the inside of the room before her eyes land on Jack. Her face lights up as she points a smile in his direction, and for some reason my shoulders stiffen.

"Do you need something, Margo?" I ask, drawing her attention away from Jack.

"I was just making sure that you were decent. The last time—" She smirks as her eyes flit over to Jack and then back to me "—I seemed to have come in at an inopportune moment when you had a guest in here."

Jack tilts his head, and I feel his gaze on me. I usually tell him everything—but admitting to your best friend that you buy sexual favors from high-paid escorts isn't something that I want to readily divulge to him.

Damn that Margo. She's doing this to get under my skin, but the fucking joke's going to be on her because I refuse to let this chick see me sweat.

I take a long drink and eye her over my glass. "Well, I'm glad that you've learned barging in without knocking is rude as fuck. At least you've learned one thing from me today."

She bites the corner of her lip. "I've learned plenty today."

"Glad to be of service. I always aim to please." I raise one eyebrow, daring her to say more in front of Jack, but she doesn't.

Instead, she glances down at the silver watch on her wrist. "You have a lunch meeting at twelve thirty and your car service is downstairs waiting."

I set my glass down. "Thank you, Margo. Be sure to bring your tablet and a notepad to take notes."

"I'm going?" I fight back a smile as I hear the surprise in her voice.

"Of course. That's what assistants do—they assist. I'll be ready in five and I expect you to be as well." I allow a hint of a smile to play along my lips as she stands there gaping at me. "That will be all, Margo."

I can tell that she doesn't like me dismissing her like common help, but something tells me that she doesn't want to make too big of a scene in front of Jack, so she doesn't mouth off before she turns and walks out of my office. The princess is definitely not used to anyone bossing her around.

This little game of ours is going to be fun.

The second the door closes, Jack scrubs his hand down his face. "Fuck. This isn't good."

"What?" I ask, unsure of what he's talking about.

He locks eyes with me. "Are you sure you haven't already fucked her?"

"No!" I argue. "I haven't touched her."

"Maybe not yet, but you will. I can see the way you two are looking at each other. It might be a hate fuck, but it's going to happen, and it's going to ruin everything we've worked for. She's part of her father's deal. Please, use the head on top of your shoulders because it has the smarter brain. It'll tell you that the best thing for business would be to *not* slip your dick in this chick."

I understand why he's flipping out. We have a lot of money riding on this, and with him being my company attorney, screwing this up will cause him a shit-ton of work on top of all the money King Corporation will lose. But he has to know that money and making sure that the company my father built succeeds is far more important than a piece of ass.

"Don't worry, Jack. I've got it all under control. I promise not to fuck the hired help." I put the crystal stopper back in the scotch decanter. "Now, let's head to lunch and see if we can get that bastard, Buchanan, to sign this deal."

I slap Jack on the back as I pass him and we head out to seal the deal and get Margo Buchanan the hell out of my office.

Chapter III
TENSION

Margo

I cross my legs feeling Alexander King's cool gray eyes, which are set beneath a pair of dark eyebrows, taking in every inch of my exposed flesh. Even when I catch him staring, he doesn't seem the least bit apologetic. Rather than look away like most men would do in his position, he gives me one of those smart-ass smirks that I've grown accustomed to over the past few days since I started working for him, and he continues to stare at me blatantly.

The man is infuriating, and to make matters worse, he's impossibly good-looking. If I hadn't seen him in person, I would swear every picture I've ever seen of him had to have been airbrushed because no man ever looks that perfect all the time. But, sadly, Alexander is the exception. Everything about him draws me in. His Roman sculpted nose, chiseled cheekbones, and masculine jawline covered in a light beard— all of it fits exactly what I find attractive in a man to a T. It's a shame he's such a rat-bastard. Beauty is wasted on the wicked.

Infiltrating Alexander's business and seducing him in order to gain access to all the information my father needs is a far more difficult task than I had originally anticipated. Most men are all too eager to please me, but not Alexander. He's hell bent on making me miserable and teaching me what he deems as my place in this situation—below him. He has no idea that I'm not like most of these ridiculous Manhattan twits who run around here. His infamous name and hoards of wealth don't do a thing for me. He won't be able to walk all over me and use me as he does every other woman in our social circle. I'm pretty sure when I stood my ground earlier today it rattled him a bit, showing him that perhaps he's met his match with me.

"So, Ms. Buchanan, how do you like the job so far?" The deep voice beside me asks.

I turn toward Jack Sutherland, who I've quickly learned is one of the attorneys for the King Corporation and second in line for the biggest manwhore in Manhattan, behind none other than Alexander King. I can see why women throw themselves at Jack. Like Alexander, he's beautiful with his curly brown hair, hazel eyes, and adorable crooked grin. Though it seems to be a running theme that all well-polished men with model faces and insanely hot bodies are assholes. I swear there's a handbook somewhere that all attractive men are given, teaching them it's a must to be an egotistical womanizer who jump when any opportunity to stick their dick in something comes their way regardless of the consequences.

My mother constantly accuses me of trying to be the female version of Robin Hood. She thinks that I look for ways to punish men like these two for the sake of all womankind. I, on the other hand, always correct her and tell her that I simply won't allow jerks like Alexander King to gain the upper hand with me.

I will never allow a man to use me again. Once was enough of that bullshit.

Besides, someone needs to put these guys in their place from time to time.

I give Jack my most flirty smile, doing the best I can to win him over. God knows I don't need him breathing down my neck for being here like Alexander did earlier. "It's been a real eye-opening experience. There's obviously a lot for me to learn since this is my first job, but I tend to catch on to things very quickly."

Jack's eyes dart down to my mouth for a split second before he reconnects his gaze with mine, and he grins. "I love a woman who's a quick study. Where did you graduate?"

"Harvard," I answer, and it causes him to raise his eyebrows.

"Really? Wow. That's impressive. What was your major?"

"I double majored in finance and pre-law and graduated with honors. I wanted to keep my options open."

"Wow. I must say, Ms. Buchanan, that's amazing. Old King here had better be on his toes when it comes to you. You seem like a highly intelligent woman." I revel in his compliments as I thank him because I'm damn proud of my education. I earned that completely on my own merit.

I love my mother to pieces, but I never wanted to be like her when I got older. She's beautiful, which is exactly what caught my father's eye years ago. My mother married into wealth, became accustomed to the lifestyle, and when my father divorced her, she was desperate to find another wealthy man to take his place. I always told myself that I wanted to be a woman who stood on her own two feet—a woman who didn't need a man to complete her or her bank account.

And believe it or not, in this day and age, a determined woman intimidates the shit out of most men.

My deep-seated drive to succeed came out in full force today. It gave me the courage to rattle the unshakable Alexander King this morning. Of course I knew the little show he put on for me with the skanky bottle-blond hooker was meant to send me running for the hills, and while it turned my stomach to see such a disgusting display, I decided I wasn't going to make getting rid of me so easy for him.

"Do you think you'll make a permanent home with us at King, or are you using the position as a mode to gain experience?" Jack asks, jerking me away from my thoughts.

I glance over at Alexander, who is watching me intently as if he's studying his prey. It's as if he's just waiting for me to say the wrong thing so he can attack.

"So far I love how kind everyone has been to me. This would be an amazing company to work for long-term. I guess we'll have to wait to see if I screw up around here before I can make any predictions on how long I'll stay. Mr. King may fire me."

Jack chuckles. "I doubt he'll be allowing you to go anywhere anytime soon. You're already far too important for him to ever entertain the idea of letting you go over simple on-the-job mistakes."

"That's very kind of you," I tell him as I glance over at Alexander again. "Hopefully, he decides to keep me around for a while."

The cool smile playing on Alexander's lips is difficult to read, but if I had to guess from our previous conversation, that annoyingly charming expression only reiterates his feelings from earlier. He won't get rid of me, but he's going to do his damnedest to make sure I leave on my own. Well, I have news for him.

Game on, motherfucker.

Chapter **IV**
UNEXPECTED COMPLICATION

Alexander

Sitting across from Dan Buchanan in this upscale restaurant, I take in his stern expression that's intended to intimidate me and smile. Buchanan means to display worldly knowledge with his gray hair and multitude of wrinkles, but I know better. This man may have been a shrewd businessman at one time in his life, but not anymore. Being the sole contractor for building mini-bird helicopters for the U.S. military, he's allowed the wealth he's earned over the years to cloud his sound judgment making in both his personal and business finances, which is exactly what landed him with a company that's about to fold. I've done my homework on him, just like I do on all my targets. It makes the kill that much easier when I know their weaknesses.

Jack slides the contract across the table to Buchanan. "Here's the contract of sale, as requested. I figured we'd get the paperwork exchange out of the way so we can enjoy lunch."

Buchanan's weasel-dick attorney, Seth James, picks up the document and examines a few lines of it. "We'll look over it and let you know."

"Keep in mind," I interject, "that I already own nearly half the stock in Buchanan Industries. I'm close to being a majority shareholder, and I assure you that will help sway the board in my favor when they see my plan of action to save this sinking ship of a business."

Buchanan slams his fist down on the table. "Selling our technologies to another country is out of the question."

I lean forward, resting an elbow on the table. "Regardless of your personal feelings in the matter, selling parts of the business is what's best, and that is exactly what's going to happen."

"No," he growls. "I won't allow that to happen. I'll find a way to buy my stock back from you."

I set my gaze on him. "That's not going to happen. You can't afford it and you've already exhausted all your lines of credit to keep the company running long enough to fill the last order you received from the Navy for mini choppers. Face it, Mr. Buchanan. It's over. Your fate now rests in my hands."

Buchanan and I continue to stare each other down. I love the challenge in his eyes. Neither of us saying a word while our colleagues, plus his daughter, watch us intently—all of them feeling the tension too. Buchanan absolutely loathes me. I can tell, and I fucking love it.

He doesn't want to let his baby go. I get that. It's been his company for a very long time now, but he needs to understand that it cannot be saved. He's in far too much debt, and he just needs to come to the realization that I'm going to end up with it to do as I please.

This is the most tense lunch I've ever attended even though Jack lectured me about keeping this meeting social.

"Good afternoon," the male waiter dressed in a fitted black suit greets us when he approaches the table. "I am Gerald, and I'll be your waiter this afternoon. May I start you off with some drinks?"

"Scotch on the rocks for me," I say when he directs his attention to me.

"Water, please," Margo answers when the waiter's eyes expectantly zero in on her.

"I'll have a scotch as well, and be sure to bring out bread with lots of butter," Buchanan orders and then dismisses the waiter after everyone else has requested their beverages.

"Daddy!" Margo complains. "You know what the doctor said. Diabetics need to lay off the bread."

Buchanan gives his daughter a half-sided smile, and it immediately brings the tension around us down a notch. Perhaps it wasn't a bad idea to bring her along after all. "I know, darling, and I have been, but a man needs to splurge every now and again. It keeps us sane."

Margo rolls those magnetic blue eyes of hers and sighs. "I really don't get why you men always want to do things that are so bad for you."

"It's in our nature," he lectures. "All men have their own way of cutting loose."

Her gaze darts over to me. "Isn't that the truth."

It's hard not to laugh like a schoolgirl with the pure satisfaction I feel knowing that I'm getting to her, but I try to remain stoic without much luck. A ghost of a smile hints at my lips.

"Alexander, did you see this?" Jack asks as he slides his phone over to me.

An email from Yamada Enterprises' president sits on the screen. My eyes race over the words, knowing Jack wouldn't be showing me this now if it weren't important since this is our interested buyer in the Buchanan deal.

I sigh heavily. "Gentlemen, it seems that you'll have a bit of an extension in reviewing the contract. My business contact for the deal has requested that I meet with him face to face while he is in the states vacationing in Las Vegas. Mr. Sutherland and I will be leaving at the end of the week and will return on Monday—"

"I can't do that, Alexander," Jack says next to me. "It's my . . . cousin's wedding and I just can't miss it."

My lips twist. This isn't like Jack. First off, he's never interrupted me in the middle of something, and second, when did he start giving a fuck about some random cousin who he's never talked about until now?

"Who cares," I say. "I'm missing my sister's twenty-fourth birthday party. This is business. Skip it."

Jack frowns. "I can't. There's no way I can get out of this one."

Before I have a chance to fire off more reasons of why Jack should stop being a pussy and go to this meeting, Margo's voice cuts between us. "I'll go with you. I am your assistant, after all."

My eyes widen. The thought of being alone in Vegas, of all fucking places, with this woman, causes my dick to twitch. I can't be around her that long and not fuck her. It'll drive me out of my mind.

"That's a great idea, Margo," Buchanan chimes in. "You can make sure whoever is getting this company is worthy. It would be nice for you to make a few contacts."

I hold up my hand. "Wait, just a minute. This is my deal, and I don't think—"

"It'll still be your baby," Margo purrs next to me. "I promise not to interfere in any way. I just want to learn. After all, you're known around this city for being able to charm the pants off anyone you set your sights on. I think I can learn a lot by watching you in action."

"Oh, you'll see me in action, all right." I purse my lips and cut myself off, not wanting to say crude things to her in front of her father and fuck up this deal.

Fuck.

I sigh while both Margo and her father watch me intently, waiting for me to give in and take the enemy along with me. The information Margo could gain from this trip could be devastating to the deal, but I doubt they'll be able to negotiate a better deal for Buchanan Industries with Yamada Enterprises. I have nothing to worry about by allowing her to tag along, and it'll make Buchanan still feel comfortable that he has gained the upper hand on me because his sweet ball-breaking daughter is his little spy.

"Fine," I concede. "Margo can go, but once we get back, we put this deal to bed. Agreed?"

Buchanan nods. "Agreed. I'll have my answer for you by then."

I roll my shoulders and relax a bit in my chair. Spend the weekend with Margo in Sin City—no problem. I can get through this.

COUNTDOWN

Margo

Why couldn't Alexander King be a pudgy, fifty-something, bald man with bad breath? It would make it a whole lot easier to pretend that I don't feel the weight of his stare on me every time I go into his office if he were hideously ugly. As it stands now, it's hard for my body not to respond to him. It's like I have this visceral reaction to him whenever I'm in his presence, and that scares the shit out of me.

His advances had backed off a bit from a couple of days ago when I caught the hooker blowing him in his office. Thank God. But I can tell he's ready to make good on his promise to have me beg him to fuck me. He thinks fucking him will break me—that I'm some little twit who wears her heart on her sleeve—and that pisses me off. *He* pisses me off.

The countdown to Vegas is on. In just one day, I'll be on a private plane heading across the country to the biggest adult playground in the world. I don't know how being alone with him for an entire weekend is going to go. He was probably right. I'll want to either fuck him or kill him with my own bare hands, but I guess it will be the latter.

"Margo?" Alexander's voice rings through the intercom sitting on my desk.

"Yes, Mr. King," I answer with as much professionalism as I can muster.

He quickly rattles off a list of tasks for me. "I need the daily stock report on Buchanan Industries, a dinner reservation for two at Per Se for seven tonight, and my coffee cup is empty."

Out of all the things that he asks me to do, getting his coffee irritates me the most. Why in the hell do I have to fetch it? Are his legs fucking broken?

I sigh before plastering on a huge smile that will come through in the tone of my voice as I press the speaker button. "Right away, sir."

The stock report and coffee are the easy things on the list, but securing a table at Per Se took some finagling. After I had disclosed exactly which Mr. King was requesting the table, it went rather smoothly. Seems his name has quite the pull.

I carry the report and coffee into his office. He holds his hand out for the paper as I set the mug on his desk.

I hope he fucking chokes on it.

I begin to turn away, but his voice quickly halts me. "I didn't dismiss you yet, Margo."

My nostrils flare as I spin back around to face him. "Will there be anything else, sir?"

Alexander pushes himself out of the chair and smoothes his red tie, attracting my attention to the definition hiding behind that blue buttoned-down dress shirt. I've noticed that when he's working in his office, he removes his jacket. It almost makes him appear casual and more approachable, but I know better. He's still an uptight asshole with or without the jacket.

He walks around the desk and stops in front of me before leaning back against the expensive-looking mahogany desk. "Are you all prepared for our trip to Vegas?"

I nod. "Yes. I mean, I will be once I finish packing—"

He shakes his head and a strand of dark hair falls across his forehead. My fingers itch to reach up and shove it back into place. I wonder if it's as soft as it looks.

Stop it! You cannot be thinking about touching this man. He is the enemy and a complete asshole. Get a hold of yourself. Don't allow hormones to take control.

"I don't mean your personal items, Margo. I meant do you have all of the necessary tasks designated to the support staff to cover in our absence."

I bite the inside of my lower lip as it occurs to me that doing that hadn't crossed my mind. "I didn't think that was necessary since tomorrow is Friday. We'll be back in the office by Tuesday, so I just planned to return calls then."

Alexander studies me intently as he taps his index finger against the smooth wood of his desk. "Time is always of the essence—it's even more valuable in my line of work. One missed tip on an investment could cost billions."

I swallow hard as the complexity of my mistake becomes clear. "I'll make sure Jack's secretary fields all of my calls and notifies me if something is urgent."

I have to keep shit together and up my game. While working for King Enterprises isn't my real career aspiration, I can still learn a lot while I'm here—things that can help me once I've found my job niche.

He straightens the cuff of his shirt. "Have a car pick you up tomorrow promptly at eight. The private jet leaves at nine. Apparently the Yamada family has requested my presence at a pool party at the Hard Rock at two, and I'll expect you to accompany me."

My eyes widen. "You can't possibly expect me to attend a meeting in a swimsuit! That's . . . no . . . it's ridiculous."

"It's not up for discussion." His voice rings with authority. "You want this job—you play the fucking game and be a good fucking sport while we meet with my business contacts."

I open my mouth to lash out and tell him that there's no way on God's green earth that I'll be parading around in front of him in a bikini, but the moment he arches his eyebrow, I quickly decide against it. My father will be so pissed if I screw this up. He's counting on me to schmooze this contact of Alexander's so that they'll go to my father directly and make a deal for whatever part of Buchanan Industries they're after.

"Fine, but just don't expect me to become one of your paid whores while we're there. This is just business."

A playful smirk flirts across his full lips. "I like this tough act of yours—the way you're fighting against me. It will make the moment your lips are wrapped around my cock that much more enjoyable, Margo."

I release a bitter laugh, and it fills the inside of his office. "Those suave lines may work on the women you're used to dealing with, but I assure you, it'll take more than a few pretty words and a bunch of heady stares to turn my head. I don't date assholes."

"But do you fuck 'em? That's the question of the hour, isn't it? I don't ever remember promising you that we'd date. I said we'd fuck. Dating versus fucking is two very distinctly different things."

I narrow my gaze. "That's never going to happen."

"We'll see."

We stand there staring at one another. Neither one of us says a word. I don't know what it is about this man, but he brings out the competitive nature in me like no other. We are at an impasse—both wanting our ways. I need information to help my father, and he wants to destroy me with sex, causing me to tuck my tail between my legs in embarrassment. I don't see either one of us conceding, so the best that I can hope for is whatever happens in Vegas to tip the scales in my favor and allow me to get the inside advantage that I need.

Chapter VI
BROTHER KNOWS BEST
Alexander

I glance down at my watch and sigh. Diem being late shouldn't surprise me. After all, I've known her for officially twenty-four years this weekend, so Diem being late for her own birthday dinner is a given. That girl couldn't be on time to save her life. Dad knew that about her too, which is why he left his business to me. He knew Diem was too much of a free spirit to ever be mixed up in the corporate life.

As I pick up my cell to call her again to ask her where she is, she comes bounding up to the table with the biggest smile on her face, making her green eyes brighten and accentuating the emerald shade of the dress she's wearing.

"You're late," I scold her.

Diem waves me off dismissively as the maitre d' pulls out the chair for her. She tucks a blond strand of hair behind her ear before she makes eye contact with me. "Stop being such a stiff. I wasn't that late. Besides, I have a really good excuse this time."

Staying mad at my baby sister is virtually impossible. It's odd how she got on my very last nerve when I was younger, but after my father died that annoyance fell away and all I wanted to do was protect her. I had to become the man of the family at twenty. When my bitch of a mother decided taking care of an ill man with cancer and her then fourteen-year-old daughter was no longer *her thing,* I became responsible for Diem.

"What's the exciting news?" I give in and ask because I can tell by the expression on her face that she's bursting at the seams to tell me something.

Her smile widens. "I sold a painting!"

"You did?" Now the little shit has me grinning like a fool. "That's excellent news. Which piece did they buy? The self-portrait?"

Her eyes widen and the smile drops from her face. "How did you know?"

I lean back, pleased that not only do I have a mind for business, but an eye for art as well. "I know good work when I see it, and that was your best work to date. It finally made me realize that sending you to that ridiculously expensive art school wasn't a complete waste of money."

Diem rolls her eyes at me. "Don't even act like the money was ever an issue. Besides, going to that school was my dream."

I sigh. "I know it was, and even though I don't say it often enough, I'm proud of you. I'm glad you have aspirations and goals, even if they don't necessarily align with the educational direction I wanted for you."

She unfolds the white cloth napkin on the table and drapes it across her lap. "Not all of us mere mortals can become cut-throat business moguls like you."

I smirk at her sassy tone as I reach into the inside pocket of my jacket and pull out the blue box containing her gift. "I shouldn't give you this for that little quip, but because I don't want to hear you complain that I didn't get you anything . . . here you go."

I slide the box across the table toward her. "Happy birthday, Diem."

She places her hand on the box while her shoulders slump forward and her mouth draws into a pout. "Are you sure you have to go away this weekend? My party is going to be epic."

"Afraid so," I tell her. "Yamada is in the States, living it up in Vegas, and I have to meet up with him to secure a deal I'm working on."

She raises her eyebrows. "Now I know exactly why you don't want to cancel. You and Yamada back together again? I smell trouble brewing."

I chuckle and shake my head. "Trust me. Those days are long over with. Besides, I'm taking my new secretary to make sure things stay strictly professional and I don't get distracted."

"Margo Buchanan? The Feisty Princess? She's your new secretary, right? I think taking her will cloud your judgment, and I know she'll definitely be a distraction to Yamada."

"The Feisty *what?*" I furrow my brow. "How do you know about her?"

This is news to me. How in the hell does my baby sister always seem to be in the know about everything in this town?

"Everyone calls her that." She pauses for a beat and then shrugs. "Jack told me about her working for you. The whole Upper East Side is buzzing about it. I remember Margo from high school. She was a grade ahead of me. She's beautiful, smart, and vicious when it comes to getting what she wants but loyal to the core in respects to the people she loves, or at least that's what the word is. She's kind of like the female version of you."

Diem giggles, and I hate the fact that my sister seems to know more about Margo than I do. I don't like thinking about Margo because it either pisses me off or makes me horny as hell every time I do.

I need a subject change.

My lips twist. "I don't think I like you and Jack talking so much."

"Why?" she fires back.

"Because, Diem, he's my best friend, and it's . . . I . . . it's just asking for trouble." I grab the glass of water in front of me and take a big gulp, unsure of why I'm allowing myself to get all tongue tied.

"We're just friends, Alexander. It is possible for a man and a woman to just hang out from time to time without anything else going on."

"No, it's not."

"You're taking Margo to Vegas so doesn't that make her your friend?"

"No, it doesn't. She hates me. We definitely are not friends," I tell her.

Diem frowns. "You should do something about that if you want this business arrangement to work out with her. You know Dad always taught us that you catch more bees with honey."

Diem's right. Father always said that, and he was known around this city for being a fair and honest man. Unfortunately, I couldn't use his methods when I took over. I was far too young at twenty to be taken seriously at running a billion-dollar company, which is why I had to be tough—flex my muscle—and show people that I wouldn't be fucked with.

I lean back in my chair and loosen my tie a bit. Maybe my sister has a point. Being a total dick to Margo doesn't seem to be making any headway. "What do you suppose I do? Concede and let her win—let her think I'm a pushover? I can't do that, Diem. It's not in me to allow someone to get the best of me."

She shakes her head. "I'm not saying to instantly become a pussy. I'm just saying to lighten up a bit. I know how you get when you think someone is your enemy. You become set on destroying them. Margo might not be as bad as you have her made out to be in your head."

"Or she could be much worse," I answer instantly.

"I doubt that. No one is a bigger badass than you." Diem winks and then laughs. "I think you should just try to be a little nicer. Break through her walls a little and show her that you pay attention. It'll make this business deal a lot more pleasant for both of you. This should be stress-free because you already have Yamada in the bag. Nothing Margo Buchanan can do will change that so you might as well learn to get along with her."

My fingers run across my bearded jawline and I sigh. "When did you get so smart?"

She grins. "Turning twenty-four will do that to you. Speaking of that, let's see what you got me." Her fingers work nimbly to tear open the Tiffany's box to reveal the diamond charm bracelet I bought for her. Her fingers slide over the engraving as she reads it aloud. "Love you, Squirt."

She wrinkles her nose.

I laugh, loving that she still hates the nickname I gave her when we were just kids but won't throw it back at me because of all the sparkly diamonds surrounding the name.

I pick up my drink. "Happy birthday, Squirt."

Chapter VII
NO ESCAPE

Margo

Right on time, the black Town Car pulls up to take me to King's private jet. Riding in private planes is nothing new to me, seeing as how my father's company specializes in building aircrafts. It is, however, the first time I've ever taken a cross-country flight accompanying a man who I absolutely loath.

My cell rings and I dig through my handbag to find it. I smile when I see Mother's name flash across the screen. "Hello, Mother."

"Gah," she sighs into the phone. "How many times have I asked you to call me Lily? You know I don't like people thinking that I'm old enough to be your mother."

I laugh. "I hate to be the one to break it to you, but I think the tabloids exposed that secret when you were pregnant with me twenty-five years ago. I'm sure it was the story of the year . 'Most Beautiful Woman on the Planet Gives Birth.'"

"Stop your teasing," she scolds. "Stretch marks are nothing to joke about."

I roll my eyes at my crazy, beautiful mother. To the world, she is Lily Doyle, who some might say at one time was the most beautiful woman in the world seeing as how she was Miss America and then later crowned Miss Universe. People loved the story of how she came from the wrong side of the tracks, so-to-speak, and worked hard to earn a philanthropy degree because she wanted to help the less fortunate. She became America's Sweetheart.

"Good news, Jean Paul is in Paris this week filming some new ridiculous bit for his television show, which means I'm free all week. Let's go shopping! I'm in need of some new shoes." The excitement in my mother's voice is infectious. Jean Paul is husband number five, and from what I can tell, a very nice man, but he's always working. That seems to be okay with my mother, of course. She doesn't mind spending his money while he's away, and as much as I would love to drown in the world of Manolo, Jimmy Choo and, my personal weakness, Christian Louboutin, with her, there will be no time this weekend for that.

I sigh. "Rain check, Mother. I'm getting ready to board a flight to Vegas with Alexander King for work."

"Honey, I love you, but I absolutely don't understand you. Why on Earth do you waste that beautiful face and body that you've been blessed with on the completely dull world of business? You could've been the next big thing if you'd gotten into modeling. Out of all the things you could take from your father . . . the need to be mixed in all those suit-wearing meetings is the worst thing ever. It totally interferes with our girl time."

"I know, but I promise when I get back, we'll do something."

"Promise?" she asks. "It's been far too long, and I miss my baby girl like crazy. Your father has all your time occupied lately with this silly nonsense of invading the King Corporation."

"It's not silly, Mother. Alexander King has my future legacy in the palm of his hand. I have to find a way to stop him from taking away what will be mine someday. Staying close to him is my only option until I can figure out a way to get Buchanan Industries a deal that can save it. But I promise that as soon as I get back, we'll shop until you drop."

"Okay." She sounds satisfied with that answer. "Try to at least have a little fun while you're in Vegas. Please, don't be a stick-in-the-mud and stay in your room the entire time."

"I won't—"

"Margo, I know you. Promise me that you'll loosen up."

"Fine, but I'm sorry to say there won't be any wild stories to report when I get back."

"You are completely no fun, Margo. You have to loosen up. At least try to pretend you're twenty-five and not fifty-one like me because we both know that even I act younger than you."

I laugh. "I will try to not be a complete fun buster."

"That's my girl. Drink one for me.

"Okay. Goodbye, Mother." I laugh and hang up the phone just as the car pulls up next to King's private jet.

The driver opens my door and I take a deep breath, willing myself to put on my best bitch face and give Alexander a taste of what it's like when a woman is in charge and knows exactly what she wants.

Inside the cabin of the plane, the lone flight attendant on board greets me. Her blond hair is pulled back into a French twist on the back of her head while her bright red lipstick is a stark contrast to her porcelain skin. She has a very Gwen Stefani kind of style.

The attendant smiles at me, and I instantly relax because she appears friendly. "Good morning, Ms. Buchanan. I'm Abigail, and I'll be with you through the duration of this flight. If you need anything at all, don't hesitate to ask. Mr. King has requested that we stock the cabin with your favorite things so there's a good chance that we'll have anything that you might need."

"Um, okay. Thanks." I stumble through my answer completely dumbfounded.

This surprises me. How would Alexander King know the first thing about what I like? He doesn't really know me in the slightest and yet, somehow, he thinks he knows what my favorite things are.

I bet there's not one thing on this plane that's actually special for me. I don't know what kind of game he's playing, but I will not allow him to butter me up.

Alexander's gaze lands on me as I stride down the aisle and take the seat directly facing him instead of taking a different seat somewhere else on the private jet. He smirks at my boldness to meet him head-on and I raise my eyebrow as we stare each other down.

It's funny how we've grown accustomed to trying to one-up one another in the last week since I've begun working for him. As much as I hate to admit it, we are a lot alike. Both of us are headstrong, determined, and have this innate need to always win.

The cabin is silent for more than half the flight, and it's almost as if we're playing some weird quiet game—neither of us willing to say a word for fear that we may lose the standoff going on between us. Occasionally, he'll glance up, and I'll direct my gaze in any other direction other than at him. I mean, I'll admit, I've been checking him out. He's gorgeous, and I can't help but appreciate the view. Any woman stuck on this flight like me would do exactly the same thing. She's a liar if she tells you any different.

"Excuse me, Mr. King. Would you care for another scotch?" Abigail asks him shortly after he swallows down the last drop of amber liquid.

"Yes. That'll be fine, Abigail," he replies coolly and then gives her a polite smile which causes her to blush.

"Right away, sir." The attendant turns to me. "Are you sure I can't get you anything, Ms. Buchanan? I have Fiji water and strawberry yogurt."

I tuck a loose strand of hair behind my ear. "Wow . . . um . . ."

I hesitate. Is it simply a coincidence that Fiji just happens to be my favorite brand of water along with having my preferred flavor of yogurt?

"If you don't want those, we also have Diet Coke and Payday bars," Abigail counters.

Diet Coke I can see, but Payday bars? That's a pretty random item to keep on a plane. Especially since, judging by the looks of how fit Alexander is, he wouldn't eat such an unhealthy snack. But I guess it is possible. The man seems to drink like a fucking fish so maybe he's not all that healthy and his absurdly toned physique is just genetic.

Gah! If it is, that just gives me something else to hate him for.

I smile at Abigail as she waits patiently for me to make a selection. "I'll have a Diet Coke, please."

As soon as we're alone, Alexander's intoxicating gray eyes bore into me. "Are you not pleased with the items that I have arranged for you?"

My brow furrows. "How did you know what I like? Do you have spies watching me to ensure that I'm not digging into your business a little too much?"

He chuckles. "You act as though you still believe me to be afraid of you, Margo. I thought by now we've figured each other out. I don't seem to rattle you, and you damn sure don't affect me."

"So what's with all my favorite things on this flight?" I fire back.

He shrugs. "I'm observant. There's not much that I don't notice about the people around me, and let's just say that I've taken a very big interest in what you're up to. I like to know what makes people tick. It makes it easier for me to break them."

I stiffen my shoulders. "I've got a newsflash for you, Mr. King. I don't break."

"Everyone has their breaking point, and sooner or later, I'm going to find yours, Princess." He smirks, and I hate it when he does that. It's a sexy expression, especially on him, and I hate that I find him attractive. He is such a smug bastard. "I see the way you look at me when we argue. I turn you on even though you don't want to admit it. You and I are very similar creatures. We both love a challenge, and we both like to always be in control."

I raise my eyebrow, still not believing anything that he says. "I thought you said you didn't have spies."

He licks his plump lips slowly, causing my eyes to flick down to his mouth. "What can I say, your reputation precedes you. Everyone knows that the Feisty Princess of Manhattan always demands her way."

My mouth gapes open. "How dare you call me that? I hate that name."

Alexander smiles. "You should learn to embrace it. A name like that means people are scared of you."

I curse the day some dumb jock in high school dubbed me that after I very colorfully turned down his eleventh attempt at asking me very bluntly to blow him. If you ask me, he deserved a punch him in the face. But sadly, the name still follows me around, even now.

I laugh bitterly. "Right. Like how you embrace yours? The Naughty King, *really?* Doesn't it bother you that half the women in this city think you're the biggest manwhore on the East Coast?"

"Not at all," he replies smoothly. "The women who call me that were fucked over by me in more ways than one, and I promise you, they fucking enjoyed every last minute of it. That's why they love to keep my name on their lips. As for the other half, they're just envious of the first."

"You are a pompous prick."

His eyes harden. "I may be, but I always do what suits me best. Women complicate the shit out of everything, and I don't have time to play their silly little games."

It's appalling how he views all women as *complications*. "Is that why you hire prostitutes? Are you really that afraid of being human and showing some compassion that you'd rather pay for sex than deal with the emotional ramifications that typically comes with it?"

"I don't see how that's any of your business, but yes. When women see me, they see a meal ticket. Why would I ever want to entertain their silly fantasies that they may be the one to make me change my ways and commit not only myself but also half of my fortune to them? No fucking way that's ever going to happen."

I roll my eyes. "Not all women think that way."

"Are you telling me that you don't?"

"No," I answer automatically. "My family is already wealthy. Why would I need to marry for money?"

"For the same reason a lot of women do. Soon, I'll be taking your father's company. How long do you think it'll take before your family's fortune runs out? Doesn't that scare you?"

"No," I repeat. "That's not going to happen. My father—"

"Yes, it will. Neither of you can stop the inevitable from happening. The contacts we're meeting in Vegas are long-time business associates of mine, and there's nothing you'll be able to do to steal them away from me, which is why it doesn't bother me to bring you along."

I open my mouth to fire back in my defense, but he keeps going, cutting me off.

"Honestly, if I were you, Margo, I would probably just quit now and work on finding a wealthy schmuck to marry. You've got a nice ass and decent sized tits, so I'm sure you won't have a problem securing a cushy future as long as you don't mind fucking some old, ugly motherfucker."

I grip the armrest of my seat and dig my nails into the cream-colored leather. It takes everything in me to not jump up and smack the ever-living shit out of this man.

I take a deep breath and count to five in my head before I blow the air out slowly through my nose. This helps me refocus and not fall into the little game he's playing with me.

I swallow hard. "I'll keep that in mind, but I would much rather spend my time figuring out ways to take you down."

"Suit yourself. But I'm warning you, Ms. Buchanan, I don't play fair." There's a wicked gleam in his eye, and there's no telling what he's planning to do to torture me, but I have to be ready for any move he tries to make.

My father is counting on me to figure out a way to save his company and my family's future.

Chapter **VII**
PROVOCATEUR
Alexander

No matter the time of day, the lights in Las Vegas are always putting on a show. The limo pulls up to the Hard Rock Casino, and I glance over at Margo as the driver stops the car.

She hasn't said much to me since our heated little discussion. Every time we talk, I seem to piss her off, which is exactly what I want to do. I want to become the itch festering under her skin that she's dying to scratch. The more she hates me—the more she'll think about me and how much she can't wait to be rid of me.

So why do I feel like a bastard and have this urge to apologize?

I shake my head to purge myself of the crazy thought. I need her out of my fucking hair. Her presence distracts me, and that's not good. I need a clear head for business. This weekend is going to be pure torture.

The minute the driver opens the door, I step out and then turn with my hand out to assist Margo. My eyes dart down to her sexy long legs, and I wonder if she knows how much she turns me on with those damn skirts she flits around in all the time. I wonder if she does it intentionally to drive me out of my fucking mind. The whole naughty businesswoman look she has going on works well for her. Even when she wears those little black-rimmed glasses, she's still hot as hell.

We're immediately greeted by a short, pudgy man wearing a black suit with his black hair slicked back like he's a 1940s mobster. "Good afternoon, Mr. King. My name is Coleman, and I'll be your personal concierge during your stay. Allow me to escort you to your room." After a quick snap of his fingers, two bellhops rush to the back of the car to retrieve our luggage before following us into the hotel.

The elevator doors ding before opening, and I stop myself from placing my hand on the small of Margo's back. I cannot allow myself to touch her because whenever I do, strange things happen to me. The last time we touched was in my office when she grabbed my cock and told me that I was the one who was fucked. She rattled me. I hadn't expected her to do that so it threw me off for a brief moment. But now that I know what she's capable of, I won't allow her to ever gain the upper hand again. I have to be careful and keep her at a distance.

Silence surrounds us once we're shut inside the tiny space and begin ascending, but it's not awkward. Either Margo and I are doing our best to ignore one another or we're at each other's throats. There isn't any middle ground between us where we can just be casual. Diem's right. We can't go on like this. I need to work on being friendlier. Having her favorite things on the plane was a small start, but I'm going to have to step it up a notch and dial my personality down a bit. The last thing I need is to fight with this woman in Yamada's presence. He'd have a fucking field day with that shit. I don't need him thinking that she has the upper hand in this situation.

The elevator dings and Coleman smiles. "Ah, here we are. Right this way to the Provocateur Suite."

Margo's shoulders stiffen as she halts in her tracks. "What happened to the Paradise Tower Penthouse that I booked?"

Coleman frowns. "We emailed you earlier this morning to notify you that the Paradise Penthouse would be unavailable for your stay this weekend. Our last guests . . . well, let's just say they put the room out of commission for a bit. It's in desperate need of repairs, and since this was a last-minute booking, I'm afraid the only penthouse that we have available for your duration is the Provocateur Suite."

Margo shakes her head, causing her black curls to bounce around. "You can't honestly expect me to stay there with my boss. I didn't mind sharing a traditional penthouse, but this is unacceptable."

"I'm sorry, Ms. Buchanan. Like we explained on the phone at the time of your reservation, this weekend we have several major events and conventions, and we are completely booked."

Margo sighs and her shoulders slump. "Okay. Since I really don't have a choice in the matter, but—" she swings around and points her gaze directly at me "—I expect you to remain professional."

I hold up my hands in surrender. "I don't have the slightest idea of what you mean. It's a room for Christ's sake, Margo."

"It's not just *any* room. It's the sex slave suite," she whispers harshly.

My eyebrows jerk up in surprise. I was definitely not expecting this curveball. "This room is right down your twisted little path, but I swear to God if you spend the weekend tying up random women in a place that we have to share, you might not leave with your balls intact," she fires at me.

A grin spreads across my face. Her spunk is absolutely the hottest fucking thing I've seen in a long time. "Margo, the only woman I plan on tying up this weekend is you."

I know I just said I shouldn't touch her, but I don't think that's going to be possible. Especially not while being reminded of sex every time I turn around in the room we're sharing. She's too damn sexy, and I won't be able to resist the temptation.

Margo's nostrils flare. "Don't count on it, King."

We stand there staring each other down. Both of us determined to be the one who comes out the victor this weekend.

Coleman clears his throat next to us. "Okay, then, why don't I show you to the suite?"

I roll my shoulders and straighten my tie but never take my eyes off Margo. "Lead the way, Coleman."

"Right away, Mr. King. This way."

We follow behind him in silence. This woman knows how to push my buttons like no other. If I'm being honest, I like that she challenges me. I've never had a woman do that before, and in an odd way, it's refreshing. She's not like all the other fucking doormats who typically surround me and do whatever I say just because of who I am.

The moment the door opens, I can tell that this is unlike any other penthouse I've been in before, and that's saying a lot considering how much I travel. The walls are deep red while masculine black leather furniture fills the space. A large stocked bar with all the top-shelf liquor one could ever desire sits near the entrance.

To the left, Coleman walks us over to one of the master suites, which is a room with three queen-sized beds pushed together complete with holograms of women writhing on the bed. This is indeed a place where sexual fantasies are meant to be explored.

We pass back through the living room area into another room that contains a padded exam table like you see at a doctor's office, but there are steel hoops bolted to it. Obviously, this table is intended to have people tied to it. One black tiled wall has more steel hoops attached to it, and there's a steel birdcage that's big enough to fit an adult into that sits in the corner. Next to the cage is a large wooden 'X' that's attached to the wall with loops made for tying someone to. A tall, black bookcase sits on the opposite wall. A couple of boxes that are clearly vibrators, sexual lotions, whips and every other thing you can think of to use in a fuck room fills the shelves.

"This room is another part of what makes this suite so special. It's fully equipped and has sexual enhancers that will increase the enjoyment. Any items that you do choose to use will be discreetly added to your bill. Attached you will find the second master suite—" Coleman motions toward the bedroom, but I can no longer concentrate on what he's saying.

All I can think about is how much I want to tie Margo to this table and explore every inch of her body. Having this man in here with us is a distraction to what I really want to know.

"Leave us," I order Coleman.

He bows his head. "As you wish."

As he opens the door, he instructs the bellhops to leave our luggage at the entrance before they all exit without another word.

I turn my focus back to Margo. Her wide eyes tell me that even though she won't admit it, being alone in this room with me scares her. She feels this weird sexual connection between us too. I know she does. She just won't give in and admit it. If we'd just fuck, I'm sure all this weird tension would disappear and we could both focus on what we actually came out here to do.

I swallow hard and then glance at the two master suite doors that are on the opposite sides of this fantasy room.

I motion from one room to the other. "Lady's choice."

"That's gracious of you considering that's not how you typically operate. By the way it looked in your office the other day, it seemed like it was all about your choices first," she mutters as she turns away from me toward the room that we hadn't toured yet.

Before I realize it, I'm snatching her wrist, stopping her mid-step and forcing her to look at me. "How do you know that when I'm with a woman I'm *not* paying for that I don't put her first?"

She raises one eyebrow. "You're too much of a selfish prick to put anyone's needs before your own."

My pulse thunders beneath my skin. "Maybe I need to change your perception of me then—show you just how giving

I can be when I want to. This suite—it's the perfect place for us to fuck and get it out of our systems. Don't you agree? Just imagine all the ways I could make you come while I have you strapped to that table."

I can't deny that just being in here and seeing all the props has me picturing what it would be like to tie her up and spank her ass before feeling her pussy wrapped around my cock.

Her head falls back slightly as she lets out a low sarcastic laugh. "I would never fuck you. You are *not* my type."

I lick my lips as I close the distance between us until her chest presses against me. "A man with a big cock who knows how to use it is *every* woman's type, and believe me, baby, I'm the best fuck you'll ever have."

I can no longer hold back. The sweet smell of her perfume and the very essence of her surround me and the need to have her—possess her—consumes me. My hands wrap around her waist and then slide down her perfect ass to find the hem of her skirt. The tips of my fingers graze the bare flesh on her legs.

Her entire body shivers, but she never takes her eyes off me as she takes a deep breath. "Prove it."

She doesn't have to tell me twice. I seize the opportunity and slide my hand up her back so I could tangle my fingers into her hair. I slam my mouth against hers with so much need it's almost overwhelming. Her lips part, allowing enough room for my tongue to snake into her mouth, and she moans.

I'm such a fucking goner.

She tastes like heaven, and I'm too much of a sinner to resist devouring every inch of her. Tonight, I will own her body. Tonight, I will make her mine.

FALLING
Margo

He's taking what he wants without apologies, and it's so damn hot.

His hands are everywhere: in my hair, on my ass, cupping my face while he deepens our kiss. Alexander King definitely knows how to touch a woman and set her skin on fire. When his lips attack mine, I throw my hands in his hair to try to immerse myself in him. Alexander wraps his arms around me, tugging me closer while never breaking our kiss.

He grabs the material at the bottom of my tucked in blouse and pulls the fabric free of my pencil skirt. One by one, he pops the buttons open with his skilled hands and when he frees the last one, he slides the material off my shoulders, allowing his fingers to trace my bare skin before my shirt falls to the floor. The hem of my skirt creeps up my thighs as Alexander slides it to get better access.

He presses himself against me. The roughness of his trousers against me causes a tingle to erupt all over my body. My panties grow instantly wet as he presses against the sensitive flesh between my legs while unzipping my skirt, loosening it so it falls in a pool around my ankles.

I stand there in nothing but my red, satin lingerie and black Jimmy Choos before him. He steps back, appraising me from head to toe with hungry eyes. I should feel self-conscious about him staring at me like this, but I don't. He makes me feel wanted and powerful by staring at me like I'm the most mouthwatering thing he's ever seen.

Alexander licks his lips and then drags his teeth slowly over his bottom lip as he closes the distance between us.

His toned body presses into me, and he grips my hips, yanking my pelvis against his and allowing me to feel his erection through his slacks. "You are the sexiest fucking thing I've ever seen. I'm going to enjoy this, and I promise you will too if you give yourself over to me completely."

Before I can say anything else, he crushes his lips to mine, plunging his tongue inside my mouth, and making my knees go a little weak from the sheer intensity of it. An ache builds between my legs, and I realize that I've never been this turned on in my life. There's no way I can put a stop to this now. I need him inside me too damn much.

My fingers snake into his hair, and I love the fact that he has just enough length for me to grab onto.

Strong hands slide down my ass and then cup the back side of my thighs. My legs wrap around his waist as he hoists me up with ease. He walks toward the table in the middle of the room and sets me down, pressing himself firmly between my legs.

I writhe against him and the soft material of his slacks allows his hard cock to rub against my most sensitive flesh. My entire body craves the relief only he can bring me. The smoothness of his well-manicured hands moving across my skin causes goosebumps to erupt over every inch of me. My breasts ache as he moves around to my back and unhooks my bra, freeing them for his pleasure. A warm trail of kisses leave fire in their wake as he works his way down my neck, nipping, teasing and promising passion as he moves past my collarbone. He takes one of my nipples into his mouth and I suck a rush of air through my clenched teeth.

Alexander opens his mouth and sticks his tongue out as I watch him swirl it around the taut pink flesh. I wrap my legs around him tighter and work my pelvis up and down.

This man has me so ready.

"You want this as much as I do." His hooded eyes flick up in my direction. "This is going to be fun."

He bends down and reaches for something under the table. The rattle of chains startles me. I guess I hadn't noticed them under there during the tour, but to be honest I was so uncomfortable standing in this room with Alexander that I didn't pay much attention to the small details. Before I know what's going on, he wraps a cuff around one of my wrists and then quickly follows with another shackle.

I furrow my brow. "What the . . . ?"

Alexander's face lights up with a wicked grin. "It's time to play."

My eyes widen as he locks my other arm into place as well. "You're tying me up?"

He nods and pushes me back with a firm hand, forcing me back on my elbows. "I want control."

Alexander's fingers find the wet spot on my underwear. "Mmmm. So wet. That's fucking sexy. I don't think I've ever wanted to taste something so badly."

"I . . ." My mouth hangs open, unable to complete a coherent thought as he grabs the silky material on my hips and rips it with ease before he tosses the scraps of satin that were once my panties to the floor.

I bite my lip as I sit on the table before him completely exposed for his viewing pleasure. His gray eyes slowly trail over every inch of me, taking his time to appreciate the view.

He pushes my knees apart again as he slides between them and then teases my top lip with his tongue. "Do you want me to touch you?"

His hand slithers up my thigh, and for the first time in my life, I'm at a loss for words. I squeeze my eyes shut, still fighting against giving him possession of me, as he wants. I'm all for having sex, but him taking complete control . . . well, that's just not my style.

"Beg," he commands. "Beg for it like a good girl, and maybe . . . *just* maybe, I'll give you what you want."

The man is infuriating. I'm finally giving in and allowing him to ravage my body and now he wants me to beg? Get fucking real.

"No," I say with authority in my voice.

"No?" His warm breath tickles my cheek as he breathes against my neck. "I need to hear you plead, Margo. If you want to come, then you need to say *please.*"

His finger slides slowly against my clit and my entire body trembles. I hate the way every inch of me aches for him—craves his stupid, electrifying touch.

"Fuck you," I whisper, trying my best to keep it together and stay strong as I teeter on the edge of an orgasm. "I beg for no man."

"You'll beg for me, Margo. I can promise you that." He kisses a warm trail down my neck as he continues to work my clit at a frustratingly slow pace. "I can keep this up all night. How long do you think it'll be before you concede and I'm fucking you senseless right here on this very table? Hmmm?"

He pushes his thick finger inside me, causing me to moan. "Oh, God."

"Tell me how much you need me to fuck you. Beg, Margo. Let me own you."

He works his finger in and out, curving up at just the right spot each time to cause my entire body to tingle. I throw my head back and moan as I rub against the heel of his hand.

"Such a greedy girl." He teasingly nips my shoulder before whispering, "You know what I want to hear. Say it and I'll give you what you want."

My brain keeps telling me that I should fight him—that giving into him will show weakness—but my stupid body is all too willing and ready. I want him. I want him to do all the things he's promising to me. I want him to make me feel good.

His thumb flicks over my clit, and I whimper.

Oh. My. God. This is more than I can handle. How in the hell am I supposed to resist him when he has me teetering on the edge so quickly?

"I'm waiting, Margo," he growls.

His demanding words cause me to shiver, and combined with how damn good he's making me feel with his hand, I'm willing to do just about anything he asks in the heat of the moment.

I snap my eyes open and bite my lip. "Please."

"Please, *what?*" he probes as he circles his thumb around my throbbing nub.

"Fuck me, please. Make me come." The begging tone of my voice appalls me, but I know that my brain has completely allowed my body to take control here. Desire clouds me to the point that I can barely think straight, let alone worry about how embarrassed I should be for begging this man for what I want.

"Good girl." Alexander bites his lip as he brings his hands up to cup my face so he can gaze deep into my eyes. "I've wanted to taste you ever since you stepped foot into my office."

His words make me shiver again with excitement.

He lightly kisses my lips. "I'm going to make you come so hard that you won't even remember your own name."

Alexander steps back and begins unbuttoning his shirt, and my fingers itch to help push it open so I can see his body, but my wrists remain shackled, limiting my movement. If I'm being honest, I've imagined what he'd look like naked more than a few hundred times. I bite my lip as his perfectly sculpted abs come into view when he drops his white dress shirt onto the floor.

Holy Mary mother of Joseph! Alexander's body is better than I imagined in my wildest dreams. His chest definition exceeds that of the most lickable men in magazines, not to mention he has biceps that last for days and the sexy 'V' cut into his hips that dips down into his pants.

I think I'm about to lose my mind. Can this man be any hotter?

He smirks when I don't take my eyes off him. "Just think . . . you haven't even seen the best part of me yet."

This man is absolutely wicked and entirely too sexy for his own good. He's the perfect example of a man who knows what he's blessed with and isn't afraid to be cocky about it. Confidence is such a turn on.

Almost like a strip tease, he unzips his pants and then shoves them down, along with his boxer-briefs, leaving them in a pile on the floor. My eyes widen at the sight of his completely naked body. He wasn't kidding when he said that he had a big cock. I'm not one who typically refers to a man's appendage as beautiful, but that's exactly what Alexander King's penis is. It stands proud in all its silky glory, and my fingers ache to touch it.

King turns to the cabinet and grabs a condom before opening a package containing a small silver bullet vibrator. After testing to make sure the vibrator works, he stalks toward me with both items. "There are a lot of toys in there. Do you think we should try them all?"

The thought of my body as his playground long enough to test out everything on those shelves causes me to shudder. I don't think I'll be able to handle it. I'm nearly ready to combust, and he's barely touched me. There's no way I'd survive.

Alexander sets the condom down and then presses his lips to mine. "Relax, Margo. Tonight's all about you. I won't do anything you don't want me to. You can tell me to stop anytime you'd like."

I want to scream out for him just to touch me again. No one has ever left me teetering on the verge of an orgasm for so long before. This man is about to drive me insane.

His tongue seeks entrance into my mouth, and I melt into him. "Spread your legs." I do exactly what he asks and watch as he kisses a trail down my body, throwing my legs over both shoulders as he drops to his knees. He grabs my ass, yanking my pussy closer to his mouth.

His tongue flicking across my clit sends an electric surge through me and I hiss. "Jesus."

"No, baby, it's just me," he murmurs before he pushes a finger inside me and licks my slick folds. "Mmmm. You taste just as delicious as I expected."

Alexander continues to work me into a frenzy, and the urge to reach out and grab a handful of his thick hair to hold him against me is strong, but my bound arms won't allow it. The heat of his tongue against my throbbing clit is almost more than I can handle. All I can do is lie on this table, exposed, and wait on his mercy. Only he can give me the pleasure that I desire to calm this ache building inside me.

The sound of the vibrator echoes around the room. Relief floods me because I know the moment he touches my clit with it, I'll finally be able to come. I hold my breath as he traces the outside of my lips with it, but he's careful to steer clear of where I need the sensation the most.

My head drops back as he kisses the inside of my thigh. I need him in me, filling me, to cure this burning desire that's rocking me to the core.

"Alexander . . ." His name comes out in a breathy whisper, as he presses the vibrator into my entrance. "I'm so close. Please."

"Told you that you'd beg." His gray eyes look up at me, and I can tell he's smiling, but it's impossible for me to fire back a snarky comment. The next thing I know, he's licking and sucking my clit like it's his only job in the world while he continues to use the toy.

My pussy has never been this stimulated, and it's pushing me to the edge already.

"Oh. My God. That's it. Keep going," I plead.

Both legs resting on his shoulders begin shaking uncontrollably and an intense tingle erupts in my core and then spreads over every inch of my body. I squeeze my eyes shut and I swear to God that I see fireworks as I come hard just like he promised. My entire body jerks as I scream out his name, but he keeps going, prolonging my pleasure to the point that it feels so good that it actually hurts.

Just when I don't think I can take another second, he stops his delicious torture and stands as he switches off the vibrator.

With quick movements, he releases both of my wrists from the shackles before pulling them one at a time to his mouth. He inhales deeply like he's trying to commit my scent to memory as he presses soft kisses to my flesh.

He stares down at me with a grin. "I love seeing that satisfied look on your face but don't get too comfortable. We're just getting started."

Oh, my.

My heart flutters with anticipation. If this was just the appetizer, dinner might damn near kill me.

He threads his fingers into my hair and pulls me into a deep kiss, allowing me to taste myself on him. This kiss makes me feel so desired that, for a moment, I can't imagine why I refused his advances. I should've allowed this to happen from the first moment he offered to fuck me.

He pulls back and stares into my eyes. "Stay."

The warning that flashes in his eyes tells me that disobeying his command is not an option. I still need him like crazy so I don't even debate not doing as he says.

I find myself biting my lip as I stare after Alexander as he makes his way back over to the toy shelf. His ass is divine. It's round with just the right amount of bubble, and I just want to get my hands on it. Some women are all about the arms, others the backs, but my weakness is a toned male booty. Alexander's is so tight that I bet you could bounce quarters off that thing.

My eyes roam over the well-defined muscles of his back as they stretch and move while he pokes around at all the other items on the shelf.

There's a glimmer in his gray eyes as he turns to me with a blindfold in one hand and a riding crop in the other.

I shake my head as he begins to stalk toward me. "No. You are not tying me up and spanking me. That's so fucking cliché."

That cocky smirk returns, making him even more fucking attractive. "How can millions of people be wrong about the enjoyment of the combination?"

I fold my arms. "What some people find pleasurable is just wrong then."

"How do you know that's true? I bet you've never even tried it." He raises one eyebrow in challenge.

"I . . ." I what? There's no defense here, considering he's right. Dammit, I hate that.

Alexander smiles. "Thought so. Off the table."

"Alexander . . ."

"Off the table." The authority in his voice rings around the small room.

He's so damn bossy. If I still weren't horny as hell, I would tell him to go take a flying fucking leap, but seeing as how I've come this far, I might as well play along.

My pride has already been tossed out the window. What else do I have to lose?

I hop off the table and train my eyes on Alexander as he closes the distance between us. "What now?"

"Close your eyes." With gentle hands, he covers my eyes with the black mask. "I've always heard that if you take away one sense that it will heighten the others. Let's test that theory, shall we?"

The warmth of his hands sliding down my body causes my mouth to drift open. The tease of his skin on mine has my body in overdrive. When his hands grip my hips, he spins me around and bends me over the table that I was just chained to.

"Grab the other side of the table and don't you dare let go."

A lump in my throat builds as the image of the crop flashes in my brain. This man is about to spank my bare ass. I should stop this—tell him this isn't happening—but I can't bring myself to do it.

While the logical part of my brain is screaming at me to end this and stand my ground and remember that Alexander King is the enemy, another part is squealing with delight as it awaits the delicious torture that he's about to inflict.

Before I have too much time to think about it, the distinct snap of something being hit sounds, and almost instantly, there's a small tingle on my right butt cheek.

"Hurt?" he asks with an inflection in his voice that implies his curiosity.

"No," I answer honestly. "But—"

He doesn't give me time to further protest. The second swat comes just as unexpected as the first.

"Ah . . ." A cry slips from my lips. It isn't one of pain, but of pleasure, and that surprises me.

Stupid traitorous body. I can't believe it's actually enjoying this.

"You liked that one, didn't you? Another?"

No.

"Yes!" I hiss.

My stupid body has completely taken over now.

Smack.

Then comes the sweet burn that follows just like the last two times, only this time was a little harder.

I toss my head back and moan.

Smack.

This one wakes me up as pain sears through me.

"Ah. Shit. That hurt." I yank off the blindfold and spin around to face him. "We're done."

Alexander shakes his head and then presses against me. "We are so far from done, Margo. You are my greatest challenge—one I'm determined to conquer."

"You—" I start to tell him this is over, but at that very second, he rakes his teeth over his bottom lip, and all I can think about is having that mouth on me again.

Without invitation, I throw my arms around him and attack him with my lips. There's no resistance from him because suddenly Alexander's hands are everywhere, tracing, teasing, and exploring every inch of me. It's like he can't get enough of me and I love the way that he makes me feel.

I'd be lying to myself if I say I haven't wanted this with him since the first time he threatened to fuck me. No man has ever aroused me this much. His take-charge attitude draws me in. It's animalistic and sexy—a complete turn-on.

Alexander King is hard to resist.

"You don't know how hard it was for me to be patient. I feel like I've waited a lifetime to have you just like this. I've even had dreams about tasting you," he growls. "You're exactly my favorite type of woman, and I can't wait to get my cock deep in that sweet pussy of yours."

His naughty words make my blood pump even faster.

He slides his hand between us and flicks my still throbbing clit. "Alexander . . ." I say his name almost like a whisper.

"Do you want me inside you?"

I throw my head back and moan as he continues to tease me. "Yessssss!"

"Then tell me, baby. I want to hear some naughty words come out of that beautiful mouth."

"I . . ." I pause. God, I so want this. I just hate the fact that he's asking me to beg, and what's worse is that I'm so turned on by him that I'd just about say anything he damn near wants. I need the relief that only he can bring me.

Alexander licks my top lip. "Say it, Margo."

I close my eyes but quickly reopen them so he knows I mean what I say. "Fuck me."

A devilish smile creeps onto his face. "I knew you were a naughty girl deep down."

He kneads my breasts while rubbing the tip of his cock against my clit as he continues to study my face. He reaches for the condom, and I seize the opportunity to wrap my hand around his cock and stroke him while he opens the wrapper.

He licks his lips and watches me work him. "Your hands on me feel so good." He hands me the thin piece of rubber. "You do it since you're so good with your hands."

I pinch the tip as I roll it down his thick cock. Pure lust fills Alexander's gray eyes are they roam over my naked body. His mouth drifts open when I spread my legs wider for him.

This man has me completely turned on, and I'm doing things that I normally wouldn't do.

"I'm such a fucking bastard for taking you like this. It's not right considering our situation, but I can't seem to stop myself. You are a very desirable woman, Margo Buchanan." Alexander leans down and kisses me again.

My toes curl inside my stilettos as I wrap my legs around his waist, pushing him toward my entrance. "I'd be lying if I said I didn't want you too."

A low growl emits from his throat as he penetrates me with the head of his cock. "Holy fuck! I wasn't expecting you to be so fucking tight. Amazing."

I slide my hand up his back. "I won't break. I don't want you to be gentle. I want you to fuck me and make it count."

Alexander bites my bottom lip and pushes his shaft inside of me all the way down to the base. He pulls back and then slides into me again.

I whimper wanting him to move faster inside me.

"Patience, baby. You feel so fucking good. If I don't go slowly this will be over before either of us is ready."

He grabs my waist and picks up the pace, pumping into me faster and harder. Sweat slicks his back as the slapping of our skin echoes around the room. I stare up at his face, surprised to find his gaze on mine. It's like he's trying to commit my face to memory as he fucks my brains out.

"Mmmm yeah. So fucking perfect. Sweetest pussy I've ever had." The words tumble from his lips and knowing that he's feeling just as good as I am causes another orgasm to rip through me.

"Alexander!" I cry as he works me into a frenzy.

"Oh. Oh. I'm coming. Oh, God," I moan as my body erupts in complete euphoria.

His movements become more rigid and intense as he works hard to find his own release.

"Goddamn, baby. Shit," he says before he growls as a shudder tears through him as he comes hard.

He buries his head in the crook of my neck. Both of us still breathing hard and he's still buried deep. "That was . . . fuck, that was amazing."

I smile as I twirl a wild strand of hair poking out from his head. "I agree."

Alexander raises his head and looks me in the eye. "I don't know how in the hell I'm supposed to remain strictly professional with you now. You're fucking addictive. I already want to do that again."

I close my eyes as the realization of what just happened between us hits. "This is going to complicate the hell out of things."

He nods. "Yes, but we're going to have to find a way to figure things out and coexist. We still have a business deal to get through."

The reminder of why we're actually here is like a splash of cold water on the face. No matter how amazing sex with Alexander King is, it can never happen again.

Chapter X
MR. YAMADA

Margo

I study myself in the mirror of this ridiculous hotel suite and wonder if anyone can tell that this is the face of a woman who just fucked her boss?

Shit.

I'm not sure what in the hell just came over me. One minute I was in the hallway completely composed and fending off his advances, and then the next thing I know we're kissing and I instigated his advances.

The moment he put his hands on me in the sex room, I lost it. They were so strong, so sure and felt too damn good. It was amazing for once to have a man who wasn't afraid to take control and pull me outside my rigid box. I would've never allowed a man to do the things that he did to me—restraints—but Alexander's forwardness and sex appeal got to me. I gave in during a moment of weakness and became just another easy lay for him, giving him full control. I've never experienced that, and if I'm being honest, it was very liberating.

I just hate that it was Alexander King. He's supposed to be my mortal enemy. Not the man who opened me up to exploration and a sexual revolution.

What in the hell am I going to do now?

A knock on the door startles me out of my thoughts. "Margo? Are you ready?"

I smooth my hair away from my face but don't dare open the door. I'm not ready to face Alexander just yet. "For what?"

"It's nearly two. I'm scheduled to meet with my contact at the pool. I'll wait for you if you're nearly finished getting ready," he says, and it instantly causes my shoulders to slump.

I stare down at my still nude body wrapped in a fluffy white hotel towel. "Go ahead without me. I'll be down in a bit."

"Margo . . ." There's hesitation in his voice. "Are you okay? You sound off."

I don't answer because I can't find the right words to express the things going through my mind. On one hand, I'm feeling amazing because I've just had the most mind-blowing sexual experience, but on the other, I'm completely torn in a way I didn't expect. Sadness for the loss of something that I know will never happen again. Being with Alexander had to be a one-time thing. It can never happen again. Sleeping with him was never part of the plan. I don't do random sex. My heart gets too invested, and I refuse to be just another notch in Alexander King's insanely long bedpost.

"Margo?" When I still don't bother to answer, the handle of the bathroom door rotates just before it swings open, revealing a shirtless Alexander wearing a pair of black swimming trunks.

"I didn't say that you could come in here," I scold him and then tighten the towel around me.

He tilts his head, and his gorgeous gray eyes bore into me. "I thought we were long past formalities at this point."

A shiver shoots down my spine. "Just because we've seen each other naked and . . ."

He lifts his eyebrows and finishes my sentence for me. "Fucked?"

I straighten my shoulders. "Yes. That. It doesn't mean that it's going to happen again or that things are suddenly different between us."

Alexander pulls his plump, bitable lips into a tight line. "So you want to just forget it ever happened and go right back to hating each other?"

I nod. "That's exactly what I want."

He lets out an exasperated sigh before running his hand down the back of his neck. "Fine. Then get your ass ready and get down to the pool. We have business to attend to."

I flinch at the sudden change in the tone of his voice, but I like that he's in agreement and doing exactly as I ask. When I open my mouth to tell him to fuck off and that I'd be down when I'm good and ready, I quickly close it when I see a flash of pain in his eyes before he turns and walks out of the bathroom.

I sigh the moment I hear the door slam when he leaves the suite.

This situation is all kinds of fucked up.

After getting myself together after a quick shower, I make my way down to the pool party that the Hard Rock calls Rehab. The scene before me causes me to raise my eyebrows. This place is something straight out of the Spring Break handbook. There are bodies everywhere—all of them dancing to the techno beat spun by the DJ.

This is seriously where King is meeting a business contact? Good luck talking business out here.

When I get through security, I merge into the crowd. Several pairs of hungry male eyes watch me intently as I pass by, and suddenly I wish I would've let Alexander wait on me. I don't like feeling like a piece of meat on display.

One dark-haired man with a set of toned abs and wide smile grabs my wrist as I pass by. "Damn! You've got the nicest set of tits I've seen all day."

I fight the urge to smack him in the face because I know that technically I'm out here for business purposes and getting arrested for assault wouldn't be a good look.

"Not interested." I attempt to twist out of his grasp, but there's no such luck.

The man tightens his hold and attempts to jerk me against his chest. "Let me feel those titties on me."

"Get off me!" I shove my arms between us and push with all my might, but he's too big and I can't force him off.

"Play nice, baby," he says, and the distinct smell of beer wafts into my face.

Before I have a chance to say anything else, the man flies back and Alexander steps between us. Alexander's hands ball into fists at his side as his entire body tenses.

"If you know what's good for you, you'll walk away. Now." The low growl in Alexander's voice emits such a warning that the man instantly throws his hands up in surrender and backs away without another word.

Alexander stands still, shielding me until he's sure the man is gone, and I have to admit that I'm grateful for his presence.

He slowly turns toward me. "You all right?"

I nod. "Yes. Thank you for that. I don't know what I would've done if you hadn't been here."

"Don't worry, Margo. Nobody will dare touch you while I'm around."

His confident words cause butterflies to erupt in my belly. It makes me feel safe knowing that he's looking out for me.

"Oh, shit. Did you see that?" The voice comes from a small Asian man who looks like he's straight out of a rap video with his gold chains and baseball cap. He slaps Alexander's shoulder and laughs. "Dat madafucka just got punked. I think he shit his pants. He better not come back for seconds because Yamada might just have to step in and he doesn't want any of this."

Alexander rolls his eyes and then turns toward the man. "Next time he's all yours, big guy."

The man turns toward me and lowers the gold-rimmed sunglasses down the bridge of his nose. His dark eyes drink me in from head to toe before he flicks his gaze in Alexander's direction. "Are you with dis fine piece?"

Alexander sighs. "Yamada, this is Margo Buchanan. She's my assistant."

"I bet." Yamada laughs and then pushes his glasses back over his eyes. "Just like old times, King. You bring all the fly honeys to the party."

That takes me back. Old times? It sounds like Alexander's relationship with Yamada goes far beyond a business one. How in the hell am I supposed to possibly find a way to infiltrate their business relationship if they are as good of friends as they seem to be?

"Don't look so serious, Dime Piece," Yamada says to me. "This is a party. Lighten up. We need to dance."

My mouth gapes open as I look at Alexander, but he's no help. He simply shrugs. "There's no stopping him when he's on a mission to party. Just go with it."

Yamada grabs my hand. "Come with Yamada. I'll show you a good time."

I glance back at Alexander while this odd little man leads me along, and he just simply grins and waves before the crowd swallows him up.

"Why do you keep referring to yourself in the third person?" I complain as he weaves us through the crowd.

He turns toward me, pulling the sunglasses down the bridge of his nose and peering at me over the top of them again with an expression that I can only describe as dumbfounded. "Because that's what all the badass madafakas do."

For a split second, I don't know if he's actually serious or not, but when he winks at me, I can't hold back a chuckle.

Yamada smiles, clearly pleased with my lightened mood, and then pushes his sunglasses back up. "Now that's a killer smile. Let's go shake it so I can show off that the hottest chick in this place is grinding on me."

This man was so not what I was expecting when I imagined coming out here to meet Alexander's business contact. I guess what I expected was a man that was, well, something more along the lines of my father—an accomplished older man.

Instead, I get a younger guy who's busy twerking in front of me at a crowded pool party.

I'm not sure I can take this guy seriously when it comes to anything business related, but he seems to be a damn good time. I'm going to have to rethink how I'm going to get in good with this man. For now, I'm going to dance because that seems like what he wants to do.

Yamada pops up and faces me. "Now that we're alone, we can talk."

I'm still dancing in time to the beat when I ask, "About what?"

"How long you know King?"

"Not long, but I've always known of him. Manhattan isn't as big of a place as people think." I tuck a loose strand of my dark hair behind my ear and figure this is my chance to get a little information too. "You two seem close. How did you meet?"

"In college," he answers before doing a spin. "I met him when I came to America to study. He was floored by my awesomeness, and we've been friends ever since."

"Wow," I say, honestly surprised. "That's cool that you two have stayed in touch."

He shrugs. "When Yamada makes a friend, it's for life, and now we're business partners."

We dance for a few more beats before he asks, "You fuck him yet, or does Yamada still have a shot?"

My mouth drops open and my eyes widen.

"Aw, shit. You did. I can tell by the look on your face. That's okay, you're only the second woman King has ever been able to beat Yamada to."

That piques my curiosity. "Who was the other?"

"Jess," Yamada answers. "His girlfriend from college. You know, the bitch who screwed him over and broke his heart."

I raise my eyebrows. "I didn't think he had one of those."

Yamada tilts his head. "What? A heart?"

I nod and keep dancing with him.

He shakes his head in response. "You obviously don't know him then, because he has one of the biggest hearts I've ever seen. I call him a pussy all the time for wearing it on his sleeve like a bitch. He needs to toughen up."

Little does Yamada know, Alexander King has done an excellent job of making me, along with most of the women on the Upper East Side, believe that he's a ruthless prick. I think I know him a little better than Yamada at this point.

"I think he's plenty tough. Matter of fact, I think he's a pompous ass," I admit.

Yamada throws his head back in a fit of laughter. "I like you. You and Yamada will get along just fine."

I glance over at Alexander, who has found a seat at one of the bars. It's like I can feel his eyes on me, studying every move I make. I'm positive that pushing him away like I did earlier was the best choice for my sanity, not to mention my heart, but it doesn't stop my stupid body from being drawn to him. It's going to be a lot harder to ignore his advances now, especially since I know what it's like to be with him. It'll be difficult to turn down those intense promises of pleasure because he does a damn fine job of delivering.

I spend the rest of the afternoon dancing and drinking with Yamada, while my brain works on trying to figure out the complex puzzle that is Alexander King—a puzzle that according to Yamada, I don't have the first fucking clue about.

Chapter **XI**
ROUND TWO

Alexander

I lay in the middle bed of this crazy room, trying to relax. I haven't even had the energy to change out of my board shorts or throw on a shirt. Hanging out at Rehab all day and watching Margo while she pretended I didn't exist, was fucking brutal. The image of her spread out before me, moaning my name in ecstasy while she came stayed in the forefront of my mind. All I could think about was how much I wanted to experience that again. How I wanted to fuck her again. How I wanted my name on her lips as she loses all control.

It makes me hard right now just thinking about it.

But Margo wouldn't so much as give me the time of day. Instead, she spent the afternoon laughing at every joke Yamada told and ignored me. Even when I asked her a direct question, all I received were short one-word answers.

It sucks knowing the fact that I'll probably never have her again, which is completely fucked up considering who I am. I'm Alexander King. I'm not supposed to give a shit about women.

Perhaps fucking her was a bad idea because it sure as hell didn't get her off my brain. It did the complete fucking opposite. Now I can't think of anything else, and it's driving me insane.

The only logical thing I could do was drink—drink to forget.

"Alexander?" Margo's voice on the other side of the bedroom door pulls me away from my thoughts. "Are you nearly ready to leave for dinner?"

Fuck. I was out longer than I thought, but I'm still drunk. There's no way I'll be able to make it.

"I'm not going," I mutter loud enough for her to hear.

"But, you have to go. Yamada—"

"Will get over it," I finish for her. "Call him to cancel."

I roll onto my side and close my eyes, but the sound of my door flinging open and Margo's high heels clicking across the floor causes my eyes to snap open. "Margo? What are you—?"

Without permission, she leans over the bed, grabs my arm and yanks. "Come on. Get up. You can't cancel this meeting. I—"

Quickly I reach out and pull her down on the bed with me, causing her to shriek, not caring a bit if I wrinkle the bright-blue dress she's wearing. "You what? Need this meeting to try to get to know Yamada better?"

She squirms in my arms as she pushes against my chest. "Dammit, King, let me go. If you're not meeting with him, then I will."

"It's not going to work, Margo. You might as well stop trying. Yamada's *my* friend. He would never sell out on me. You're wasting your time."

She stops fighting for a split second and stares me in the eye. "I have to at least try. I have to at least go for what I want. Don't you understand that?"

Her words resonate with me so much. I've lived by the motto of getting what I want for years now. "More than you know."

She pushes me away and scrambles out of the bed. "I'm going. With or without you."

The clicking of her heels against the marble floor echoes around the room. I don't know where she thinks she's going, but she's not going to meet with my contact alone. No way in hell will I allow that to happen.

I'm up in a flash, crossing the room, and the second she grabs the door handle, I wrap my fingers around her wrist. "You're not going anywhere."

Her back tenses as I press my chest against it. The feel of the heat of her skin is almost more than I can take. I clutch her hip with my other hand and pull her ass against my cock. I want her to feel how hard I am to show her that I want her again.

Her head falls back slightly, sending her floral scent swarming around me, and there's a pant in her voice. "Don't tell me what to do."

I swipe her hair to the side, exposing her smooth flesh, and then whisper in her ear. "I'm your boss, baby. You'll do as I say."

I press my lips against the soft skin under her ear before I playfully nip it, needing desperately for her to give in to me.

The tension in her body loosens as she leans into me. "Damn you. We can't . . . You said—"

I grin, knowing that she's about to fold. She's flustered and I'm about to work that to my advantage and not give her a chance to pull herself together and refuse me.

"Fuck what I said before." I can no longer resist the urge to taste her. My tongue darts out and I trail a line down from below her ear down to her shoulder. "I need to fuck you. I can't get the thought of how good your pussy felt wrapped around my cock out of my head."

I knead her tit through her blouse, and she whimpers. "I hate what you do to me."

"No, you don't." I spin her around to face me and then cage her against the wall with my body. "You love it. You crave this just as much as I do, but you won't allow yourself to admit it."

Her breathing picks up speed and her chest heaves. "No."

"No?" I raise an eyebrow as I lean in and lick her top lip, causing her to shudder. "If you really meant that, then you wouldn't react so much when I touch you."

"You're such an egotistical asshole," she murmurs, but I can tell it's just her defense mechanism in full effect trying to fucking fight me tooth and nail.

"Come on, Margo." I reach down, grabbing behind her right knee, and hitch it around my hip. "I'm damn good at everything I do. Besides, being cocky is part of my charm. You know I'm the best lay you've ever had."

My heart thunders in my chest. She fits against me perfectly. I slide my hands down her back and rest them on her hips, where they rest so comfortably it's like they were made for my hands to hold on to. I have to have her again—experience the feeling of euphoria one more time.

My cock is rock hard in my shorts and it's driving me out of my mind knowing that only two thin pieces of fabric are holding me back from fucking Margo's brains out right here against this door. I grind myself against her and her mouth drops open.

I reach between us and stroke her clit through the silk panties she's wearing. "Mmm. So wet. This makes my mouth fucking water."

"What are you doing to me?" She moans. "I'm usually in control."

"That's what makes this exciting—letting go. No matter how much you try to fight it, you want me inside you just as much as I want to be there. Look at how your body reacts." I apply more pressure as I continue my slow teasing circles that won't bring her anywhere near climax. Her head falls back and bumps against the door as her fingers grip my biceps so tight I'm sure her nails will leave imprints.

"Alexander . . ." There's a plea in her voice. "We shouldn't. This is wrong."

I lean in so close that I can feel the warmth of her breath on my face. "Nothing about pleasure is wrong, Margo. I know that you hate me, but say yes to this. I need to have you at least one more time and then, I swear, I'll never ask again."

She bites her bottom lip as she debates my request while I continue to work my thumb against her. She won't be able to say no to this—say no to me.

Margo moans and then licks her lips. "This changes nothing between us. We are still enemies, and I plan to find a way to get my father's company back from you."

A grin spreads across my face as I realize that I've won. "I'd be disappointed if you didn't try."

My eyes drift down to her pouty lips and then back up to refocus on her gaze. There's hesitation in her eyes mixed with a hint of lust.

My fingertips find their way to her face, where they trace the smooth skin along her jaw. My cock throbs in anticipation. This woman seems to have that effect on me. "Margo—"

"Just shut up and kiss me before I change my mind," she whispers.

She doesn't have to tell me twice. I crush my lips into hers and my hands frantically begin to unzip her dress.

We shouldn't be doing this. We both know it. This . . . it's not good for business, but I just can't seem to fucking help myself. I've never wanted a woman so much that I was willing to throw all the fucking rules out the window just to have her. It's like none of it matters—everything I've worked for—when I'm around her. She drives me out of my mind with that smart mouth of hers—the way she stands up to me and tells me exactly what's on her mind. She's upfront—that's a trait to be admired because it's rarely seen anymore.

"Fuck. I want you," I tell her before I shove the dress off her shoulders and it falls in a pool around her feet. I deepen our kiss, loving the delicious taste. "So fucking bad it hurts."

My hungry eyes trail over every inch of her body. The black bra and matching satin panties are almost more than I can handle. I need them off.

Now.

When I unhook her bra, her puckered nipples rub against my solid chest. It makes me even more eager now that she's pressed against me. I don't think I can take my time with her. I want her too much. Without permission, I rip the thin fabric and toss it to the floor before I go back to attacking her lips. I fully expect Margo to yell at me for destroying yet another pair of her underwear, but she doesn't. She's just as caught up in this kiss as I am and only responds by shoving my shorts down. My cock springs free and it presses against her bare flesh. Margo throws her hands into my hair and holds me in place as our tongues tangle together.

I knew she wanted this just as much as I do.

Margo whimpers as my finger finds her swollen clit again for a moment before it glides inside her. "Mmm, you're so turned on. Feeling just how ready you are makes me want to fuck you hard and fast."

She groans as I work my finger in and out of her. "Alexander . . ."

I love hearing my name spill from her lips. It's nearly enough to cause me to blow my load on the spot. I can't believe how fucking turned on I am from just knowing that I'm making her body feel so good.

Margo claws at my back as I work her into a frenzy. The only thing better than this will be when my cock replaces my finger and I pound her into submission. "Your pussy is so fucking greedy. Do you feel how it's milking my finger, begging for my cock?" My tongue darts out to taste her lips. "You're so ready for me. Do you want me to take you? Right here? Right Now?"

"Yes," she pants.

The way she's panting causes my balls to tighten. I like hearing her practically beg me for it because it means she's losing control just like I am. Uptight Margo would never beg me for anything, but horny Margo seems much more open to bending to my will.

I trail my nose against her jaw, inhaling the scent of her before I whisper in her ear, "If you want my cock inside you, ask me for it. Ask me to fuck you. I need to hear you say it."

My thumb rubs circles over her swollen clit and her head falls back, bumping against the door. "Oh, so close."

"Say it," I command. "Ask me, and I'll make you feel so fucking good."

"Fuck me, Alexander," Margo says in a breathy voice.

I nibble on her bottom lip. "Good girl."

I hoist her up against the wall, unable to stop myself and press my bare shaft against her wet pussy. "I can't wait another fucking second."

My own breath catches the moment my bare cock glides into her warmth, allowing it to wrap around me. Her pussy squeezes every inch of my cock as I push in balls deep.

"Holy fuck," I say against her mouth. "You feel so fucking good."

I pull back slowly and then fill her again, giving her time to adjust to me. Margo whimpers against my lips, and I push into her one more time. The little noises she's making combined with how good she feels, are deadly. I won't be able to last. This time when I pull out of her I slam back in.

"Jesus!" Margo cries out. "Yes!"

Her cry only excites me more as I begin slamming into her. "Mmm, Margo. You like it hard, don't you? I knew you were a dirty girl."

I fuck her hard and fast against the door while she continues to claw at my back and scream out with delight. It feels so fucking good, and it doesn't take long for my balls to tighten.

"Oh, Alexander. Oh, God. I'm coming. Don't stop! Don't stop!" Margo cries out as she comes hard around my cock.

Watching her fall apart sends me over the edge and I pull out just in time to drop her legs to the ground and come all over her thighs. I pant hard as I lean my head against the wall over her right shoulder to catch my breath.

What in the holy fuck am I doing? I never fuck a woman more than once, and I for damn sure don't risk fucking one that could cost me billions of dollars. Why am I allowing this girl to get to me and fuck with my head? It's like I'm a fucking crack addict and she's the best hit I've ever had. I can't get enough, no matter what the cost.

I need to tell her to get the fuck out of this room and fire her ass. It's the only way I'll be able to make sure I don't slip up again.

I pull back and open my mouth, fully ready to turn back into a huge asshole, but the sight of Margo's bright-blue eyes narrowed at me causes me to snap it shut. I wasn't expecting that expression, considering I'd just given her one damn fine orgasm.

"You are such a bastard," she snaps.

I raise my eyebrows and pull back a bit. "Most women thank me for what I just did for you."

"Thank you?" She shakes her head and releases a bitter laugh. "Alexander, I should punch you in the face for ruining my Versace dress."

My gaze drops down to the floor, and I see her dress still in a pool by our feet only now it has my come on it from when I pulled out of her.

I smirk, unable to stop myself from finding a little humor in the situation. "Great sex requires sacrifice, and I'm afraid your dress paid the ultimate price."

"Ugh!" She growls as she shoves my shoulders back and steps away from me. "You're unbelievable." She bends over and snatches the dress off the floor. "From now on, stay the hell away from me. This will not be happening again."

I stare her down, meeting the challenge in her eyes. "Margo, don't kid yourself. If I want you again, all I have to do is touch you and you'll give in. Your body has already proven twice that it can't resist me."

She pulls her lips into a tight line. "Never. Again. Alexander, do you hear me? This—whatever it was—is over. Done. When we get back to New York, I'm going to figure out a way to bury you. You can count on it."

I give her my most wicked smile, showing her that her threats mean nothing to me. "I look forward to your sweet ass attempting to destroy me."

Her nostrils flare and I can tell she wants nothing more than to lay into me. Instead, she takes a deep breath, squares her shoulders, and flips me the middle finger.

I laugh and then chide, "Mature."

Margo jerks open the door while she's still bare ass naked. "Fuck you."

"I thought you just said we weren't doing that again?" I tease.

"You . . . I . . . Ugh!" That's all she manages to get out before storming out in nothing but her stilettos and slamming the door behind her.

I drop my head into my hand and then run it over the top of my head. What the actual fuck just happened? That spiraled out of control quickly and I didn't even have to say a damn word. I guess I don't have to ask her to stay away from me, after all.

The sharp ring of my cell cuts across the otherwise quiet room, not giving me the time to think about what in the hell just happened. I pull my shorts back up before walking over to the nightstand and smiling as I see the name of the caller flash across the screen.

"King," I answer.

"Where are you, asshole? Yamada's been waiting on you all night. First you blow off dinner and now drinks at the bar?" There's irritation in his voice.

"Look, man, I'm sorry. I had too much to drink today so I'm staying in for the night, but I promise tomorrow we'll party."

I know that I flew out here to spend the weekend with him and secure the deal with our companies for the Buchanan deal but going out to find random women to party with doesn't sound appealing.

"Okay. Fine. But, I'm holding you to tomorrow. You better bring your 'A' game because it's going to be Yamada and King just like the old days. Getting' bitches and gettin' laid."

I chuckle. "You got it, buddy. Tomorrow, Vegas better watch out."

"Make sure you bring Dime Piece back with you. She's got a rockin' body, and I wouldn't mind—"

"Goodnight, Yamada."

I quickly cut him off before he has a chance to finish whatever dirty thought was brewing in that twisted little mind of his. Besides, it pisses me off for some reason when he talks about how sexy Margo is. I know he's harmless, and I can't believe I'm admitting this, but the idea of another man looking at Margo makes me jealous as hell.

This is going to be a fucking problem.

Chapter XII
HOLY SHIT

Margo

Stupid. Stupid. Stupid. That's the word I've been scolding myself with since last night. I can't believe that I had sex with Alexander King . . . *again.* Even after I forbid myself from ever doing it again, the moment he put his hands on me in his room I was a goner.

I hate that the man has so much power over my body.

When he texted me early this morning to demand my presence in the common area of our suite for breakfast, I replied with a friendly fuck off. Not the most mature thing to do, I know. Normally, I play it cooler when dealing with assholes like Alexander, but for some strange reason, he's able to get under my skin like no one else and cause me to lose my typical level head.

I spent most of the day in my room with the door locked trying to figure out ways I could avoid Alexander while still maintaining a close presence to figure out a way to get between him and Yamada. From what little bit of background I know about their relationship, it seems that they go way back, but hopefully their bond has a weak point I can break into.

The hotel phone rings, pulling my attention away from my thoughts and I answer on the third ring. "Hello?"

"Dime Piece! Are you coming to my party tonight?" Yamada's upbeat voice laced with his heavy accent shoots across the line.

I lift my eyebrows. "Alexander didn't mention anything."

"King said you hate him right now and wouldn't come even if he asked, but I knew if Yamada invited you up to his penthouse, you couldn't turn that down."

I roll my eyes and laugh to myself. Yamada really is convinced that he's quite the ladies' man.

Yamada's also wrong about Alexander. Alexander didn't tell me about the party because he knew I would jump at the chance to spend a little one-on-one time to pick Yamada's brain. Alexander kept this from me on purpose. He knows how badly I want to talk with Yamada. Alexander wants to limit my access to the man who whill have a huge hand in the destruction of my father's company.

King has another thing coming if he thinks he can keep me from my main objective while we're here.

"So, are you coming or not?" Yamada asks.

I lift my chin. "I'm in. What time does it start?"

"It's already in full swing, so get your smokin' self up here. I'm in the Real World suite. I'll send my security down in thirty minutes to escort you up."

"I'll be ready," I tell him.

"Great. See you then, you sexy thing." I hear the smile in his voice, and I can't help shaking my head.

Out of every type of business partner I imagined Alexander King to have, Yamada was definitely unexpected.

When I pass through what I have officially dubbed 'The Room That Shall Not Be Named' on the way to the common area of the suite, I shudder the moment my eyes land on the table. The things that man did to my body on there are unspeakable in the best kinds of ways. It's hard to admit the man that you love to hate can make you feel so incredibly good.

A quick rap on the door makes me quicken my pace. I open the door and find two very large official looking men in black suits—one white guy with short buzzed blond hair and the other a light-skinned black man with braids—each of them at least six-foot-five or better because they dwarf me by at least a foot.

The man with braids gives me a polite smile. "Good evening, miss. We're here to escort you to Mr. Yamada's suite."

I nod stepping out into the hallway with them and closing the door behind me. The ride up in the elevator to Yamada's penthouse is quick, but I find myself fidgeting with the hem of my black dress, trying to squeeze an extra inch from the length to cover more thigh. This is the shortest one I brought, and suddenly, I wish I wouldn't have picked this one to wear to a place I know Alexander will be in attendance. I don't need the temptation of having him come on to me. Lord knows that I can't seem to resist his advances, so I need to make sure I steer clear and don't set myself up for another encounter with him.

When the elevator dings and the doors open, the men lead me down the hallway. They pause at a set of double doors and use their keycard to gain entrance into Yamada's suite. It doesn't surprise me that this suite is the biggest one in the hotel.

Wall to wall bodies fill the large space as music pumps through the air. People are dancing to the beat while sipping on drinks like the place is one of Vegas' hottest nightclubs. I follow the security team closely as we wind our way through the crowd. Yamada seems very eccentric and over-the-top, so this place totally fits him.

The crashing sound of bowling pins smashing into one another catches my attention, and I raise my eyebrows when I find a full-fledged bowling lane in the suite just a little ways down from the hot tub that's filled with bikini-clad women.

Turning the corner, I see a large white sectional crammed with people. My heart freezes in my chest the moment my eyes land on Alexander, who has two women strategically placed on either side of him. He hasn't spotted me just yet because I follow his line of sight and his gaze is fixed on Yamada, who is standing in front of him wearing a flat bill baseball cap turned sideways, low-riding jeans, and a white buttoned-down dress shirt that's undone to reveal a T-shirt underneath. Yamada seems to be telling a story of some sort because he's throwing his hands around causing Alexander to laugh. I stop in my tracks and just stare. It's the first time I've ever actually seen Alexander look relaxed and happy, and it's breathtaking. The casual outfit he has on of jeans and a T-shirt looks amazing. He's never looked more handsome, and from the outside looking in, he looks like a carefree spirit—one I wish I knew instead of the asshole I fucked . . . twice.

"Sir, Ms. Buchanan, as requested," the blond security guy says, interrupting Yamada's joke.

Alexander's eyes immediately snap in my direction, and the jovial expression that I was just admiring has completely been wiped off his face. His posture even changes and instead of leaning forward toward his friend, he relaxes back against the couch and throws his arms around the women on either side of him, pulling them snug against his sides.

My nostrils flare. That asshole. What's he trying to do—make me jealous? Ha! Well, I'll show him that it doesn't bother me one tiny bit.

I'm here for one reason: To get close to Yamada. I will not allow Alexander King to distract me no matter how ridiculous he looks draped over some random bottle-blondes.

Yamada turns to me and holds out his arms. "Dime Piece! I knew you wouldn't refuse Yamada! Come give Papa some love."

I hold back a laugh and an eye roll as I step into his embrace and hug the guy back. "This party is really something. Do you know all these people?"

Yamada pulls back and then places his hands on his hips as he surveys the filled space. "No, but the bitch—"

"Bitches love Yamada," Alexander cuts him off. "I'm sure you've told her that one already."

I curl my lip at Alexander. "He can tell me again if he wants. You shouldn't be a complete asshole and cut people off like that. It's rude, and you've got a bad habit of doing it."

Alexander's eyes narrow at me. He hates when I belittle him. This grumpy look he's giving me is the same one I get every time I tell him something he doesn't want to hear.

Yamada bursts out in a fit of laughter. "Yamada's in love. Any woman who stands up to King earns my respect." He grabs my arm. "Come on. Let's go get you a drink."

He pulls me through the crowd to where he has two bartenders working what appears to be a full bar. "What are you drinking?"

I bite my lower lip. "I don't typically drink, so just a diet soda or water would be fine."

Yamada tilts his head and stares at me like I've just sprouted wings. "What? Are you one of those Christian-y types or something?"

I shake my head. "No. I just like to keep my head on straight. People always seem to do crazy things when they drink."

The corner of Yamada's mouth lifts into a half smile. "That's kind of the point—to let loose and have some fun."

His words ring through my head and I think back on the phone conversation I had with my mother just before I boarded the plane. I did promise her that I would have at least one drink and not be a complete stiff while I was out here. What's the worst that can happen?

I push up to the bar and the cute dark-haired bartender looks my way with a smile on his face. "What can I get you?"

"Can I get a screwdriver?" I ask and the guy nods and gets to work making my order.

Yamada's smile widens. "That's the spirit." He turns toward the bartender. "Make that two. We're getting fucked up tonight!"

Three drinks later, Yamada and I are dancing to some crazy techno sounding song that I've never heard, but with all the alcohol coursing through my veins, I'm not bothered that I might look like an idiot.

Yamada sings along—complete with doing the rap to the song that completely comes out of nowhere. He flings his hands and points his fingers while spitting out the fast-paced words just like the guys do on the videos.

"You're pretty good at that," I lean in to tell him. "You should be a rapper or something."

He smiles. "That's exactly what Yamada's going to be, waiting for his one shot to be discovered."

"Why don't you make your own video and put it on YouTube or something? You have the money."

He nods. "Yamada might just do that while he's here in the states. Good thinkin,' Dime Piece. Beautiful and smart. No wonder you have King tripping all over himself."

I roll my eyes before I nod my head in the direction of the couch where we left Alexander sitting with the two women. "Clearly, he's not. He couldn't care less about me."

He puts his hand on my shoulder. "Don't let that show over there fool you. Trust me. The Barbie Twins are a cover—for his own benefit—to make you think that he's not thinking about you,when, in fact, he is. He just isn't ready to admit it to you or himself yet that he cares."

"You can't possibly know that."

"But I do," he assures me. "He warned me that you were off-limits."

I shake my head. "That's only because of my father. Alexander's afraid that I'm here to try to mess up the deal the two of you have going for parts of my Buchanan Industries."

"That's not it. Trust me. Alexander knows that nothing you could do would pull my loyalty away from him."

That hurts, knowing there's nothing I can do to make Yamada change his mind about my father's company. I guess it's time to face the facts. Alexander has won this war. It's not fair and it's wrong in so many ways, but there doesn't seem to be anything I can do to stop Yamada's company from making a deal with Alexander.

I sigh and drop my head. "I'm such an idiot. I'm a project to him—nothing more—and I'm stupid for letting him in my pants. I'm usually a lot smarter and don't allow myself to lose control. He said he was going to torture me until I quit. I guess fucking me and then showing me that I mean nothing to him is his tactic to get me to do that."

Yamada tips my chin back up with his bent index finger. "Don't discount yourself like that. The last girl King warned Yamada to stay away from was Jess, and he was madly in love with her. The guy turned into a jealous maniac whenever another man even thought about breathing in her direction. I haven't seen him act that way—all possessive and shit—toward another woman since then—not until this weekend with you, that is."

I furrow my brow. "What are you saying?"

Yamada sighs, and his eyes soften a bit. "He's different with you. King can be an asshole—everyone knows that—but you have to be able to see past all that to see the real him."

I glance over at Alexander, who is watching Yamada and me intently. His words about seeing the real Alexander waft through my head as I remember how happy Alexander looked when I first spotted him tonight. Is it possible for me to even get to know that guy? Would he ever be like that with me?

The short answer to that is no. It's never going to happen. Alexander sees me as the enemy and nothing is ever going to change that. For some reason knowing that fact causes my stomach to twist.

I take a deep breath. Being in this room while I break down can't happen. I won't allow Alexander King to see me cry. That implies weakness and I need to maintain a strong front when it comes to him.

"I'll be back," I tell Yamada before I take off in search of a restroom.

My eyes burn and I have no idea why in the hell I'm allowing the situation with Alexander to get to me at this very moment. Must be the damn liquor that's flowing through my veins. It's causing my emotions to surface at the most inopportune time.

When I finally find the bathroom, I rush through the door and place my hands on the counter. I close my eyes as I count down from ten to calm myself. Mother taught me as a little girl to do this when I felt my emotions getting out of check. It has always helped me to regain control and refocus on the situation with a level head.

"Three . . . Two . . . One . . ." I count aloud but the sound of the bathroom door opening causes my eyes to snap open. "Someone is in here."

"I know that." Alexander's deep voice cuts through the room as he closes the door and locks it, closing us in the tiny space together. "Are you okay?"

"I'm fine." I sigh as I stare at him through the mirror when he walks up behind me. "What are you doing in here?"

He raises one eyebrow. "Is it wrong that I came in to check on you? You've had a lot to drink. I wanted to make sure you weren't in here puking your guts out."

I turn to face him and fold my arms over my chest. "So what if I was. It's not like you care."

He flinches. "Do you really think that I'm that big of an asshole that I wouldn't come to check on you? While we're out here, you're my responsibility to keep safe."

"No. I'm not. I can take care of myself," I fire back.

"I'm aware that you're fully capable of handling yourself, but that doesn't mean that I don't . . ."

"Don't what?" I prod.

"Care, all right? I'd care if you were all alone in here sick. " He pinches the bridge of his nose and shuts his eyes for a brief second. "I'm not a dick all of the time."

"Just most of the time, then?" His omission causes me to smile. Maybe I need to give Yamada some credit. He might not be so far off the mark, after all.

Alexander shakes his head as he closes the distance between us and backs me up against the counter. He drags his teeth slowly over his bottom lip as he reaches up and cups my face. "Why can't I leave you alone?"

The question seems more rhetorical than directed at me, but I'm curious as well.

"Why didn't you come to breakfast this morning?" he asks as he stares into my eyes.

"I couldn't bear the thought of seeing you after last night. I was angry at myself for letting things go that far with you . . . again, after I promised myself that it wouldn't," I admit.

He nods like he fully understands where I'm coming from. "We really do need to try to stay away from each other."

I let out a shaky breath and try to pretend that being so close to him, feeling the warmth of his breath on my face isn't sending my body into overdrive. "Any idea how to make sure that happens?"

"Touching is a bad idea. It leads me to think about that sweet pussy of yours. And how good it feels when I'm inside you. We should avoid doing that if we don't want to end up fucking again, but that might be complicated." He traces my jaw with his thumb. "I've tasted your sweetness, and I know what I'd be missing out on by denying myself, and I never tell myself no if it's something that I really want."

I swallow hard as his gray eyes remain locked on me. "What are you saying?"

"I'm saying since I'm sure by now that you know there's no swaying Yamada away from me with whatever plan you came out here with, we might as well enjoy the rest of the weekend . . . and each other."

My brows furrow. "You want me to be your fuck buddy for the weekend?"

His shoulders rise in a noncommittal shrug. "If you must put a label on it, then yes. I want you to willingly give yourself to me for the weekend, whenever I want to fuck."

"No," I instantly respond and push him back a bit so that there's more space between us. Having him so close clouds my judgment. "I told you before we came out here to not expect me to be one of your paid whores. I don't work like that."

"Who said anything about paying you? You've fucked me twice already for free."

My nostrils flare as I pull back and smack him with all my might. "You're such a bastard."

The spot on his cheek where I made contact turns scarlet, and he raises his hand to rub the spot. "So that's a no then?"

I flip him off. "That's a hell fucking no."

I don't give him another minute to say anything else before I storm out of the bathroom. The party is still in full swing, but I don't feel like having fun anymore. I'm mad as hell. It's one thing to make a mistake by sleeping together, but it's an entirely different thing when he insinuates that I'm an easy slut.

That bastard will never get into these panties again.

Yamada stands in front me, blocking my path as I head toward the door. "Whoa there. Where are you running off to?"

"I'm going back to my room."

"Why?" Yamada asks. "King pissed you off, huh?"

"He's an asshole." It's all I can manage to say.

Yamada smiles. "He is, but you already knew that. He's testing you."

I flinch. "Testing me? For what?"

He shrugs. "To see how much of his bullshit you will put up with before you leave him. He's trying to push you away so that he doesn't have to open up to you. It's a defense mechanism. Every woman he's opened up to has left him." I stare at Yamada with my mouth agape, which only causes his smile to widen. "Come on, Dime Piece. Don't look so shocked. Yamada is not only devastatingly handsome with an amazing personality, but he's an intelligent madafucka too with a minor in psychology."

I stand there flabbergasted. "So you're saying that I should stay?"

"Yes," he answers. "Show him that he doesn't intimidate you, and that you'll stand your ground."

I sigh deeply. He's probably right. It's not like I'll never have to see Alexander again after we leave Vegas. I'm still his employee. I'll need to stand my ground and prepare myself for when I see him at work so that he knows that I'm not someone he can shove around and bend to his will.

"Okay, but I think I'm going to need another drink," I say.

"That's the spirit," Yamada praises before grabbing my hand and towing me back through the crowd. "I've got to take a leak. Go get that drink."

As soon as Yamada walks off, I step up to the bar and order a shot of tequila, needing to drink myself into oblivion if I'm going to coexist in the same room with Alexander.

I sense him before I feel him, and there's no question who has just flanked my side. Alexander's chest pushes against my arm. His spicy cologne fills my nose and my mouth waters.

Gah! Stop it! Even his damn scent is sexy.

"I'm surprised to find you still here," Alexander growls into my ear. "I figured you'd be holed up in your room down in our sex den."

I turn and level my stare with his. His eyes hold so many questions—ones I'm sure he's waiting for me to answer—but I'm not going to give him what he wants. Instead I decide to do a little teasing of my own. "Yamada's argument for me to stay was *very* compelling."

He obviously wasn't expecting that response because he raises both of his eyebrows and he licks his lips nervously. "And what, might I ask, did he say to you?"

I shrug. "That's between Yamada and me. We're really bonding, you know. I'm sure it won't be long now before he considers me a friend too and cuts my father a deal instead of you."

Instead of getting mad like I expect, Alexander chuckles. I grip the counter a little tighter than needed be to keep myself from smacking his condescending face yet again.

"Margo, I really wish you would stop trying to outdo me in everything. You'll eventually learn that I always win. It's silly for you to keep expelling energy on any other outcome. I get my way in all things."

I roll my eyes. "That's not possible. Everyone loses at some point or another."

Alexander smiles. "Not me."

"Well, neither do I," I say just as the bartender sets my shot down. I instantly pick it up and throw it back.

"Whoa. You might want to slow down there, lightweight, or you really will be throwing up later."

I scowl at him. "Don't tell me what to do. Besides, I can probably hold my liquor better than you can.

He smiles. "Is that so?"

I give him a curt nod. "Absolutely."

Okay, so maybe I was exaggerating a bit here, but I refuse to let him get the best of me.

"Well, you'll just have to prove that to me then." Alexander holds up five fingers to the bartender and then points down to my empty glass before looking back at me. "To make it fair since I'm quite a bit bigger than you, I'll drink two shots for every one of yours."

The bartender sets five tequila-filled shots in front of us, and Alexander does two of them immediately and then flips the glasses upside down on the counter before pushing another shot over to me. "Now we're even. Ready to prove me right? First one to puke, loses."

"You're on." I pick up one of the shots and tip it back with ease. "Hope you're prepared for that pride of yours to get crushed when I kick your overconfident ass."

Alexander takes the other two shots, but his eyes stay trained on me the entire time. "And just so you know, I'm not one of those romantic bastards who will hold back your hair when you're praying to the porcelain god."

I wrinkle my nose at him. "I don't plan on doing that anytime soon."

The sound of bowling pins falling catches Alexander's attention and his eyes light up. "Come on. Let me kick your ass at bowling too."

After three games of bowling, I find myself genuinely having a good time hanging out with Alexander. The more we drank, the more fun I had, even though I'll never admit that to him. He's actually pretty entertaining when he drops the world's biggest prick act.

"We need more drinks," Alexander announces after he bowls the last ball, winning his second game out of the three we played. "I believe I just won our little competition. I'll be back. Let me know if you want me to kick your ass again when I get back."

I laugh, staring after him as he walks away to get more drinks. His ass in the dark-washed jeans he's wearing looks amazing.

I plop down in the chair as I wait on Alexander to bring the drinks, and Yamada appears in front of me. "Looks like someone's having fun now."

I shake my head and attempt to scowl, but a smile keeps popping up. "No. I'm having zero fun."

Yamada's expression is one of disbelief as he sits down next to me. "Then what was all the laughing Yamada heard over here?"

"Oh, that." I wave him off dismissively. "That was just Alexander wiggling his ass a little before he took every shot to distract me. It was so ridiculous that I couldn't help laughing."

"Shot number seven for the lady and thirteen and fourteen for me," Alexander says as he approaches Yamada and me with three shots.

Everything around me is a little cloudy and I know all the liquor is messing with me big time, but I'm doing my best to pretend that it's not.

"The two of you are going to regret this tomorrow," Yamada says in sympathy as Alexander and I clink our glasses together and down the liquid. "Everyone's leaving and Yamada is ready to go out on the town. Let's find another place to party and find trouble."

"I'm game," Alexander says as he extends his hand to me.

"Why not," I answer taking his hand and allowing him to help me up.

The moment I'm on my feet, Alexander wraps his strong arms around me and buries his face in my hair, inhaling deeply. "You smell so fucking good. Are you sure you want to go out? We could just go back to our suite . . ."

Heat instantly pulses through me while my body craves nothing more than to go to our room to go crazy on each other. But even in my drunken state, I know that's a bad idea.

I press my hand against his chest. "No. We're going out."

Alexander sighs and presses his lips to the sensitive flesh just below my ear. "If that's what you want. But—" he pulls away, but reaches down and threads his large fingers through mine and grins "—I'm not letting go of you tonight. No other man is going to have you if I can't."

My heart does a double thump against my ribcage as Alexander leads me out of the penthouse behind Yamada. That might be the nicest and most romantic thing anyone's ever said to me. Who knew Alexander King was capable of that?

The sound of the maids running the vacuum somewhere in the hallway wakes me and my head instantly begins to throb. Thank God for heavy hotel curtains that block out the sun, but I still don't dare open up my eyes.

The bed I'm in bounces a little and I instantly freeze. I pull in a deep breath through my nose to steady myself and peel open one eye to spot a shirtless Alexander King sprawled out next to me.

I grimace and cover my face with my hands.

Oh. My. God. How could I let this happen?

I continue to mentally scold myself as I try to remember exactly what happened last night, but everything is such a blur. The last thing I remember was Alexander winning at bowling and him whispering possessively in my ear that made my knees a little weak and then leaving to go to a club. That's it.

Hopefully, we just fell asleep in the same bed together. I lift the covers and stare down at my completely naked body. I'm guessing we had some hot, sweaty sex again. But I was too drunk to remember it and too drunk to force my body to listen to my head and not give in and fuck this man again.

Shit.

I grab the blanket with my left hand to pull it back so I can slip out of this bed before he wakes up. A single ray of sunlight cuts through the small opening in the curtain and shines on my hand, causing a brilliant sparkle to catch my attention.

I stare down at my hand and my mouth falls open as I spot a diamond wedding band on my ring finger.

"Holy shit!" I yell.

What in the holy hell is going on? My eyes focus on the ring as I desperately try to remember how this got on my finger last night because it's definitely not a gag ring judging by the size of this thing. It's a fucking monster and looks pretty real to me.

Alexander rolls over and rubs his face while he asks in a groggy voice, "What the fuck?"

My eyes practically bulge out of their sockets when I notice Alexander's left hand has a ring on it too. I grab his hand and yank it closer to my face to inspect it. The sound of screams echo around the room, and it takes a second for me to register that it's me who's doing it.

"Ah. Shit, Margo. My ears," Alexander complains.

"Look at this!" I order as I hold his hand up in front of his face so his eyes can focus on the ring on his own hand.

Alexander immediately sits up straight as a board in bed, suddenly wide awake, and his face contorts in disbelief. "What the . . . how . . . YAMADA?!"

The sound of bare feet slapping against the tile floor comes barreling towards us. When the bedroom door flies open, Yamada stands there wearing nothing but a pair of tighty-whities underwear and a black silk robe and a huge smile. "Happy honeymoon, madafakas!"

End of Part One

A SEXY MANHATTAN FAIRYTALE: PART TWO

Michelle A. Valentine

Chapter I
DUM-DA-DA-DUN

Margo

I STARE AT THE WEDDING photo in absolute horror. "Oh, my God. Yamada was a witness? And is he wearing—" I lean in and take a closer look "—an Elvis costume?"

Alexander leans over my shoulder while I sit at the island in the kitchen of our suite, his spicy scent wafting around me as he gets a better view. "Shit." He pushes himself back upright and straightens the dark blue tie he's wearing. Even in a dress shirt, the man makes my mouth water.

I gaze up to see a pair of gray eyes trained on me. "Please tell me this is all a sick joke. Please tell me that we aren't really married."

"No joke, Dime Piece," Yamada says as he walks into the common area of the suite with a set of brunette twins wearing matching schoolgirl outfits—one under each arm. "Yamada was there, and it was the dopest wedding ever! Wasn't it, ladies?"

The two women giggle and nod in agreement. One even runs her finger suggestively over Yamada's scrawny bare chest beneath the silk robe he's still wearing. "Whatever you say, baby," the woman purrs.

Yamada grabs the woman's hand. "No touching in front of Dime Piece. Might make her jealous. Poor girl will never get a taste of a night with Yamada since she's married to King now."

The woman jerks her gaze to me, and I swear to God she hisses at me. I raise my eyebrows, and Alexander shakes his head.

"We need to talk about what happened last night, Yamada," Alexander tells him and then adds, "*Alone.*"

"Okay," Yamada says and then gives each of his companions a kiss on the cheek. "Time to go, lovelies."

"But we want to play with Yamada some more," one of the girls whines in a voice that mimics a toddler as Yamada turns them both toward the door.

He opens the door and ushers the girls out, patting each one on the butt as they pass him. "Sorry, but Yamada's a man in demand. Bye girls."

"Yamada . . ." the girls' voice cuts off as he shuts the door in their faces.

He turns and gives us a mischievous grin. "Bitches love Yamada."

Alexander rolls his eyes. "I have no idea why."

"Don't be a hater." Yamada struts into the kitchen and opens the door on the stocked refrigerator, reaching in for a bottle of juice. He twists the cap off his apple juice and then halts when he turns to take in the expression on Alexander's face. "Why are you not the happiest madafaka on the planet right now? You're married to the hottest chick Yamada has ever seen. What's there not to be happy about?"

Alexander folds his arms over his chest. "This isn't funny. What the hell happened last night?"

Yamada swallows and then shrugs. "We were all having fun. The two of you were fucked-up and when we passed a wedding chapel . . ."

"And let me guess. You convinced us in our drunken state that it would be so much fun," Alexander finishes for him.

Yamada's face pulls into a lopsided grin. "You didn't take much convincing."

Before Alexander has a chance to respond, the front door pops open and the same bodyguard with the braids who walked me up to Yamada's party last night sticks his head through the door. "Sorry to disturb you, Mr. Yamada, but we have a situation. The women you escorted out are sitting in front of the elevator demanding to speak with you about when they can see you again. Would you like us to physically remove them from the property, sir?"

"Let me talk to them." Yamada shakes his head, muttering as he heads toward the door. "This happens every time."

"Yamada . . ."Alexander calls after his friend but gets no response as the door closes us alone in the suite.

Alexander turns around and rests his back against the counter in the kitchen area of our suite. The material of his pressed shirt strains against his bicep as he lifts his hand to pinch the bridge of his nose while he squeezes his eyes shut. "I can't believe I allowed you to con me into this. How could I be so careless?"

This causes me to jerk my eyebrows up as my eyes widen. "Me? You actually think I *want* to be married to you?"

His eyes snap open. He holds up his left hand that's still bearing a wedding ring and points to it. "Obviously, you do. You don't honestly expect me to believe that Yamada came up with that shit by himself. He had to get the idea from somewhere."

"Excuse me." I lift my hand to interrupt. This man is completely out of his ever-lovin' mind if he believes that. "Being married to you is the last thing on my wish list. Why would I ever subject myself to something like that?"

Alexander releases a bitter laugh. "Right. I know you're smarter than that, Margo, so cut the act."

My mouth falls open. "What *act*? My thorough disgust at the thought of being your wife isn't for show—that I can assure you. My disdain for you is quite real."

He stares at me through narrowed eyes. "I'm sure you'd like me to believe that, but Princess, I'm on to your game. Once Jack figures out if we're legally married, I'll have him slap you with an annulment so fast it'll make your head spin. When I told you to marry some schmuck for money, I didn't mean me!"

The moment those words leave his mouth, things begin clicking into place. My hungover brain obviously isn't quick enough this morning to figure out that if, in fact, we are married, it means there was no time for any pesky contracts like a prenuptial agreement. Alexander King is screwed, and he knows it. He's now at my mercy.

Oh, how the tables have turned.

Since he paints me to be the evil mastermind of this plot, I might as well go along with it.

I lick my lips and peer into the beautiful eyes of the man I love to hate. "I must say, Alexander, this new development changes things drastically between us. Don't you think?"

"This changes nothing," he growls. "This marriage is a mistake. No judge in the world will award you shit if you press the issue. Besides, we don't even know if the marriage is legal." He snatches the picture of the so-called wedding off the table and panic rolls through his voice. "A minister wearing a fucking Kiss costume can't be a legitimate man of the cloth capable of marrying people legally, right?"

While I have to agree with him on that, there's no way I'm about to let Alexander know that I'm having a hard time believing this whole thing is legit.

"Maybe you're right . . ." I tilt my head. "And maybe you're wrong. Are you willing to take a chance and find out? If our marriage is legally binding, I won't let you off easy."

There's a long pause of silence between us, and I can tell the wheels are spinning inside that brain of his, He's trying to figure a way out of this situation.

"What will it take for you to walk away from this quietly?" Alexander's nostrils flare, and I can't help smiling. Pissing him off is my new favorite pastime.

I turn on the barstool that I'm occupying and cross my legs in the direction that Alexander is standing. It's finally nice to feel like the one in control of this situation. For a while there, I felt like trying to save Buchanan Industries was a lost cause, but now things have definitely changed in my favor.

"You know exactly what I want," I tell him.

He raises his eyebrow. "Forget it. I have too much riding on this Buchanan deal. I'll take my chances with Jack eating you alive in court."

"Suit yourself. Everything that went on here this weekend will prove that you were a willing participant. Besides, your college buddy was your best man. Yamada wouldn't let someone coerce you into something that you weren't willing to do. I'm sure it won't be too hard to convince a judge to see things my way." I shrug and then push myself off the barstool. "I think I'll go ahead and start with a call to our family attorney. I'll have to start planning how I want to spend my newfound fortune of half your money."

"I don't know what planet you're living on, Margo, but that isn't going to happen." His gray eyes harden. "You can't afford to take me on."

"What's yours is mine, darling. So it seems to me like I can, thanks to your sprawling wealth."

His nostrils flare. "You are such a bitch. I can't believe for one moment that I—" He quickly cuts himself off and clenches his hands into fists by his sides. "Pack your shit. We're going back to New York. Now."

I fold my arms over my chest. "You can't tell me what to do."

Alexander smirks. "Being your husband earns me that right. Now pack."

I open my mouth to tell him to take his orders and shove them right up his bossy ass, but before I have a chance, he turns and walks toward his room, slamming the door behind him.

The second I'm sure that I'm alone, I drop my head and rub my forehead to try to soothe the pounding headache that's still raging inside. How the hell could I allow myself to get this out of control last night? I have so much riding on saving the family business. Being married to Alexander might fuck everything up.

Chapter II
CHANGE OF PLANS
Alexander

THE ROAR OF THE JET has been the only sound I've heard for the last hour. Margo hasn't said a word to me since we left Las Vegas. Hell, she hasn't even so much as glanced at me either. Whatever little connection we shared this weekend is now long gone. Reality has definitely set in that we are enemies and nothing more.

I allowed myself to forget that this weekend. I gave in to temptation and had her over and over.

It had been a long time since I'd laughed—let loose and just had a good time. The combination of liquor and Yamada tends to put me in a carefree state, but I never let my guard down around women. Margo Buchanan is irresistible, and I'm not exactly in the habit of telling myself no, which is how I landed myself in this situation. I couldn't get enough of her.

"Another scotch, Mr. King?" Abigail asks, pulling me out of my thoughts.

"Yes, but make it a double this time," I instruct her before she scampers off to fulfill my order.

I lay my head back against the headrest and close my eyes, only to be instantly alerted to a ringing phone. I answer on the second ring. "King."

"Madafaka! You left without telling Yamada good-bye?"

I roll my eyes. I knew he'd be pissed at me for taking off like that, but I couldn't spend one more minute in the penthouse cooped up with Margo's tempting ass. That woman and her sexy as sin body drives me out of my mind and causes me to lose all control, so I knew I had to get out of there before I did something foolish. I will not break down and give in to her demands, no matter how hard my dick gets.

But Yamada doesn't need to know that was my reason for taking off so quickly. "I'm sorry, my friend. I had urgent business I had to attend to back in New York."

He chuckles on the other end of the line. "You left because being alone with Margo scares the shit out of you. You forget how well Yamada knows you."

The tie around my neck feels too tight, so I pull it away from my skin to relieve the sudden choking sensation. "I assure you, that isn't the case."

"Uh-huh. Then you have no problem flying out to see Yamada on his private island on Thursday."

"A private island? When did you buy a fucking island? That's not really your scene."

"Everywhere Yamada chooses to be is Yamada's scene. Besides, it was a good investment. Everyone loves the British Virgin Islands. This place has a resort on it and a full staff. There are some fly honies that work there. We'll have a good time. No visitors on the island while Yamada's there either."

I rub my temple as I groan. "Now isn't really a good time. I have to sort out this crazy Vegas wedding you got me wrapped up in."

"Now is the perfect time," he chimes in. "We never talked business in Vegas. If you want Yamada Enterprises in on the Buchanan deal, then we sit down before Yamada goes back to Japan. Oh, and bring Dime Piece too or no deal."

"Yamada . . ."

"No is not an answer Yamada will respond to. You want to talk business, you come Thursday to see my new island. Yamada's Booty Paradise has a nice ring to it, no?" A female giggle cuts over the line and Yamada chuckles and then shushes her. "Got to go, King. I'll text you the island coordinates. See you Thursday."

"No. Wait. Yamada—" Silence is all I'm met with, and I curse as I hang up the phone.

A few seconds later, he sends coordinates to one of the small pieces of land in the British Virgin Islands via text.

I scrub both hands down my face. I'm not blind as to what Yamada is trying to do. His matchmaking between Margo and me isn't going to work. I'm not interested in a relationship, and Margo hates my guts, so I know she doesn't want one with me either. Earlier today, she clearly showed her disdain about being married to me. I know she won't appreciate Yamada's meddling with our lives any more than I do.

I jerk my gaze over to Margo. She chose to take the seat across the aisle instead of bravely facing me as she did on the way out here. In her current seat, her head faces away from me, causing me to take note of her striking profile. Her dark hair is pulled back in a low-set ponytail and those dark-rimmed glasses that she tends to wear around the office covers her eyes. Even when she doesn't seem to be trying to attract my attention, she always manages to capture it. She's really one of the most beautiful creatures I've ever seen.

Too bad she's also one of the biggest bitches on the planet.

"Bad news." She whips her head in my direction and meets my gaze. "It seems that Yamada has requested my presence at a private island this week."

Margo clutches her chest in dramatic shock. "That sounds *so* horrible for you. A private island? You *poor* thing. How will you ever survive?"

The sarcasm isn't missed in her voice, and it only makes me want to burst her little attitude bubble. "Trust me. It will be a complete fucking nightmare, especially since he says that I have to bring you along."

I fully expect her to get pissed and start shouting about all the reasons that she can't possibly accompany me to this island, but she doesn't do that. Instead, a wicked smile crosses her face. Instantly, that irritates me off. I don't like that she's pleased about this one damn bit.

"I don't know why you're so happy about this," I grumble.

That only causes her smile to widen. "Just means that Yamada is starting to like me too. I told you that he would be my friend."

My nostrils flare at that thought, but I know that no matter what Margo Buchanan believes, Yamada would never take her side over mine.

"When do we leave?" she asks.

"Yamada apparently owns one of the islands next to the British Virgin Islands, so it'll take us about six hours to fly there. Then we'll need to get a helicopter or boat to take us over to wherever this place is. If I want to make a deal with Yamada, then we have no other choice but to go. Once Yamada gets his mind stuck on something, he tends to get his way."

"Looks like the game is still on when it comes to Yamada," Margo muses.

It's time to remind her that I'm still the boss in this situation. "Don't get your hopes up, Princess. Yamada will never sign a deal with you over me. He's *my* friend."

She lifts her eyebrow. "You're not the only one who got an invite to chat, King, so it looks like he's my friend, too."

Dammit. I hate that she's right. Yamada does like her or else he would have never been so welcoming once he figured out that he wasn't getting into her pants. That also means this could be big trouble for me if she can figure out a way to sweet talk him in to doing a deal directly with her father instead of me. It will cost me far too much money and I won't allow that to happen.

When we land at the airstrip just outside the city, Margo rushes off the plane. She demanded that I order a car to be waiting for her because she refused to be trapped with me any longer than she had to. She doesn't even glance in my direction as she heads toward it.

Guess the fucking honeymoon's over.

I shove myself up from the smooth leather seat and button my jacket as I make my way off the plane. The late afternoon sun hits me full force as I step outside, causing me to whip out a pair of sunglasses from my inside pocket and then slide them on my face.

It's then that I notice Jack leaning against the limo with his arms crossed as he waits for me. Even though his sunglasses shield his eyes, the smirk on his face tells me that I've opened myself up to a never-ending line of jokes about my random Vegas nuptials. "Your wife isn't riding with us?"

I shake my head. "Don't start your shit."

"What?" Jack says with a slight chuckle as I slide into the limo first with him following right behind me. "I'm not allowed to ask about your wife?"

"She's not my wife," I snap.

This only causes Jack to laugh harder. "Sure, she is. It's legal and everything."

"Fuck." It's the only word that comes to mind. I'm totally fucked here. "How bad is it?"

Jack raises his eyebrows. "Well, if the two of you didn't consummate your marriage, I'm sure we could've had a quick annulment, but—" I pull my glasses off and give him my best you know me better than that look which cuts him off. "That's what I thought. We fight it. I'm not exactly a divorce lawyer, but I'm sure we can bring on a few other attorneys who specialize in high-profile cases to help. We might stand a chance."

"A chance?" There's a catch in my voice. "You have got to be fucking kidding me! You're telling me that after being married for one fucking day, it possible Margo Buchanan can take me to the fucking cleaners? This is fucking insane."

"Buddy, what's insane is you marrying a woman who's out for your blood. What possessed you to do it? I mean, I know she's hot, but was fucking her really worth all this trouble? What the hell were you thinking?"

I pinch the bridge of my nose. "I don't know."

I wish I could blame marrying Margo solely on Yamada, but I know that wouldn't be exactly fair. Being with Margo this weekend was exciting. She didn't take my shit, and I find that insanely attracted. Hell, maybe Jack can plead a case of temporary insanity because the woman causes me to lose my damn mind. Yamada said it didn't take much convincing for me to marry Margo, and in my gut, I know that's probably true. I drank enough liquor to kill a horse, so I know the logical part of my brain was not functioing, and my dick did any major decision-making.

I lift my head and stare out the window as the car cuts through traffic, getting us closer to Manhattan. "How quickly can we get this resolved?"

"Well, that depends," Jack replies.

"On . . ." I prod as I whip my gaze in his direction.

He sighs. "On whether or not Margo Buchanan cooperates."

I release a bitter laugh. "She hates me, so that won't happen."

"That's too bad. Dragging things out can cause problems. If the board catches wind about your fly-by-night nuptials, they may begin to question your integrity."

"My *integrity*? Are you fucking serious? This little mishap with Margo has nothing to do with my ability to run King Corporation. This business means more to me than anything else." I shake my head, reeling from the disbelief that Jack's even bringing this up. "I would rather slice off my own hand than do something to damage the empire my father built."

"I know that, but the board . . . they don't know you like I do, and well, you've amassed quite a reputation in this city when it comes to women. The board may perceive your rash decision to marry Margo and then immediately divorce her as you being a bit . . . flighty."

I raise one eyebrow. "Me . . . *flighty*? I'm an emanate professional. Why does who I fuck and accidentally marry bring my character into question?"

Jack shrugs. "It could cause them to question your decision-making skills—your ability to see what's best for the company in the long haul—and they may band together to try to go against you on things."

"That won't matter. I own a majority of this company. If they don't like the direction I take this business—tough. It's *my* fucking company."

"It is," Jack agrees. "I'm not bringing this up to be a prick, but I just want you to be aware. The board can make things a whole lot more difficult if they fight you on every little thing."

I run my fingers down the back of my neck and take a deep breath. Fuck. If only I could rewind time and go back to the first moment I fucked Margo and let my guard down, then none of this would be an issue right now. I screwed up, and now I have to deal with the consequences of giving in to my dark desires and taking Margo, even though I knew it could fuck everything up.

I meet Jack's stare. "So what should I do? If Margo refuses a quick annulment, there's no way I can keep this quiet and keep the word from spreading across this city. You know how people talk around here."

"Play nice with her," Jack says as if it's the simplest thing in the world. "Find out what it will take to appease her and give it to her so she doesn't fight you on this divorce."

"I can't do that!" I protest. "She wants me to bail out Buchanan Industries so her family's company won't go under, but you and I both know that if we do that, we'd lose millions on that deal. We can't afford to do that."

"Then you'll have to find a way to meet in the middle. You both are going to have to give a little to find common ground in this situation."

I scrub my hand down my face. This is horse shit. I hate the fact that she basically has my balls in her purse, ready to zip them in tight and cause me excruciating pain. I so badly want to bash my fucking head against the window as straight-up punishment for allowing shit to get out of control like this.

This—the whole allowing someone to gain the upper hand on me, especially a female—is not like me. I'm typically in control.

My cell rings and I fish it out of my jacket pocket before checking the caller ID. I sigh as I hit the green button, ready for the whine fest that I know my baby sister is about to inflict on me for missing her birthday party this weekend. "Yes, Diem?"

"Are you back in town yet?" she quizzes.

"Just landed about ten minutes ago," I tell her. I decide then that I might as well open the door for her temper tantrum for being absent this weekend. "How was your birthday party?"

"It was wonderful," she replies in a tone I only remember her using after watching some sappy romance movie. Most people would call it dreamy. I call it delusional. Diem is very much the hopeless romantic type, so this mood of hers tells me that she's met a guy.

I pinch the bridge of my nose. What shitty timing for this to happen. With me being so wrapped up in the whole Margo scandal and trying to close this deal with Yamada, I won't have time to properly investigate whoever this man is like I typically do. As her brother, I find that it's my duty to make sure whatever asshole is sniffing around my sister is good enough. Unfortunately, Diem tends to pick the loser artist types who I fear are after far more than her model good looks. Like me, people try to get their hooks in Diem for what our father left us, and it's up to me to protect my free-spirited, trusting sister from motherfuckers who would use her.

Time to cut to the chase.

"Who's the guy?"

"Does a man have to be involved for me to be happy?" Diem instantly fires back.

"Come on, Diem. You can't bullshit me. You know the drill. Who's the guy?"

She's quiet for a few moments and then says, "I'm not telling you."

"Diem . . ." I say her name with a bite of warning in my voice. "You might as well do this the easy way and just tell me. Don't make me have Jack start looking into who this mystery guy is you obviously don't want me to know about."

Jack's eyes immediately cut over to me at the mention of his name. I see a flicker of unease on his face before he quickly turns his head to stare out the side window. Jack hates when I send him out on personal missions like this for me—that's no secret—so I'm sure the idea of tracking down my kid sister's new love interest isn't something that he really wants to do. But I know Jack. He's loyal, and he'll do it if I ask him to because, not only does he work for me, but he's also my best friend.

"Don't do that," Diem begs. "I promise I'll tell you all about him when I'm ready, but for now, allow me to keep this to myself. Please, Alexander."

Her bravery to maintain this secret takes me aback because Diem isn't typically like that with me. Sure, she bucks against my will most of the time, but it doesn't take me long to get her to bend. She knows that I get what I want no matter what. So this little show of defiance catches me off guard, but the idea that she's finally growing a little backbone makes me proud in an odd way. It doesn't make me worry any less, though.

I sigh. "Fine. I won't push for now. But so help me, Diem, if this asshole hurts you in any way, I will end him."

"Thank you." The pleased tone in her voice rings through loud and clear.

After I tell her good-bye, I end the call and lean my head back against the headrest. I hope Diem knows what she's doing and doesn't do anything rash with this guy until I've had time to run a full background check on him. I don't have time to worry about my sister right now though. I have to focus all my energy on figuring out how to get out of the fucking mess I've gotten myself into with Margo. I can't believe I'm married to the fucking Feisty Princess of Manhattan. How in the hell did I allow this to happen?

Chapter III
MOTHER KNOWS BEST

Margo

IT TAKES EVERYTHING IN ME not to bash my head against the expensive marble counter as I sit at the island in my mother's ridiculously huge kitchen. I'm trying to figure out a way to tell her that I married a total rat-bastard this weekend on accident. Seriously, when Jean Paul renovated his Upper East Side apartment, he spared no expense when it came to this kitchen. It makes sense because he does occasionally film segments of his television show in here.

"That man takes such good care of me." Mother busies herself with punching reheat on two of the pre-cooked meals her husband prepared for her in his absence. "He won't leave for a trip if he hasn't left food for me to heat up while he's gone." She turns to face me with a dreamy expression on her face. "I really think I've found a good one this time, Margo, honey. This one is a keeper."

I love my mother, but it takes everything in me not to roll my eyes and blurt out 'that's what you said about the last four.' My mother is a hopeful romantic, always believing in soul mates and fate and all that hokey nonsense.

She takes in the expression on my face and then shakes her head, causing her long dark curls to bounce around her shoulders. "Don't give me that look."

My mouth drops. Sometimes I forget how good she is at reading what's on my mind even if I don't make a move to voice it. "I didn't say anything."

"You didn't have to. I'm your mother, Margo. I can read how much you detest the idea of love by the expression on your face. I'm pretty good at that, you know. Matter-of-fact, I once had this clairvoyant tell me I was a natural at reading auras."

The sound of the microwave dings, signaling that our food is ready and interrupting her train of thought. She lifts one of the plates of grilled chicken to her nose. "Ah. This smells wonderful. Jean Paul is a man of many talents, cooking being one of them." She wiggles her eyebrows suggestively.

My face twists. "Ew. Mother. Please. I'm your child, for God's sake. I don't need to hear about your sex life."

She sets a plate in front of me and then waves me off dismissively. "Oh, please, darling. You're a grown woman. It's not like you are too young to hear about this."

I wrinkle my nose as I cut into the chicken in front of me. "There's never going to be an age when I'm old enough to discuss sex with you."

Mother pulls out the barstool across from me and takes a seat before she begins to cut up her food. "Speaking of sex, I took the liberty of Googling Alexander King while you were off gallivanting with him last week."

I raise one eyebrow as I swallow down the food in my mouth and do my best not to choke. "Why would you do that?"

"I had to see exactly who my daughter was spending all her time with."

This time, I do roll my eyes. "Don't let his beautiful face fool you. He's not pleasant to be around."

"The hot ones never are, dear. That's what makes them so fun. They're a challenge." A smile pulls at the corners of her mouth. She's no doubt reliving some memory of a time she spent with some old asshole boyfriend as she takes a sip of her water. "Tell me, was that trip to Vegas all work or did you manage to get some playtime in with the notorious Naughty King?"

For a moment, I debate whether to lie to her. I could stick to the story that absolutely nothing happened between

Alexander and me, but knowing how well she can read me, she'll see right through me.

I readjust in my seat. "I would like to say that it was all business . . ."

"But?" she prods.

"It wasn't," I answer honestly.

Her smile widens as she leans in, clamoring for the juicy bit of gossip she can tell is about to spill out of my mouth. "Do tell. And don't leave out one sordid detail."

I close my eyes and wrinkle my nose. There's no way I can hide what happened in Vegas from her. Besides, she's the one person in this world I can trust with this secret. "I slept with him."

"That's my girl!" she exclaims and then instantly launches into a question. "How was it?"

"Mother!"

"What? Inquiring minds, darling. Are you going to see him again?"

I lift one shoulder in a noncommittal shrug. "I don't want to, but I'm afraid I'll be forced to."

She nods. "That's right. The whole spy mission your father has you on. I nearly forgot about that. If you really don't want to see Alexander King anymore, just quit and tell your father that you're done being his little tattletale. Lord knows how hard it is to be in close proximity to an ex-lover. Your father should understand and not make too much of a fuss over the situation."

I sigh. "It's not that simple, I'm afraid."

"But it is. If you're afraid to tell your father, I'll call and tell—"

"My issues are much bigger than handling Daddy."

She bunches her brow, clearly confused. I can see the wheels turning behind her eyes as she tries to figure out what I'm hiding. "Then what is it?"

"I married the bastard on a drunken whim," I blurt out before I lose my nerve.

Her eyes widen. "Say again? I'm not sure I heard that quite right. It sounded like you just told me that my only child ran off to Vegas and got married for the very first time without me present."

My lips twitch and finally pull down at one corner. "It's not like I planned for it to happen. Hell, I don't even remember it."

"Oh, dear." Mother sighs. "Does your father know?"

I nod. "Of course he does. He thinks this is excellent leverage to have on Alexander."

We sit in silence for a few moments and then Mother says, "Maybe this isn't such a bad thing."

That's not exactly what I was expecting her to say. "How can you say that? Being married to Alexander King is one of the worst things I can ever imagine happening to me in my life."

"Are you sure about that?"

I push my half-eaten plate of food away before folding my arms across my chest. "Of course, I am. He's a pompous asshole, and I can't believe I allowed myself to get in to this situation."

"See, dear, that's where I think this marriage might not be such a bad thing."

Clearly, my mother is allowing Alexander's disgustingly good looks to blind her to the truth of how awful he is. "You're not grasping the—"

"I understand just fine." She cuts me off and then levels her gaze on me. "I'm not sure *you're* seeing that maybe fate has a way of intervening, even if you don't believe what's happening is the best thing. If you let your guard down enough to marry him, drunk or not, he can't be all bad, can he? There has to be some small part of you that enjoys being with him or else you would've never gone through with a quickie Vegas wedding."

I open my mouth to argue—to explain that the liquor completely impaired my judgment when it came to Alexander, but that wouldn't exactly be the truth. I had sex with the man two times before I even had a drink of alcohol. I have no excuse for that. Alexander King is a very intoxicating man, and it pisses me off that I find it so hard to resist him.

Chapter IV
HARD BALL

Margo

MY PALMS SWEAT AS I sit at my desk, waiting for the moment Alexander comes marching through the door. I don't recall the last time I've been this nervous. That man just has a way of pushing my buttons, even when he's not around. I seriously entertained Mom's idea of quitting, but I know Daddy would kill me if I gave up on saving the company, so here I am.

All night long, I ran scenarios through my head of what it would be like to see him today. I have loads of fiery dialogue just waiting to assault him the moment that cocky mouth of his opens and he says one cross thing to me.

The soft ding of the elevator stopping on this otherwise quiet floor catches my attention. I practically leap out of my seat, not wanting to be in a position to be talked down to if it is Alexander.

It's only seven. Most of the employees don't start rolling in for at least another forty-five minutes, but I know that Alexander is always the first one at the office every morning.

I hold my breath as I hear heavy footsteps head in my direction.

Our gazes meet as soon as he rounds the corner and turns into my office. He's always so put together, and today is no different as he waltzes toward my desk in his perfectly pressed black suit. I stare into Alexander's gray eyes, ready to begin our verbal sparring match, but I never get the chance to say a word. He turns without so much as a word to me and storms into his adjoining office, slamming the door shut behind him in the process.

My mouth drops open. So much for my thought-out plan of attack.

I plop down in my chair and do my best to pretend the man, who is now my husband, isn't on the other side of that door, avoiding me at all costs.

Asshole.

I flip off the door but refuse to go chasing after him to demand answers. If he wants to play 'let's pretend last weekend never happened,' then so be it.

Game on.

He will not control my thoughts any longer. I won't allow it because I've done nothing but obsess about him since I arrived back in New York. If I haven't been daydreaming about the way his hands felt on me, then figuring out a way to take him down has consumed me. I wish he weren't such a fantastic lover. Maybe then, I could jerk my head out of the fucking clouds and stop thinking about Alexander King in toe-curling sexual positions.

I sigh and check the clock on my computer screen. It's nearly twelve, and there still hasn't been a peep out of Alexander. Not even for his coffee—which is odd since he always seems to take great pleasure in having me fetch on his command.

I'll be damned if I break the little silence game we have going on between us. I refuse to allow him to believe he has an inch of power over me. I still want him to think I'm ready to stick it to him at any moment for not having a prenup in place before he married me.

I return my attention back to the statistical figures for King Enterprises that I've been able to get my hands on. All morning, I've been looking for traces of unethical practices that can help me in my pursuit to take Alexander King down with a bit of blackmail. Unfortunately for me, nothing of use has turned up. To my surprise, this company seems to do everything by the book.

The phone on my desk rings, and I snatch it off my desk the moment Alexander's name flashes across the caller ID. "Yes, Mr. King. Is there something I can do for you?"

"I need a car brought around in exactly fifteen minutes," he orders without as much as a greeting.

I don't appreciate the bossy tone in his voice, so I decide to throw a little dig of my own at him. "Of course, sir. Is there anything else you need from me? Your messages, coffee, divorce papers? Oh, wait, I forgot that we need to tie up many loose ends before we close that deal."

The last one has me biting my lip to hold back a snicker. I don't even have to see the expression on his face to know that one has him seething.

"Margo . . ." he says my name with a warning, but I've decided I need to keep going—keep pushing his buttons.

"Do I detect some anger? Is that any way to speak to your wife? We are still in that newlywed phase, after all."

"Margo," he growls. "Get your ass in this office so we can discuss this matter privately. We don't need the entire fucking office knowing our goddamn business."

I raise my eyebrows while a smirk crosses my face. "No need to get touchy. I—"

Click.

Before I can throw out anything else, Alexander stops me in my tracks by hanging up.

The smile still rests on my face as I push myself up from my desk. I like the idea of having this egotistical man by the balls. His reputation of dicking women over precedes him in this city, so I love the idea that I've one-upped this man.

Now all I have to do is march in there and keep up this bitch persona. The only chance I have of keeping him at bay is to continue to piss him off. If he despises me, then he'll stay on the other side of that desk and not attempt to use those magical hands on me. Lord knows, if he touches me, I'll lose all self-control, and I cannot allow that to happen. This is my one shot at forcing Alexander King into not taking over my father's company. It's also one of my last chances to put distance between the two of us and regain control of my heart before it falls for this wicked man.

Chapter V
THE BARGAIN
Alexander

I ADJUST MY TIE FOR the third time and take a deep breath, readying myself to enter into battle with Margo. I hadn't planned her to be here early this morning, so when I walked in and saw her sitting at her desk, I froze and not one damn word would come out of my mouth. I figured silence was best until I could figure out a way to convince her of my plan. I spent some time last night figuring out how I could spin this situation to make me look good to the board.

The door swings open, and I lean back in my chair and steeple my fingers in front of me. If I've learned one thing about Margo, it's that she's a shark like me. Any sign of a little blood and she'll attack, so it's best to put on a good front and pretend that I'm not the least bit rattled.

Margo struts through the door with her chin tipped up, and I can tell by the heated expression on her face that getting her on my side will not be an easy task.

"Sit," I order her.

She shakes her head. "I think I'll stand."

Her little act of defiance doesn't surprise me. She hates being ordered around.

I want to lash out and say a million things that I know will get under her skin and piss her off even further, but I quickly think back to what Jack said. I have to stop fighting with this woman and get on her good side so she'll cooperate with not only the divorce process, but also with the other little plan that I have in mind.

I take a deep breath and push myself to be more pleasant with her. "Would you please have a seat, Margo?"

She arches one of her perfectly manicured eyebrows, clearly questioning my sudden manners. She stares me down a moment longer but then takes the seat across from me. Margo crosses those long, sexy legs of hers, and my eyes instantly dart down to them. She's wearing another one of those goddamn skirts that does nothing but accentuate every curve beneath it. A couple of buttons on her blue blouse are undone, the valley between her tits on display.

I pull at the collar of my shirt and do attempt to stop thinking about how fucking sexy she is both in and out of her clothes. "I have a proposition for you."

She narrows her eyes at me. "This had better not be another request to be your fuck buddy. The last time you propositioned me for that, I distinctly remember smacking your face."

My tongue dances behind my teeth, ready to remind her just how much she enjoyed having my cock buried inside her—how she begged for it. But I know doing that right now won't help my case.

"Look, Margo, you're an intelligent woman, so there's no need for me to beat around the bush. I need something from you."

This catches her interest, and both of her eyebrows shoot up. "And I suppose you believe I'll just give over whatever it is you need from me."

I lock my gaze with hers. "Yes."

She opens her mouth to protest, but I quickly cut her off.

"The answer is yes because I'm willing to make you a very generous offer."

She folds her arms over her chest. "What exactly is it that you want?"

"Your cooperation," I tell her honestly.

She smirks. "You want to divorce me so soon?"

"This isn't a joke, Margo. Our little moment of drunken indiscretion could put me in some deep shit."

"And this is my problem because . . . ?"

Her flippant attitude is really getting under my skin. "If you want to save your father's company, then it should matter to you if I'm no longer the one making final business decisions when it comes to the King Corporation."

She rolls those magnetic, blue eyes of hers. "You're really reaching, Alexander."

I pound my fist on my desk, causing her to jump and release a tiny gasp. "It's true, dammit."

Her eyes search my face as she chews on that plump bottom lip of hers, and then she asks softly, "How is that possible? I thought your father left you this company?"

"He did, but there is a catch. A clause written in his will states the board has the power to overthrow my position as president if it is deemed that I was making reckless decisions in either my professional or private life," I explain.

Her eyebrows draw in and there's a flash of pity in her eyes. "Why would he do that?"

"Because I was only nineteen years old when he was diagnosed with cancer and that's not exactly a mature age for a guy to run a Fortune 500 company without some protective measures in place." I shrug. "I understand why he did it. Hell, I would do the same thing in order to protect the family empire and make sure it remained profitable. He was looking out for my sister, Diem, and me."

Margo's lips twist. "But you're thirty years old now. Does that clause not have an expiration date?"

I nod. "It ends when I'm thirty-two. Father figured since that was the age he settled down, got married, and began building his empire that I should have my head on straight by then." I lean in and set my elbows on my desk. "That's why I need your cooperation. I need to convince the board that our marriage wasn't some random drunken act so they don't question my ability to run this company. I've worked my ass off since my father's death to prove not only to the board, but also to myself, that I'm fit to fill Father's shoes. I would want him to be proud of how well I've handled everything."

Silence settles in the office. I've never really admitted to anyone why I'm so driven, but it feels good to say it out loud. I just hope that Margo understands why this means so much to me and agrees to help me out.

Finally, after she's had time to process everything I've just told her, she launches into question mode. "So you're saying that you want to stay married and that you want me to play along and make the world believe that we're madly in love?"

"That's exactly what I'm asking."

Margo nods. "What's in it for me?"

I flinch. "I thought I was pretty clear about how me staying in power benefits you."

She shakes her head. "All you said was that if I wanted to save my father's business, then I would need to help you. I'm just sitting here asking myself why I would want to do that. I know your main objective is to buy out my father's entire company and then break it into pieces to sell off like it's some worn-out toy at a flea market."

I sigh, hating that what I'm about to propose goes against everything in me. "If you help me, then I promise that in return, I will not break apart your father's company and sell it off in sections as I originally planned. Instead, King

Corporation will become a financial partner with Buchanan Industries. And as a bonus, I'll make sure Yamada Enterprises strikes up a deal with your father's company directly."

A wicked smile lights up Margo's face as she stands up and sticks her hand out to me. "You've got yourself a deal, baby."

Internally, I cringe, but I know I have to look at the bigger picture in this situation. Losing this deal with Buchanan Industries is going to hurt like a motherfucker, but losing control of my company will hurt a lot fucking worse.

I stand and then walk around the desk in order to take her hand in mine. Immediately, the warmth of her touch causes my heart to pound a little harder in my chest as my body craves to get my hands on more of her soft skin.

I lick my lips as my eyes flit down to her mouth. "I'll expect you to be at my house, suitcase in hand, by seven sharp."

"Excuse me?" Margo instantly attempts to pull away from my grasp, but I don't let her go. "You didn't say a thing about me living with you."

I cock my right eyebrow as I stare down at her. "Married couples generally live together."

"Yes, but typically those people like each other," she growls as she pulls again to break free of me.

A smirk crosses my face. "Are you saying that you don't like me?"

"I despise you," she hisses.

Whenever Margo gets into bitch mode, it triggers something in me that's so insanely attracted to her that I can barely contain myself. Before I even realize what I'm doing, I have her by the nape of the neck and am crushing my lips to hers.

At first her eyes widen, but she doesn't fight me a bit. As a matter of fact, it seems to turn her on. Because the next thing I know, her hands are in my hair and our bodies are pressed so close I can feel the curve of her tits against my chest.

I spin Margo around and push her ass against my desk. A loud crash echoes through the room as I shove all the paperwork from my desk to the floor.

I grip her hips as she shoves my jacket off my shoulders. "I've thought about fucking you on this desk since the first time I saw you." She moans into my mouth as I slide my hand between her thighs until my fingers trace the silky material of her panties. "I've missed the taste of this sweet pussy on my tongue. Just think about how fun this is going to be when we get to my apartment tonight."

I'm unable to resist the urge to touch her. She tosses her head back, and I seize the opportunity to nip at her earlobe and inhale her sweet perfume. My cock jerks inside my slacks, and I want nothing more than to take her right here. Right now.

I shove the silk material of her panties out of the way and slide my index finger against her swollen clit. "Always so wet, Margo. I love that about you."

With my free hand, I hitch her leg around my waist so I can spread her wide and work her into a frenzy.

"Oh, that's it," she moans as I continue my assault on her pussy. "Alexander . . ."

The way she says my name—all breathy while she's on the verge of orgasm—nearly makes me come in my pants. This woman has no idea how much she turns me on.

"Come for me, Margo," I order, needing to watch her as she lets go.

She lets out a cry that I'm sure the rest of the office would hear had she not buried her face into the crook of my neck. Her entire body shakes against me as I flick her click and she comes hard.

The heat of her breath warms the skin on my neck. Desperately needing my own release, I pull back and stare into her eyes. "Now, it's time for you to get on your knees for me."

As the words leave my mouth, a sharp pain slices through my bottom lip as Margo bites me just a little too hard. She shoves me away from her and then smacks me square in the face.

I rub my cheek, completely confused. "What the fuck was that for?"

Margo's nostrils flare as she draws back to smack me again. This time, I catch her by the wrist before she can make contact with my face. "Stop it! Jesus!"

She yanks her arm out of my grasp and straightens her skirt. "I don't like to be used. I thought I made it perfectly clear when we were in Vegas that I'm not going to be one of your hired hookers. If you think the deal we just made changes that, then you're sorely mistaken. Married or not, I am not some little slut for you to use whenever you feel like it."

She doesn't give me a chance to say another word. She turns on her heel and storms out of my door, slamming it so hard in the process that one of the pictures falls off the wall.

I stand there with my mouth agape like a fucking idiot. For once in my life, I'm at a fucking loss for words. The thought of using her in that manner never crossed my mind, but now that she's put it out there, having Margo Buchanan around as my live-in sex slave doesn't sound so bad.

Chapter VI
TWO'S COMPANY

Margo

AT SIX THIRTY ON THE dot, the car that Alexander promised has arrived to pick me up. On the way to his place gives me time to think. I honestly don't know how I'm going to survive living at his place. That man . . . he has a way of getting to me unlike any other person I have ever met. Every time he speaks to me, he evokes so many emotions within me. I have a hard time figuring out how to deal with them, considering my stupid body always seems to want to go against everything my highly educated brain is screaming not to do. I can't believe I kissed him.

I mean, what the hell was that in his office today, and why can't I stop liking it so much?

It's a horrible position to be in when you find your enemy insanely attractive.

The car comes to a stop, and the driver steps out of the car. This is it. No turning back now. I made a deal with a handsome as hell devil, and there's no going back.

I take a deep breath before I grab my purse and give myself a little pep talk. "You can do this. Be strong. And treat him like any other man whore who needs to be destroyed."

The driver opens the door and helps me out. I glance up at the towering building and stare for a moment at how impressive it is with its gleaming glass front. Leave it to King to own an apartment in one of the richest looking buildings in Lenox Hill.

"Good evening, Mrs. King. I've been expecting you." The voice laced with a heavy Scottish accent startles me, and I quickly refocus my gaze onto an older doorman with a friendly face. He smiles at me while his salt and pepper hair pokes out from under his hat. A few seconds pass and he tilts his head when I don't immediately respond, almost to question if I'm who he's been waiting for. "You are Mrs. King, correct?"

Hearing the name 'Mrs. King' throws me for a bit of a loop. It actually does take a second for it to register that I am, in fact, Mrs. Alexander King, and the whole purpose of me living here is to make people believe that we are indeed a married couple.

I clear my throat before I square my shoulders, reminding myself that I'm doing this to secure my rightful future and that I need to play my part in this whole happily-ever-after illusion. God knows I don't need to give Alexander any reason to argue with me. It seems that when we do that, we end up tearing at each other's clothes. "That's right. I believe my husband is expecting me."

This seems to satisfy the old man. He gives me a curt nod and then opens the door for me. "Right this way, Madame."

"Thank you . . ." I trail my words as I pass by him, unsure of his name.

"Darby," he announces while still wearing his smile.

I smile in return, completely at ease with this man who seems to be extremely friendly. I don't know how in the world the man keeps such a pleasant outlook considering he has one of the biggest pricks in Manhattan living in his place of employment. It's bad enough I have to fetch Alexander's coffee and whatever else he needs while being treated like crap. I can only imagine how unpleasant he must be toward Darby when he passes by him every day.

I make my way through the elegant lobby and listen to the heels of my shoes click on the marble tile as I head toward the elevator. When I press the up button, it occurs to me that I have no clue what floor Alexander's apartment is on.

I turn toward the front door where Darby busies himself collecting my bags from the driver and placing them on a gold plated trolley. I bite my lip, unease suddenly rocking through me at the realization of how unprepared I am for this situation.

The panic I feel must be evident on my face because the moment the doorman pushes his cart up next to me, he asks, "Are you all right, Madame?"

I tuck a loose strand of my dark hair back behind my ear. "Oh, yes. I'm perfectly fine."

Darby's quiet for a few moments. "You know, I was a wee bit nervous the first night my bonny lass and I settled into our cottage together. I believe that's normal for everyone when they get married."

"Oh, I'm not—" The elevator dings cutting me off before I babble on how I'm not going out of my mind right now when, in fact, I am.

I step inside and move to the side so Darby can squeeze inside with my things.

Darby punches the 'P' button on the elevator, so I make a mental note to remember that for next time. "I don't think you'll have anything to worry about. Alex is a good lad."

I bunch my brow together. Since I've met Alexander King, I've never heard anyone address him so informally, so this takes me aback and makes me a bit curious. "Have you worked for Alexander long?"

Darby nods. "Aye. The missus and me have worked for Alex's family for the better part of thirty years now—since Alex was a wee babe. I think that's about the time we moved to the States from Ottawa Valley. Aggie practically raised Alex and Diem, you know."

That's a lot of information to take in, but one thing definitely stood out to me about that story. "So when you say that you've worked for his family . . . do you mean that the Kings own this building?"

"Aye," he answers. "It's been in the King family for generations. When Alexander's father inherited it, he decided to turn the penthouse into his family home."

From the research I had done on Alexander, I discovered that his father was a very family-oriented man with a reputation of integrity. It was clear by all the photos I found of the two of them before Mr. King had passed away that Alexander and his father were close. So it doesn't exactly surprise me that this building, much like his company, was passed on to his son too.

When the elevator's doors open into the hall, only one door comes into view. It's painted a soft cream color and trimmed in gold accents, making it very reminiscent of a much more regal era when paired with the red carpet that also contain gold trim. Just to the right of the door is a small box that appears to be an intercom. I stand back as Darby presses the call button to alert a bell on the other side of the door.

"Yes?" an older lady's voice calls over the box.

"Aggie, I've got the new Mrs. King for ye. Care to open the door and let the lass inside?"

Within moments, the locks on the other side of the door jingle, and the door is opened, revealing a foyer fit for a palace. My eyes widen at the sight of all the marble with gold accents. A staircase stands proudly in the middle of the space, leading up to another level of the apartment. This entry takes me back to a time when I was a little girl and dreamed of being a princess living in a castle; only it's more amazing than my dreams.

"Don't be shy. Come on in." The lady who I'm banking is Aggie, Darby's wife, holds the door open for me.

She smiles as I pass her, and much like her husband, there's a very friendly energy surrounding Aggie. The blue of her maid's uniform enriches the color of her ocean-blue eyes while her gray hair sits in a low bun, showing off her round face.

Darby follows me inside, and Aggie quickly turns her attention from me to her husband. "He's done well, hasn't he, Darby? This one is a pretty one."

A blush creeps over my cheeks as I listen to the woman dote on me.

Aggie closes the door, causing the bottom hem of her uniform to swish about a bit. "Now that we're alone, we want you to know that Darby and myself know the truth about the situation at hand, so there'll be no need in puttin' on a show fur the likes of us."

I raise my eyebrows, still not sure if I should break my cover just in case they really don't know that Alexander and I didn't really mean to get married.

"Don't look so surprised, dear. There's not much that Alex keeps from us. He gave us all the details. I still can't believe that Henry put that silly clause in his will. I tried to explain that just because he was wild until he was thirty-two didn't mean that our Alex would be the same. I wish Henry were here to see just how well his son has done with running the empire he built. He would've been so proud and that little clause would never have existed." Aggie sighs. "It's just a shame Alex still has to deal with all this." She quickly backpedals. "Not that it's anything to do with you personally, dear. I'm sure you're a lovely young lady and we'll be happy to have ye here until this mess is settled. I just wish he didn't have to go through proving that he's capable of running a business even though he makes a few mistakes."

"The lad is only human," Darby chimes in. "Can't expect him to be perfect all the time."

"He's far from perfect." My eyes widen the moment I realize that I've actually said what was running through my mind. Not wanting to offend two people who clearly care for Alexander, I try to correct my mistake. "Er—I mean . . ."

Darby laughs. "No wonder he likes her. She's a feisty one."

Aggie nods in agreement. "Aye. Maybe he's found his match."

I stand there, completely unsure of what to say.

"Come on, lass. Let me show yew to where you'll be staying," Aggie instructs and then turns toward the staircase. "Darby will bring your bags up to your room. I'm sure you'll need to freshen up for dinner."

Once at the top of the stairs, Aggie leads me down a wide hallway lined with paintings. Some of the paintings are abstract pieces, while a few focus on people. Each one is more beautiful than the last. One, in particular, catches my attention.

It's Alexander.

He sits in a high-back leather chair, and the dark background causes the red tie he's wearing to pop out against his gray suit. It's uncanny how lifelike the piece looks. There's a hint of mischief in his gray eyes paired with that signature cocky grin. Even in a painting Alexander King appears to be up to no good. It's amazing how even a picture of him causes my body to do crazy things, like yearn his touch.

"These are beautiful," I tell Aggie, who's waiting patiently for me to study the pictures that I'm sure she's passed by a million times. "Are they all the same artist?"

"They are." Alexander's voice causes me to jump.

Clearly, I wasn't expecting him to be the one to answer me.

My back goes ramrod straight with the arrival of the unwelcome asshole who owns the place. The relaxed mood that Aggie and Darby had created the moment I stepped foot inside this building is suddenly gone.

Alexander comes strutting down the hall, wearing a white oxford rolled up to his elbows and the same dark slacks he had on earlier in the office. He's clearly made himself more comfortable since the last time I'd seen him today.

He stops about a foot away and then turns to stare at the portrait of himself. "It's a great likeness, don't you think? I look pretty damn fantastic, if you ask me."

I have to fight the urge to roll my eyes at his outward show of cockiness. "It's very nice work. It's too bad the artist didn't have a better subject. If they'd had someone different, then perhaps this would be in a museum somewhere."

A hint of a smile crosses his lips. "Margo, you have an uncanny ability to insult me and yet throw out a compliment. In this case, I'll allow your snide jab at me to slide, considering you've just praised my little sister's work."

"Diem did this?" I raise my eyebrows, and it hits me instantly that I remember his sister from high school. Even back then, she was an artist, which made her stand out from all the other kids, and that's how I remember her. Most kids I went to school with were obsessed with getting into top-notch colleges in order to be able to work for their family businesses, but not Diem. She was all about art and expressing herself.

He motions to the other paintings hanging on both sides of the hall. "She did all of these. She very passionate about her work, and she actually just sold her first piece shortly before we left for Las Vegas."

"That's fantastic," I answer honestly. "She's clearly very talented."

This time when he smiles, it's more reminiscent of a proud parent. It's nice to know he's not a heartless jackass in all facets of his life.

"Come," Alexander instructs. "I'll show you to your room."

He turns to go back the way he came down the hall, and I follow, suddenly aware that Aggie is no longer with us.

We pass a couple of doors. Alexander explains that one is a bathroom and that there are seven in total in the apartment. The second door belongs to his little sister who still stays with him from time to time.

"I take it that the two of you get along well," I state as we pass by Diem's room.

He shrugs. "For the most part, we do. There are times when she tries my patience, but I guess that's what little sisters do."

"Does your mother still have to break up fights between the two of you like she did when you were children?"

This question causes Alexander's body to stiffen. "My mother hasn't been in our lives for quite some time."

"I'm sorry to hear that," I tell him as the feeling of pity for the loss of a mother wafts over me. Nowhere in my research about Alexander King did it talk about a strained relationship with his mother. It then falls upon me to lighten the mood since I seemed to have brought up a touchy subject. "Well, seems to be her loss, and Diem seems to be able to create in spite of her not being around."

He nods but doesn't say another word about the topic.

Clearly talking about his mother isn't something that he likes to do. I make a mental note about that so I tread lightly on the subject stay on his good side. I want this little arrangement to go off without a hitch. In order for the board to believe that we're a happy couple, we have to maintain what I like to refer to as a pleasant working relationship.

When we come to the third door on the left, Alexander stops. "This is your room. You may decorate it however you wish while you're here. If you need anything at all, please feel free to ask Aggie or Darby. They will see to your needs. Unless your needs are of the sexual variety. In that case, I expect you to report directly to me so that I can assist you with that. I like for all my guests to be satisfied."

"And there's the asshole I know," I say. "I wondered where you'd been hiding for the last few minutes."

Alexander pulls a key from his pants pocket and then dangles it in front of me. "You know very well that I can be *nice* when I want to be, Margo. I thought I was very accommodating in Vegas."

There's no mistaking the teasing tone of his voice, and it pisses me off. I don't like the fact that I gave in to this man, and I don't like him throwing the fact that I've fucked him in my face. And I for damn sure want to make sure that he knows that he's never getting inside these panties ever again.

I narrow my eyes. "Well, don't worry about being nice to me while I'm here. I made sure to pack my own battery-powered happiness maker, so I'm afraid I won't need you to accommodate anything relating to me ever again."

That trademark grin returns in full force. "I seem to remember you making these same threats before, and we still ended up married."

"For now," I reply and then snatch the key from his hand. "That's one problem I intend to remedy as soon as possible."

He leans against the wall and folds his arms over his chest. "Well, Princess, I hate to be the one to burst whatever perfectly planned little bubble you've got going on in that beautiful brain of yours, but we're not separating until I'm sure the board buys that we were at least madly in love when we said I do and we have to pay Yamada a visit on his island this coming Thurday."

I twist my lips. I wish I could go back and punch myself square in the face during that part of our nuptials and scream 'I don't!' because now King has me by the proverbial balls, and he knows it. I just have to keep cool and not lose my head, even though the man is frustratingly gorgeous and has a body that I wouldn't mind seeing naked again. Being so attracted to him complicates the hell out of things.

I will not be lured into temptation. I still have a job to do. Winning back Buchanan Industries and securing my future must be my main focus. It's time to keep my eyes on the prize and not on Alexander's stunning physique or his promises of naughty pleasure.

"Don't worry, King. This marriage is nothing more than a business relationship for me. I'll uphold my end of the deal. By the time I'm through putting on a show, this whole damn town will believe that we're the most in love couple on the planet." I square my shoulders after my little mental pep talk and shove the key into the door. I pass Alexander and step into the room without saying another word.

Chapter VII
SHOCK AND AWE

Alexander

MARGO DIDN'T COME OUT OF her room at all last night. Aggie got worried after a while and checked on her, but she still couldn't convince her to come down to the main floor of the apartment for dinner. Instead, Aggie fixed a tray and took it up to her. She told me that I needed to give the girl time to adjust to the situation and reminded me that I'm not always the easiest man to live with.

This morning, I got the same coldness from Margo when I offered her a ride to work. I explained that it would be best to be seen coming to the office together since we're a happily married couple.

I could tell that she was reluctant, but she agreed.

I steal a quick glance in her direction in the elevator. Her dark hair is down today, flowing freely in big waves over her shoulders. It's such a stark contrast from the bright red dress she's wearing that I can't help but notice every curve on her body.

As if she can feel my eyes studying the contours of her body, she turns her head and points her gaze right at me. I don't make any apologies when she catches me either. I never say sorry unless I mean it, and in this case, I don't think there's anything wrong with staring at the work of art that's Margo's body. So I might as well compliment her on it.

"Your tits look amazing in that dress. You should wear it more often," I tell her.

She narrows her eyes. "Do you always have to be so crass?"

"Yes," I muse with a smile. "It's part of my charm."

"Who said you were charming?" she jabs back at me.

I raise one eyebrow. "I seem to recall being able to charm you out of your panties on more than two occasions."

"Well," she scoffs. "Everyone loses their mind from time to time. If anyone ever questions me about it, I'll plead temporary insanity."

"Insane with lust, you mean." I chuckle.

"Hardly," she says as the elevator doors open.

When we step out into the lobby, Darby stands near the front exit. He smiles the moment his eyes land on us. I know what he's thinking. God knows he and Aggie have voiced how beautiful Margo is enough times since they met her yesterday. Although they aren't entirely pleased with the way I ended up married, they somehow believe Margo might be a suitable match for me since she doesn't seem to take my shit. While their opinions mean a great deal to me because I consider them to be my family, I don't think they know what in the hell they're talking about. They obviously don't know the bitchy side of Margo like I do. Once they see that come out, I'm sure they'll be celebrating the day I get Margo to sign the divorce papers.

Without permission, I wrap my arm around Margo's waist and pull her tightly against me.

She begins to pull away nearly instantly. "What in the hell do you think you're doing?"

"Acting married and madly in love, of course," I reply as smoothly as I can.

She shakes her head. "There's no one here to put on a show for."

I swirl my index finger in a circle. "There are eyes everywhere. If we want to be believed, anytime we're in public we need to make our relationship appear to be real. So get ready because these hands will be on you a lot."

I can tell by the heated expression on Margo's face that she would love nothing more than to smack my hand away. The woman seems to be very fond of inflicting pain to my face with her hands. I can tell this is killing her to allow me to grope her a little in public, but before she has time to argue much more, Darby steps in front of us to open the door.

"It's almost working," Darby says. "The two of you aren't smiling. If you want the world to buy it, you'll be needin' to sell it a wee bit more."

I glance down at Margo and plaster on the biggest grin that I can fit on my face. "Hear that, sweetie. We both need to smile. We're in love, remember?"

"How can I forget," she replies with a dry tone. "How's this?"

She tips her head and stares up at me, and it gives me a moment to stare into those gorgeous blue eyes of hers. The moment she smiles, I swear to God my breath catches. I've never believed in the saying 'You take my breath away,' but it just fucking happened to me.

"You're perfect," I tell her, and at that moment, I mean it.

My honesty must surprise her because her usual sarcastic comment doesn't follow. Instead, her eyes remain locked on mine as she swallows hard.

My heart is pounding like a thoroughbred's hooves beating against the ground. I know it makes me sound like a complete fucking pussy, but if I had met Margo Buchanan in a different way, I could see myself actually being with this woman. Not only is she the hottest thing I've ever seen, but she's wicked smart and has a witty tongue. Beauty and brains like hers are a rarity. She's like finding a goddamn unicorn.

Darby clears his throat. "Your car has arrived, Alex."

I shake my head, breaking out of my daze. I can't seem to keep my head on straight when I'm with Margo, and I need to figure out a way to stop that. So much is riding on every move I make right now. I can't afford to screw anything up. My head has to be in the game at all times, or I might lose everything.

The car ride to the office is quiet. I'm sure we both have a lot of thinking to do and neither of us find it necessary to make small talk. I appreciate the silence.

When we step into the elevator to head up to the office, I tell her, "Even though this is a work setting, we still need to maintain our little act, so I expect you to play your part of doting wife."

Margo smoothes her hair down with her fingers. "Don't worry, King. I know my part and I plan to play it well, so you better hold up your end of the deal."

"I never go back on my word."

"Good to know," she says.

The elevator dings, and as if on cue, I place my hand on the small of her back. Her body shivers under my touch, and I fight back a smirk. It pleases me greatly to know that I have that effect on her.

The doors open, and since I'm much later than normal, every set of eyes in the front office is on us the instant we walk in together.

Margo stiffens, and I know she'll probably hate what I'm about to do, but I want everything out in the open as quickly as possible. I'm the kind of man who wants to break the bad news to the world instead of allowing speculation to run wild.

I lean down and kiss her cheek and then whisper, "It's best to maintain control at all times, don't you agree?"

She nods and then pulls back and smiles. "Absolutely."

That's when she does something that shocks the shit out of me. She traces my cheek with the tips of her fingers before she kisses me. I close my eyes briefly and allow myself the pleasure of tasting her lips. She's so damn addictive.

She pulls away before I'm ready, but I know it would be definitely crossing the line to fuck her in front of an audience even though my cock is growing stiff in my slacks. That's a sexual harassment lawsuit just waiting to happen.

Margo saunters away, giving her hips an extra swish as she heads toward her desk, and it causes me to smile. That naughty little minx knows how to play her part very well indeed. Hell, if she keeps that up, *I* might just begin to buy into it.

It's unusually quiet in the office, and I turn my attention back to the front office staff who are all frozen in place with their mouths agape. That's enough of a show for them.

"What are you all looking at? Back to work," I order, and they all instantly go back to pretending to be in a huge rush.

I stalk past them all, and then come to a halt when I find myself at Margo's desk. "Good work, Mrs. King."

She smiles. "Let me know if they need an encore to buy it."

I shake my head before turning toward my office. "I think we've stunned them enough for one day."

I try to stay busy for the rest of the day by finalizing a few small deals I've been working on. When it's nearly lunchtime, there's a quick knock on my door before Jack comes striding in.

He has a huge grin on his face, so I know that he's pleased to hear that people are buying into the little act with Margo. "You son-of-a-bitch. You've done it. People actually believe that you and Margo are in love. I never thought you'd be able to get her to go along with it."

I lean back in my chair and my lips pull up at one corner. "Come on, Jack. You're acting like you've just met me. You know I can close any deal. This thing with Margo is nothing but another deal."

He plops down in the chair in front my desk. "So if this is just a deal, it means that you've promised her something."

This was the part of my plan that I dreaded explaining to Jack, but I knew it had to be done. I stand up and then smooth my tie down before heading over to the bar. I flip two glasses over and pull the glass cork from the crystal decanter before pouring the scotch.

"Shit," Jack mutters as he pushes himself up from the chair. "If you're pouring the liquor before one, I know you're about to break some bad news to me. Please tell me that you didn't give in to her demands and promise her something completely unreasonable."

I sigh and hand him a glass. "What would you have me do, Jack? I can't very well lose control of my father's company."

He shakes his head. "I get that, man. I do. But couldn't you figure out something else to give her—write her a check or something? We'll lose so much money if this Buchanan deal doesn't go through."

As much as it pains me to think about walking away from the deal I've been working on for months and losing out on all the money that we stand to make, it hurts way fucking worse to think about a bunch of old, greedy bastards running the company that my father built.

Chapter VIII
PUPPY LOVE

Margo

THE FIRST DAY WE WENT public was the hardest. Since then, rumors have been flying all around the city. Gossip in this town spreads at lightning speed, especially when it involves the Naughty King and the Feisty Princess *willingly* committing to each other. If I were on the receiving end of that news, I would pity the idiots for thinking a relationship like that can actually work.

Good thing I'm not in this relationship for something as silly as love.

I don't believe in love. I've seen too much when it comes to relationships; not only courtesy of my mother, but also from the assholes I've dated. One, in particular, did a number on my heart, so I learned that in order to not get hurt, you have to keep your feelings on a tight leash at all times.

At this point, I couldn't care less if people pity me and think I'm a dumb twit who Alexander will blindside. I'm doing this for me and the company that will rightfully belong to me someday.

I find myself curled up on a chaise lounge in one of the biggest private libraries I've ever seen. Ever since I was a little girl, I've enjoyed reading. Sneaking my mother's romance novels and reading them in secret was one of my favorite pastimes. I find that as an adult, whenever I'm feeling stressed, a steamy romance seems to take my mind off reality for a bit. And this feels like the perfect place to hide out other than my room while I'm trapped here.

"Alexander? Aggie?" I hear a female voice call from the front of the apartment. "Anyone here?"

The distinct sound of heels clicking against the marble alerts me that whoever is in here is heading my way. I slide a bookmark into place and then swing my legs over the side of the seat just in time to see a four-legged ball of fur bound in my direction.

The yellow lab pup jumps into my lap and instantly assaults my face with his wet tongue. I giggle as I try to pull him off me. "My, you're a friendly thing, aren't you?" As if to answer me, the puppy barks and then places a paw on my arm. I stroke his head and smile. "You're about the cutest thing I've seen in a long time."

"Jimmy Chew!" The voice from earlier sounds in the room I'm in. "There you are!" The moment my eyes land on the woman, I instantly remember her from high school. Diem looks exactly the same, with her long blond hair and bright green eyes, only now she's a little older and more beautiful.

Diem rushes over to me. "I'm so sorry, Margo. Jimmy is obviously still in need of a few lessons with a good obedience trainer."

I wave her off, surprised that she remembers me as well. "It's no problem at all. I actually love dogs."

She smiles. "Me, too."

"His name is cute," I tell her as I continue to pet Jimmy.

Diem sits on the couch across from me on the other side of the large wooden coffee table. "Thanks. Those are my favorite shoes, so when I was thinking about a name, that was the first thing that popped into my mind."

"I think it's an excellent choice." I glance in her direction and feel the need to strike up a conversation so we're not sitting here in awkward silence. "I was admiring your paintings the other day. They are quite good."

Her smile widens. "That's very kind of you. Thank you. I actually just sold my very first piece, so I'm hopeful that's a testament to my having true talent."

"Congratulations. Alexander told me that the other evening."

Diem adjusts on the couch, and I can tell by the way she's fidgeting in the seat that she's uncomfortable. She's probably wondering what in the hell I'm doing in her family home considering we never really spoke back in school.

She licks her lips and eyes me suspiciously. "So it's true, then—the rumors about you and my brother being married?"

Looks like she knows exactly why I'm here. Word travels quickly in this city.

It shouldn't shock me that Alexander didn't tell his sister. I mean, after all, he didn't mean to marry me or make me apart of his family, so I can see why he wouldn't want his sister in all this. But it still doesn't mean it was the right thing to do. If he wants people to believe that we are actually married, then he should've told his family, just as I told mine.

My lips pull into a tight line. Confirming this for Diem might piss Alexander off, but it has to be done.

"It's true," I say with ease that surprises me.

Diem tilts her head. "That must've been some trip to Vegas. I'm betting that Yamada was involved in some way."

I nod. "I'm not positive because the details are all still a little fuzzy, but I think he was the ringleader of the whole thing."

"I knew it!" she exclaims. "Honestly, I'm shocked. I was afraid the two of you would kill each other in Vegas. Never in my wildest dreams did I ever imagine this happening, but I should've expected it. Whenever Alexander and Yamada get together, something crazy always happens."

"They seem like quite the pair."

"That's putting it lightly." She chuckles. "The two alone are something, but when you add Jack to the mix, scandalous debauchery ensues. The three of them together is like one big fat never-ending party."

"I can see that. Jack and Alexander seem a lot alike," I tell her.

"You know, I used to think that too, but Jack has really shown me a different side of himself lately. He can be a gentleman when he wants to be." A slight blush creeps into her cheeks, and I instantly wonder if Diem has a crush on her brother's best friend. "He's actually the person to whom I sold my first painting."

I lift my eyebrows. "Wow. That's awesome. I didn't take Jack as an art buff, but I'm sure the painting he bought was stunning just like the rest of your work displayed around here."

"You really are too kind, but I don't know if I would necessarily refer to the piece that he bought as beautiful considering it was a self-portrait."

"Really?" Now that adds a twist to this little story. Maybe the attraction is a mutual thing. I bet Alexander doesn't have the first clue that his little sister and his best friend seem to be into one another. "Well, it sounds to me like Jack digs the woman who painted it a lot." I give her a wink.

Her blush colors her cheeks in full force as she lifts her shoulders in a bashful shrug. "I'm still not sure about that yet, and he hasn't made any real moves yet, but I think it's because he's afraid of what Alexander might say."

"Who's afraid of me now?" Alexander's voice slices through the room, and Diem instantly stiffens.

Alexander struts into the room and stops directly in front of me, folding his arms across his broad chest. Diem's back is to him, and she's staring at me with wide-eyes, begging me silently not to say a word about what she just admitted to me.

His eyes flick down to Jimmy, who is now asleep on my lap. "I wasn't aware that you had a dog."

"Oh, he's—"

"That's because he's not Margo's dog." Before I have a chance to stumble over explaining that the cute little pup isn't mine, Diem feels the need to interject. Diem turns toward her brother. "That's what we were just talking about, actually. I was afraid of what you would say about the dog."

Alexander sighs. "You have your own apartment, Squirt. If you want a dog to keep you company, you don't have to ask my permission. You're the one who'll have to take responsibility for it."

"The thing is, the dog isn't actually for me either. He's for you."

Alexander furrows his brow. "Why would you get me a dog?"

Diem stands up, and the moment she does, Jimmy's little head pops up to watch her. She steps over to me and scoops the dog up into her arms. "I actually picked him out weeks ago before he was weaned from his mother. I thought a dog might keep you company since I moved out. If I had known you were about to get married, I might have reconsidered buying you the dog."

Alexander's eyes flick in my direction, and I instantly throw my hands up in surrender. "Don't look at me. She knew before she got here."

His gaze shoots back over to Diem. "How?"

She chews on the corner of her lower lip. "Everyone's buzzing about it. It seems that the two of you kissed in front of the entire staff of King, and they started researching the shit out of the two of you. They found notice of your marriage license online somehow."

"Shit," he growls before scrubbing his hand down his face.

"Here," she says as she places Jimmy in Alexander's arms. "They say dogs relieve stress."

"Diem . . . no . . . I don't need a dog." Alexander stands there stiffly, cradling the yellow pup in his arms.

Diem turns and sits back down. "I dare you to resist that face. His name is Jimmy Chew and he's the most adorable thing on this entire planet."

He stares down at the tiny ball of fur. Jimmy stretches his neck in order to lick Alexander's face, which causes him to smile. "He *is* pretty cute."

Diem lets out a little squeal. "See! I knew even you wouldn't be immune."

I catch myself grinning from ear to ear at the very sight of Alexander holding what quite possibly may be the most adorable puppy on the planet. It allows me to see another glimpse of that easygoing guy I spotted with Yamada the night of Yamada's party in Vegas—the guy he likes to keep hidden from me and the rest of the world.

"You didn't want people to know that the two of you were married?" Diem questions with a confused expression as she watches Alexander cradle Jimmy in his arms. "If that's the case, then you probably shouldn't have made out in front of fifty people."

"It wasn't fifty," he refutes instantly.

"Same difference," she counters. "What's the big deal? You meant to get married, right?" Alexander sighs as he takes a seat next to her. She tilts her head and studies her brother. "You didn't, did you?"

King's lips pull into a tight line and then his eyes flick to mine quickly before he turns his gaze to Diem. "No."

My mouth drops open. I can't believe he just exposed the secret he's been hell-bent on keeping. I'm tempted to say something, but stop myself, knowing that it's his secret. If he trusts his sister with it, that's his business. I just hope she doesn't go blabbing about it to the rest of the city.

"Yamada?" She only has to say his name like a question, and it seems to resonate with Alexander.

He nods. "Yes. And now it's a fucked-up mess. The board will be all over my ass because of that stupid clause Father put in his will if it gets out that Margo and I rushed into this unintentionally. Jack is afraid the board will see it as a weakness, accompanied by poor decision-making, and swoop in to contest my sole authority to make decisions for the King Corporation."

Diem's mouth drops open. "They can't do that, can they?"

"Afraid so, but Margo has agreed to help me convince everyone that we're a happily married couple."

Diem turns her attention to me. "That's really awesome of you, considering I know the two of you don't really get along so well."

I open my mouth to reply, but Alexander cuts me off.

"Don't toot her horn too much, Squirt. It's not like she's doing this out of the goodness of her heart. She's getting something out of it too."

"Just what's rightly mine and you know it," I fire back in my defense.

She lifts her eyebrows. "Oh? Well, I'm still glad she's doing it. I don't want you to have any issues with Daddy's company. I knew it meant a lot that it would be in your hands when he was no longer here. And on that note—" Diem pushes herself up from the couch. "I'd better get going so you two can get ready."

"Ready?" I asked confused as to what she's referring to.

"For the King Corporation Education Gala, of course. It's the company's biggest event of the year, and they will expect Alexander to make an appearance with his new bride. If you ask me, it's the perfect time to convince the board that you're a happy couple."

"You're right," Alexander says as he stands. "I hadn't told Margo because I didn't think it would be a good idea to have her there, but it might be best to confront the board head-on before the rumors get to them. Here." He begins to hand

Jimmy back to Diem, but she shakes her head. "Come on. What am I supposed to do with him?"

Diem smiles and begins to backpedal out of the room. "He's your dog. You'll figure it out. Good luck, you two."

Once she leaves the room, Alexander turns to me. "The gala begins at eight. I know it doesn't leave you much time to get ready, but there are new gowns in your closet that will fit the occasion. I had Aggie pick up a few for you just in case I needed you to accompany me to the gala. Choose whichever one you like."

As much as I want to argue and tell him that I'm not going, I know that in order to uphold my end of the deal, I need to play my part. A wife would be happy to attend something like this on husband's arm, so I'll have to force myself to smile.

I push up from the chaise. "I'll be ready."

Alexander nods. "Thank you." As if on cue, Jimmy barks. "I can't believe she got me a dog. She knows how busy I am."

I smile as I lean in and pet the dog. "I think it's sweet that she cares enough about you to worry about you being lonely."

Alexander's gaze locks on mine the moment I glance up at his face. He opens his mouth to say something as his eyes search my face, and this weird tension floats between us. I'm not sure what he was about to say to me, but whatever it is, he's holding back.

I'm curious as to what it might've been, but I don't ask. Instead, I step around him and head toward my room. "I'll meet you in the foyer?"

"Seven thirty sharp," he calls over his shoulder.

As I head to my room, it hits me that living in this apartment with Alexander King hasn't been anything like I expected. Everything from his relationship with Aggie and Darby to his willingness to give in to his sister has all surprised me. Maybe there is some truth to what Yamada was saying about Alexander having a heart because I'm pretty sure I just caught a glimpse of it back there.

Chapter IX
THE GAME PLAN

Alexander

STANDING IN THE FOYER OF my apartment, I glance down at my watch. What in the hell takes a woman so damn long to get ready?

Jimmy paws at my leg, begging for my attention. I bend down and scratch the soft fur behind his right ear. "I can't play right now, buddy. You be good for Aggie while I'm gone."

Diem's right. I have a hard time resisting this dog no matter how hard I try.

A sigh escapes me as I stand upright and check my watch *again*. I hate being late; it's a pet peeve of mine. I always have to be early. I'm tempted to go to Margo's room to tell her to hurry her sweet ass up, but before I can decide, she appears at the top of the staircase.

My breath catches at the very sight of her in her black gown. She pauses for a brief second, and our eyes meet just before she descends the staircase. It's like watching a scene from a movie with her moving in slow motion, as she gets closer and closer to me. She's pulled her dark hair back, and the style accentuates her gorgeous face. She's even more stunning than any time I've ever seen her before. It's truly like staring at a piece of art, but I don't think Diem could even create something so perfect. I can't pull my eyes away.

I stand there with my mouth hanging open, and it's hard for me to even find the appropriate words to say to her as she halts directly in front of me.

Margo glances down at her outfit and runs her hand over her stomach as if to smooth out the fabric that's already lying perfectly in place. "It doesn't fit exactly right, but I think it can work for a few hours."

I bite my bottom lip. "You're stunning, Margo."

Her hypnotic blue eyes flit up to meet mine, and my heart flutters in my chest. "Thank you. That's the first real compliment you've ever given me."

I tilt my head. "I don't believe that's true. I distinctly remember telling you that you had great tits."

She bends down to pet Jimmy on the top of his head before flicking her eyes back in my direction. "Why do you always do that?"

"Do what?" I ask, completely perplexed as to what she's referring to.

"Get crude with me every time we have a conversation. Every time you say something sweet to me, I almost start believing you aren't a complete asshole, but you always ruin the moment with that mouth of yours. It wouldn't kill you to be nice every once in a while."

Her words stun me for a moment. I didn't mean to insult her, and having her in a pissy mood before we leave for this event isn't ideal. God knows I don't need her bitching me out in front of the very people who need to believe we're in a real relationship.

"You're right, Margo. I'll work on that," I tell her. "I promise to tone things down a bit."

"Thank you," she replies. "It will be nice not to be sexually harassed by you every time we have a conversation."

"I'm not saying it'll never happen again. I mean, have you seen you? I can't help thinking about your body and sex when I see you. You're sexy as hell," I admit.

Redness creeps up into her cheeks, and it's the first time anything I've ever said to her has caused that reaction. At that very moment, I realize the way to win Margo Buchanan over is with flattery. My habitual filthy talk had turned her on and helped me find my way into that sweet pussy of hers, but it never made her blush. It was like it pissed her off, but she was so turned on that she allowed me to fuck her even against her better judgment. But telling her how amazing I think she looks and meaning it affects her.

"Ready?" she prompts.

I shake my head. My palms begin to sweat as I reach into the pocket of my dress slacks. The velvet box in my hand suddenly feels like it weighs a ton as I hold it out to her. "I got you something."

Her eyes widen. "Alexander . . ."

"It's just a replacement for the one I gave you in Vegas. If we are going to pull this off, then we need to pull out all the stops and make our relationship believable. If you were really my wife, the ring on your finger would be large enough for the entire world to see. I would want everyone to know that you were mine. Clearly, our options in Vegas were limited when we went ring shopping in the middle of the night."

I open the black velvet lid, revealing the fifteen-carat diamond ring that I bought her from *Jacob and Co*.

Margo gasps as her hand flies to cover her mouth. "Oh, my God. Alexander! I cannot accept that."

I pull it out of the box and hold it out to her. "Consider it a thank-you gift for helping me. It's yours to keep, and you may do as you please with it once we're through with this whole marriage thing."

I wait with bated breath for her answer. She stares down at it, and for a moment it almost feels like I'm actually proposing to her. "What do you say, Margo? Will you be my fake wife?"

"Yes," her answer comes out barely above a whisper and relief floods through me.

I would've felt like a complete jackass for getting a replacement ring if she would've ended up saying no.

She swallows hard as she takes the ring from me. "It's the most gorgeous thing I've ever seen."

"Allow me." I snap the box closed and stuff it back into my pocket before taking the ring and sliding it onto Margo's ring finger. I stare down at her hand, memorized by the way it sparkles. It actually looks even better than I expected on her.

"It's perfect," she says. "I love it. Thank you, Alexander."

I turn and then extend my right elbow to her. "Come on, Mrs. King. It's time to break every woman's heart in Manhattan."

She shakes her head as she loops her arm through mine. "You are so damn full of yourself."

I shrug while wearing a lopsided grin. "It's not being conceited when it's the truth. You know as well as I do that most of the women in this city dream about taming me. They'll be jealous as hell once they see for themselves that you've hooked me."

"So you think I'm about to walk into a pissed off beehive because you're off the market?"

I nod. "I hope you're prepared to use that witty tongue of yours to ward off all the questions you're about to be bombarded with. I need you to defend our relationship to anyone who questions it. It's vital that you're in on this charade with me one hundred percent."

She pats my forearm with her other hand as if to soothe me. "Don't worry. We've got this."

I stare down at her and smile. "Shall we?"

With that, we say our goodbyes to Jimmy and head toward the front door. I take a deep breath and mentally prepare myself for what I'm sure is about to be a very interesting evening.

Chapter X
HELL OF A RIDE
Margo

IT'S A QUICK RIDE TO the gala or at least it felt that way. Alexander and I spent the time going over scenarios of what we would say to members of the board once we ran into them at the event. If there's one thing I can say about Alexander King, it's that he likes to be thorough.

We're sitting in the back of the limo, waiting for our turn to be dropped off at the entrance, when Alexander turns to me. "Perhaps we should go over some rules of engagement while we're in there."

I turn my head to face him. "Such as?"

Alexander presses the button on his door and effectively rolls up the privacy wall, separating us from the driver.

"Kissing for one," he says coolly. "It will be expected of us once we get in there. People are going to want to see some level of affection displayed toward one another."

"I'm pretty sure we'll be able to handle some simple pecks on the cheek. Seriously, Alexander, you're overthinking this. People will buy that we're together."

"How can you be so sure?" he asks. "Maybe we better practice a couple of kisses just to make sure we're on the same page. I don't feel like getting smacked in the middle of a party if I do something to offend you. I need to know what your limits are."

I level my stare on him. "You're really asking me to kiss you right now?"

He licks his lips and then beckons me with the crook of his finger. "Come here."

As ridiculous as this idea seems, he might just have a point based on our history. When we touch, crazy things happen. Setting boundaries between us is a good idea.

I sigh and then slide over toward him. Alexander's eyes trail down my body, taking a moment to stare at my chest. This low-cut Prada dress accentuates my breasts nicely, so I can't fault him for his lingering gaze.

He tilts his head and then places his hand on the bare skin of my thigh. "Will doing this get me smacked?"

My heart thunders inside my chest. The heat from the contact of his skin on mine is sending my body into overdrive.

"No," I tell him with a breathy tone. "But if you go any higher than that, it might."

"Noted." He arches one eyebrow. "How about this?" He moves his hand from my thigh and then cups my cheek. The pad of his thumb swirls around my skin before it dips lower to brush the corner of my mouth.

My mouth drifts open, and I close my eyes as he traces my lower lip with his thumb. An ache between my legs builds. It's crazy how my body reacts so quickly with one simple touch from this man.

I don't even realize he's leaning into me until I feel his warm breath on my face. "You don't know how badly I want to kiss you right now."

"What's stopping you?" I ask, needing more of his skin on mine in that moment.

He leans his forehead against mine. "Don't tease me like that, Margo."

"Who's teasing?" My hand snakes up his chest until it finds the exposed flesh on his neck. "I want you to kiss me."

He cups my face. "What are you doing to me? Why can't I resist you?"

I bite my lip as I gaze into his eyes. "I've asked myself the same thing about a million times. I'm supposed to hate you, but I can't stop wanting you."

That was easier to admit to him that I ever thought it would be.

Alexander sucks a rush of air in through his nose and his chest heaves. He doesn't move away from me, only stretches his hand out and hits the intercom button, simply instructing, "Drive."

"Where to, sir?" the driver asks.

"I don't give a fuck where. Drive until I tell you to stop," he orders.

The words no sooner leave his mouth than both of his hands are cradling my head, holding me in place while he crushes his lips to mine. His tongue swipes against my lips, begging for entrance while the trim whiskers on his face poke me. I moan as I open my mouth and welcome him inside.

This is wrong, but I can't find a reason within me to stop. It feels too good—too right.

His hand slides down my neck and then sweeps across my collarbone before pushing the straps of my dress off my shoulders. "I want you, Margo. Tell me that you want me, too."

His admission causes my blood to pump a little faster through my veins, and his need to hear my confirmation has every inch of me on fire. This man has a way of turning me on like no other, and he's damn near impossible to resist.

I grip the collar of his crisp white tuxedo shirt and stare into his eyes as I straddle his lap. The bottom hem of my dress rides up my thighs as I press myself against the hard erection in his pants. "I need you, Alexander."

Those simple words are all the permission that he needs. Alexander attacks my lips with his once again, while his hands work frantically to get me out of this dress. The need to have him inside me to stop my building ache is intense. I lift my bottom a bit to gain access to his belt. When that's out of the way, I make quick work of unzipping his pants and reaching inside his underwear. He lifts his hips, allowing me to shove the fabric down. I take his cock into my hand. The skin of his shaft is silky as I stroke his considerable length.

Alexander watches me carefully under his long lashes as he reaches between my legs and strokes my clit through the material of my underwear. "These panties are soaked. I love that you get that way for me. Tell me, Margo. When you pleasure yourself, do you think of me?"

My chest heaves as Alexander pushes my panties to the side and slides his finger against my most sensitive flesh. If he keeps this up, I might explode.

"Oh, God." I throw my head back and allow his naughty words to ring through my mind as I enjoy his touch.

"Do you think of this, Margo? Do you long for it? Do you touch yourself and wish it was me?"

I bite my bottom lip while I curl my fingers around his cock. I can't concentrate on anything but my own pleasure and the way he's making me feel. He has me so turned on I can't see straight.

"I've missed this." He leans in and licks the soft skin just below my ear. "When I don't have you, I'm dreaming of fucking you, tasting your lips, and hearing you scream my name while you come all over my tongue."

Fire pools in the pit of my belly. I lean in and kiss him before moaning into his mouth. "Alexander . . ."

"Tell me, Margo. Do you want me inside you?" he murmurs.

"Yesss," I hiss.

He moves his hand, leaving my underwear pushed to the side and then pulls me back on top of him. The warmth of his cock against my clit feels so damn good. I rock against him a few times, coating him with my desire and allowing our skin to slide together with ease.

Alexander goes to work, trying to undo the zipper in the back of my dress. He curses when it sticks halfway down and then tugs roughly on the dress, losing all patience with taking his time in getting me naked.

The distinct sound of the fabric ripping causes my head to snap up. "My dress!"

Panic shoots through me, knowing I won't be able to go into the gala like this.

Alexander threads his fingers through my hair and locks me into place. The tip of his nose traces my jawline, breathing me in as he continues his deliciously slow torture of teasing me.

"I'll buy you a fucking new one. Don't you dare stop," he growls in my ear.

I do exactly as he commands and continue rocking my hips. He shoves the torn fabric down, allowing it to pool around my hips. His patience with my underwear seems to be gone too because he reaches under my dress and rips them away from my body.

The index finger of his right hand dips into the cup of my bra. It twirls around my nipple before moving on to the next. He bites his lip as he pushes the cups of my strapless bra down, fully exposing my breasts. His tongue darts out and licks the taut pink flesh before he sucks the entire thing into his mouth.

Every nerve in my body comes to life, and I thread my fingers into his thick, dark hair. I rock against him, needing to feel him inside me. "I'm so ready."

Alexander grips my hips, steadying me against him. "I want to feel you, Margo. I want to come inside you this time."

My mind drifts back to the time when we had sex against the door in Vegas and how amazing that felt. That also reminds me this is the second dress he's ruined during sex. He's technically my husband and I'm on birth control, so I don't see the harm in it just this once.

I nod as I play with a strand of his hair that's poking out in the back. "Okay."

He leans in and presses his lips to mine as he shifts his hips and his cock presses against my entrance. A quick thrust of his hips and he slips his dick inside me all the way up to the base.

His mouth drifts open, and he stares up at me with lust-coated eyes as he works my hips in a slow rhythm. "Fuck. So damn amazing."

We rock in time, both getting lost in our own desire—both searching for our own release.

Watching him as he enjoys my body is one of the hottest things I've ever seen. I like knowing that I can cause the asshole control freak, Alexander King, to lose all control. It's powerful and liberating and makes me feel downright sexy.

It doesn't take long before that familiar tingle overtakes every inch of my being. "Oh, that's it," I pant. "Oh, God. Alexander, I'm coming."

No sooner do the words leave my lips do I fall apart, giving in to the wave of pleasure that Alexander's given me.

He tightens his grip on my hips and works them faster and faster until he's biting his lip and sweat beads on his forehead. We lock eyes and a low growl escapes his lips as he explodes inside me, filling me full with his desire.

We stay wrapped in one another's arms, staring into each other's eyes as we try to catch our breath. I don't know what just happened, but this sexual encounter with him felt different—more intimate—and it feels like everything is about to change.

Chapter XI
MAY I CUT IN?

Margo

AFTER A CHANGE OF CLOTHES at Alexander's apartment, I'm heading back down the stairs. Hopefully, we make it to the event this time. I glance at my phone before dropping it into my clutch. We're running extremely late.

When I meet Alexander in the foyer, he takes my hand. The warmth of his fingers curled around mine feels so intimate. I'm not sure what in the hell happened between us back in that limo, but it's more apparent to me now that keeping things strictly business between the two of us is impossible. Something just happens when we're together. There's a pull—a connection—I don't understand, and I'm pretty sure Alexander feels it, too. Otherwise, he wouldn't have allowed himself to end up married to me, causing himself a whole lot of grief in the process. He's too smart for that, which is how I know the brain behind that beautiful face of his isn't making the decisions when it comes to me.

I glance down at our hands as we make our way outside to the waiting limo. I'm tempted to ask him if he's merely pretending to show me public affection for the benefit of anyone who's watching or if he's holding my hand because he wants to, but I won't. I don't want to know the answer. If he claims it's just an act, it might hurt.

Inside the limo, I expect for Alexander to pull away from me, but he doesn't. We ride to the gala side by side, still holding hands like a happily married couple.

As we pull up to the building the party is being held in, Alexander turns his head toward me while wearing a devilish smirk. "You ready to try this again, or are you ready for round two?"

A blush creeps over my cheeks. As much as I would love nothing more than to go another round with him, I know there's simply no time for that. Tonight is all about convincing the board members of King Corporation that Alexander is more than capable of running the empire his father left behind.

"As much as I'd like that, we have a job to do," I tell him. "But I'll take a rain check on that second round."

Alexander's smile widens. "Are you sure? I wouldn't want to make your battery operated boyfriend jealous."

I chuckle at his reference to my vibrator. "Don't worry. B.O.B. only wants to see me satisfied. He's probably enjoying the vacation."

"Bob might have to go. You know I'm a jealous man. I don't share, especially when it comes to you." He reaches over and slides one hand between my legs and then brushes my panty-covered folds with his thumb. "And this pussy is all mine."

His words cause me to shiver. Never have I been claimed like this before, and I have to admit, it's a fucking turn-on.

"Tonight, I want you in my bed." Alexander leans in and brushes my lips with his. "But first, we have a little business to handle inside. Are you ready?"

"Let's do this."

A few lingering paparazzi snap photos of Alexander and me as we step out of the car—all of them clamoring for a shot of us to put in the society gossip columns.

"Mr. King, is it true that the two of you are married?" one heavyset, balding man with a camera shouts, but Alexander doesn't even bother to glance in his direction.

Sure, I've been in the society papers before, but no one has ever been desperate to know so much about my personal life. It's weird that people would even care, but things are different for Alexander. He's been on the public radar since he was named youngest billionaire in the world ten years ago when he inherited his father's company. People are fascinated by handsome young men who are extremely wealthy.

Alexander reminds tight-lipped until we make it inside the building. "I'm sure we're going to get a lot of that until the shock over our marriage dies down. As soon as they find another big story to cover, they'll forget about us." He extends his elbow to me, and I loop my arm through his. "Come on. Let's get this ass-kissing over with. The sooner we can get away from these pretentious assholes, the better."

I can't help but laugh. His blunt vocabulary is actually comical when I'm not pissed at him for talking to me that way.

The ballroom is alive with Manhattan's upper-crust society, milling about in their small cliques. A jazz band plays in the corner and a few couples are dancing while everyone else lingers about gossiping or discussing business ventures. A few heads turn in our direction, and it doesn't go unnoticed that I'm clinging to Alexander's arm.

The men in the room nod as if approving Alexander's choice of arm candy for the night, but the women are a completely different story. Their expressions range from pity to contempt. I'm guessing the ones who look like they want to punch me in the face are women Alexander has slept with and aren't quite over him yet.

"I feel like everyone's staring at us," I whisper.

Alexander rubs the light beard covering his face. "Angry beehive, remember? This is where we'll need to sell it most." He gazes down at me. "I'm going to kiss you now. It's best to get this over with. Let them know where we stand, just as we did at the office the other day."

He's right. It will save me from having to explain our relationship status a million different times for the next hour.

I nod. "Okay."

Alexander pinches my chin gently between his thumb and forefinger. "The countdown clock to get you into my bed starts now."

A genuine smile spreads across my face. "Looking forward to it."

He leans down and presses his lips to mine, and the weight of all the eyes in the room judging us falls on my shoulders. The kiss doesn't last long, and it isn't more than a sweet peck, but it's enough to show everyone in this room there is definitely something going on between us.

Alexander pulls back. "Let's work this room."

And that's exactly what we do. We spend the next hour rubbing elbows with some of the wealthiest people in New York. Most of the board members appear to be pleased with the match between Alexander and me. All but one, that is.

A tall, slender blond woman with a little age on her approaches us with a smile, but I can tell right away that it's not genuine. It's a forced act for Alexander's benefit as she leans in and kisses him on both cheeks. "Alexander, darling, how nice to see you."

Alexander's posture is notably different. His stance has gone from relaxed to rigid. Something about this woman obviously puts his guard up.

The woman's eyes instantly flit over to me after she releases Alexander. "Are you going to introduce me to your date?"

His nostrils flare as he inhales deeply. "Camille, this is Margo Buchanan—my wife."

Camille's dark green eyes widen. "Your wife? Wow." She turns her attention to me and extends her hand. "You'll have to excuse my surprise. When Alexander dated my daughter, Jess, he never really seemed like the type to ever settle down. It's hard for me to picture Alexander as a married man."

I swallow down the lump in my throat. I never anticipated on meeting anyone connected to Alexander's ex tonight.

Especially not the one I've been told who broke his heart. It's difficult to digest that the man I'm starting to open myself up to and feel something for was once very much in love with someone else. I'm jealous this woman exists and probably had a relationship with the easygoing Alexander I've witnessed from time to time. It's also hard for me to grasp the reason Alexander is the way he is with women is because of Jess according to Yamada.

I want to get back at this girl for hurting Alexander, even though I don't know her at all.

I turn and lean into Alexander, placing my right hand on his chest as I address Camille. "I keep hearing that my Alexander was quite the ladies' man, but I assure you he's a changed man." I flick my gaze back up to Alexander's smile. "He has my heart completely and I have his. We're each other's everything."

"How lovely, for you." There's a hardened edge to her voice. "I hope that it stays that way."

I level my gaze on Camille and the smile drops off my face while I place my left hand on Alexander's chest to show off the ring he just gave me. "Thank you for your concern, but I assure you it's unnecessary. We're completely in love with one another and will be very happy together. Nothing will get in the way of that."

Her lips twist and I can tell that she despises me and wants nothing more than to tell me off. I don't understand why she would hold ill will toward Alexander. Her daughter is the one who dumped him. She can't possibly be upset that he's moved on with his life.

Instead of saying another word to me, Camille turns on her heel and storms away from us. The sparkly dress she's wearing trail behind her.

I turn back to Alexander. "That was odd. What's her deal?"

Alexander wraps his arm around my waist, drawing me in tightly against his side. "She wanted her daughter to marry me.

She didn't exactly approve of the tennis pro that she ran off with when she left me. He doesn't make enough money to suit Camille's standards."

"So why blame you? Clearly the split with her daughter isn't your fault."

"She knows that, but it doesn't stop her from blaming me. Jess can do no wrong according to her parents, so no matter the situation, it's always going to be someone else's fault—never Jess's."

"That's crazy," I say.

"Agreed, but that's how things work around here. You know that. Family is always going to defend their blood no matter what." He kisses the top of my head. "Let's get out of here. Kissing ass here tonight chapped my lips, and I've had enough of these people for one night. Besides, I do believe we're on a tight schedule for the rest of our plans for the evening."

One side of my mouth pulls up into a grin as I think about all the naughty things he's going to do to my body when we get back to his place. Being married to Alexander King does come with some perks.

Chapter XII
YAMADA'S BOOTY PARADISE

Alexander

I KNEW MARGO WAS STRONG, but I never realized how protective she was until she stood up to Jess's mother two nights ago. It felt nice to hear her brag about how much she was into me, even if she didn't mean it.

Time flew by after that night. It's been much easier than I anticipated to be happily married to Margo Buchanan. In fact, it's gotten so easy that the lines of what's real between us have been blurred. The first word that comes to mind when I think of Margo is no longer hate. I've become quite fond of her, and when the time comes for us to part ways, I'll actually miss her. It's not just the sex I'll miss either. I'll miss how that smart mouth of hers is always there to call me out for being an asshole, and I'll miss her audacity.

I flip her over onto her stomach, yank her to the edge of the bed, and smack her ass with the palm of my hand. She groans just like she did when I spanked her last time. She's a dirty girl underneath that tough persona.

She's the perfect example of the old saying about being a lady in the streets and a freak in the sheets.

I slam my cock back into her tight pussy, causing her to moan. I grip her shoulders and continue to pound into her, searching desperately for my release.

I have to admit that having a bedroom on my private jet comes in quite handy during long flights like this and keeps me from putting on a show for the crew.

She curls her fingers around the sheets as her entire body shakes. "Oh, God. I'm coming. I'm coming. Alexander . . ."

Hearing my name roll off her lips while she's in the midst of ecstasy never gets old. I love making her come. It's highly addictive to witness and even more intoxicating to know that I'm the one making her feel so damn good.

It's not long before every nerve inside me starts tingling, and I explode inside her, filling her full.

I lean down, pressing my chest against her back while I catch my breath. I bite the bare skin on her shoulder and then kiss the exact spot. "I swear it gets better every single time we fuck."

Margo shakes her head, causing her long dark curls to bounce around. "I wish you wouldn't refer to what we are doing as fucking. It sounds so . . ."

"So what?" I probe.

"Graphic."

I pull out of her and then lie down next to her. "What would you have me call it then? Making love?"

She props her head up with her hand and stares down at me. "Don't be ridiculous. We're not in love."

"Exactly," I say. "Which is why it makes perfect sense to refer to it as fucking. We get each other off. It's what we do. We fuck."

She's quiet for a few moments, but then nods. "I suppose you're right."

I pull her to me and kiss her forehead as she lays her head on my chest, effectively ending that topic of conversation.

I trace the bare skin on her shoulder and try to memorize the softness of it because I know sharing moments like this with Margo is a fleeting pastime.

We both lie there in silence—neither of us saying what it is that's running through our mind—both of us knowing that this thing between us is only temporary.

My cell phone on the nightstand rings, and I debate on whether I should answer the call or stay wrapped up just like this.

"Are you going to get that?" Margo asks as she tilts her head up so she can look at me.

I smile down at her as I pull away and reach for the cell on the nightstand. "King."

"Where are you, asshole? It's almost midnight. When Yamada says be here Thursday, it doesn't mean show up Friday morning."

I sigh. "I know. We got a late start. I had a few things to wrap up at the office before we headed out tonight. We'll be there soon enough."

"Okay, but I don't want this weekend to turn out like Vegas where you spend the entire time playing eat the cookie with Dime Piece." There's irritation in his voice. "Yamada expects a huge party this time."

"You got it. And I promise tomorrow we'll party, but just give me tonight alone with Margo when we get there."

I know that I flew out here to spend the weekend with him and secure the Buchanan deal for his company, but I don't want to pull myself away from Margo tonight.

"Okay. Yamada will give you your fuck night with Dime Piece, but tomorrow you assholes better be ready because Yamada has a big surprise for you."

I chuckle. "Don't worry, buddy. We'll get it out of our systems tonight. Tomorrow, you'll have our undivided attention."

"Oh, sexy, sexy. Can Yamada video you? We put that shit on the Internet and make you famous. Dime Piece could be a centerfold model."

"Good night, Yamada." I quickly cut him off before he expands his idea about showing Margo's body off to the world because I fucking hate the very idea of that.

"Is he upset?" Margo asks.

I stare down at her and run my fingers through her thick hair. "No, just seemed disappointed. I wouldn't worry too much about him, though. Yamada is pretty resilient. The man loves a good party, and it doesn't matter who it's with most of the time."

"He said you two went to college together." It's a statement, not a question. "It's hard to picture the two of you as such good friends."

I smile as I think back on the night I met Yamada. "It's hard not to like the little asshole. He has a way of making you have so much fun that you don't care how absolutely ridiculous you look while doing it. The first night I met him, he was able to talk me into doing a few keg stands in order to get noticed by a girl."

"Was it Jess?" she asks, and instantly, my body stiffens.

"How do you know about her?"

It wasn't a secret. Those who know me well knew I was in a long-term relationship with Jess, but I don't like to talk about it. Some things need to stay fucking buried because they hurt too damn much.

"Yamada . . ." She shrugs.

Figures. He never did know how to keep his mouth shut. Now, I need to figure out exactly what my friend has been telling her about me.

"What did he say?"

"Not much," she admits. "He only said that I was the second girl who you were ever able to get before him—Jess was the first, but then she broke your heart."

I blow a rush of air out of my nose. "I don't like to talk about her."

Margo chews the inside corner of her lower lip. "I can respect that. Relationships suck. Promises aren't always kept and people get hurt, which is why I decided a long time ago that I never wanted to fall in love."

"That's good that you protect yourself because love is for suckers." I trace the contours of her beautiful face and wish that I didn't believe that. "I'm glad we both can see what we're doing here for the physicality of it and nothing more."

There's a flicker of pain in her expression before she nods. "It's good we've both agreed this is just fucking then."

My heart squeezes at that thought. Suddenly, I wish I had never said that. I didn't mean to make her think that what was happening between us didn't mean anything to me because it does. While I'm certainly not in love, I do feel a definite attachment to her. It would be so easy to fall for Margo if I allowed myself to open up, but deep down, we both know a relationship between us would never work. We're both too controlling, and when I go behind her back and make this deal with Yamada to tear her father's company apart, she'll hate me even more than she ever did. I know it. That's why this has to be just fucking. That's why, as much as I want to have her in my bed just like this every damn night, it can never happen. However, I have the urge to at least let her know this time we have spent together meant something to me.

"Would it be strange to say I'm no longer excited by the thought of divorcing you?"

She shakes her head. "I was just thinking the same thing. It's weird to say that I would like to date my husband."

I chuckle. "It definitely does sound odd when you put it like that. As much as I would like to say we could try dating, I think we should wait and see how things go between us for a while. I mean, it was only last week that you hated my guts."

"That's true. Perhaps you're right."

A cocky grin spreads over my face. "I usually am."

She rolls her eyes and then pushes herself up from the bed and heads to the bathroom.

A few hours later, we're in a helicopter heading toward Yamada's island. He's going to be pissed that we're here so late, but I know he'll eventually get over it.

I've never seen a sunrise like this before. The sky lights up as the sun pops up above the rippling water, lighting up the ocean as far as the eye can see. The turquoise waters meet the multicolored sky. I'll give the little shit one thing. He picked one of the most beautiful places on the planet to buy an island.

"It's beautiful," Margo exclaimed into the microphone that's attached to the headset. "It's been so long since I've been to the beach. I'm actually looking forward to this."

"Let me guess. You were too busy earning two degrees that you didn't get out."

She nods. "Yep. That's exactly right."

I smile at her. "In that case, Princess, I'm going to make it my personal mission to see that you have a good time while you're out here."

Finally, a small island comes into view. Trees cover the tall, rolling hills of most of the place, but there are some visible paths and roads, not to mention the large resort sitting along the back shoreline.

This is the kind of place where famous people come to party out of the spotlight.

The chopper hovers over the landing pad and then steadily descends. Yamada sits in a white topless Jeep that has no doors while he waits for us to land.

When we're on the ground, the crew opens the door and helps us out. We duck as we walk over to Yamada.

"Get in, madafakas. Yamada's been waiting for you all night."

I glance over at Margo, and she shrugs before climbing into the backseat. Looks like she's learned quickly to just go with whatever Yamada has in mind.

I follow suit and climb into the passenger seat. My ass no sooner hits the seat before Yamada mashes the gas, sending us shrieking down the dirt road.

"Whoa!" I grab the dashboard and reach for the seat belt to buckle myself in. The last thing I need is to fall out of a speeding vehicle because of Yamada's crazy driving. "Have you slept at all since I spoke to you last night?"

"Sleep?" he says with a chuckle. "No time for that. Yamada was busy entertaining. Everyone Yamada knows is here to celebrate my new island. Those madafakas are still up partying."

I furrow my brow. "Who did you invite?"

"Everyone," he emphasizes. "I put the invite out to all my friends on social media, and most of them showed up."

"Jesus. Social media? You'll have every freak you've ever met here." I pinch the bridge of my nose. I don't know why I expected this to be a quiet weekend because I know how Yamada is. He's not the type who only attends a party—he is the party.

He reaches over and grabs my shoulder, giving it a little shake. "Don't worry, King. You special. Yamada saved you and Dime Piece a room. The rest of the assholes here have to sleep in tents."

I shake my head at my crazy friend.

The massive main house that we spotted from the helicopter comes into view, and my jaw drops as I take in the crowd gathered around front. Yamada wasn't kidding when he said he invited everyone. There are bodies wearing only bikinis and swimming trunks as far as the eye can see.

Yamada whips the Jeep into a parking spot right in front of the house and then pops up out of his seat. "Yamada's back, bitches. Get the music started. Time to celebrate this wedding right!"

The crowd cheers and most of the people hold up cups of beer.

My eyes widen. "What is this, Yamada?"

Yamada jumps out of the Jeep then turns to me and grins. "Best man's job is to throw parties, and who better to throw you a reception than Yamada?"

I step out of the vehicle and help Margo out. I open my mouth to tell Yamada that we didn't need a party—that our marriage was a mistake and now it's part of a business deal, nothing more—but Margo places her hand on my chest, stopping me from saying anything at all.

"That's very nice of you, Yamada. Thank you," Margo tells him and then pats me on the chest. "We appreciate it."

This seems to please him because his smile grows wider. "Welcome. Now, let's party."

He takes us both by the hand and leads us into the awaiting crowd. Most of the people among all these dancing bodies are people I've never seen before, but leave it to Yamada to throw a rager on a private island.

Some hip-hop song blasts through the speakers, and while Yamada busies himself rapping along to the song, I grind against Margo.

She smiles as she wraps her arms around my neck and swings her hips to the beat. It's the first time since Vegas that we've had fun like this, and it's nice.

After a few more songs, Margo pushes up on her tiptoes to talk into my ear. "I'm going to get a drink. Do you want anything?"

"A beer would be great. Thank you." It's a nice gesture for her to think of me.

I smile as I watch her walk off toward the bar inside the house. Who knew Margo Buchanan would end up being so nice to me. I follow behind her, not wanting her to feel like she has to fetch me a drink like she does at work. I cringe at the thought that delegating that task made her feel like a servant. It was wrong of me, and I won't ask her to do it again.

When I approach the bar, the first thing I see is a man standing next to Margo a little too close for my liking. He turns toward her and leans his side against the bar so that he can fix his gaze on her. I can tell by the way he's watching her that he's thinking about making a move, but what he doesn't know is that she's already been taken. By me.

The guy is about my height, with about twenty pounds or so on me, but that doesn't matter. If he makes a move on Margo, he'll lose a fucking arm.

The bartender takes Margo's order and then turns his attention to the guy next to Margo and asks him for his order. "Bud Light, and buy this pretty woman next to me another round of whatever she just ordered."

"No thanks," Margo says stiffly.

The guy touches her arm, and I just lose my fucking head. There's no way in hell I am going to stand here and allow another man to touch what's mine.

I shove his hand away and step between Margo and him. "She said no, motherfucker. Hit the fucking road."

The man's face turns white as a sheet, and he takes a step back. "Sorry, man. Didn't know she was claimed."

"Beat it, pussy," is all I say to cause the man to turn tail and run.

"Aww, shit. Yamada missed another King throw down. Damn, it's sexy when you get all fired up," Yamada teases. "Next time an ass kicking is brewing, come get Yamada. We can throw down."

I laugh. "Next time, they're all yours."

That seems to satisfy him because he turns and disappears into the crowd, leaving Margo and me standing there.

I pull her into my arms. "You all right?"

"Never better." She turns her gaze up to look me in the eyes and smiles. "He cares about you a lot. It's really clicking why the two of you are such good friends because I'll admit, I didn't understand your relationship at first. The two of you are very different."

"I don't know how our friendship works, but it just does."

"Sometimes people have a way of worming themselves into your heart whether you want them to or not."

I continue to gaze into her eyes, and I can't help but feel a little hopeful that she means me even though I shouldn't. It's wrong of me to want her to feel something for me because I know that I'm about to break her heart. But I'm a selfish bastard and I'll hope for it anyway.

I lean in and press my lips to hers. "I'm glad we're here together."

"Me, too," an all too familiar voice purrs from behind me.

I whip around just in time to see a blast from my past standing there in nothing but a black string bikini.

"What are you doing here?" Even I can hear the shock in my voice as I drop my hands from around Margo's waist and pull away from her.

"I had to come and see for myself if the Naughty King is married." Jess tilts her head, swinging her long, blond ponytail. She looks just the same as the last time I saw her—drop-dead gorgeous. But that wicked smile of hers doesn't fool me. This woman broke my heart—she taught me that no woman could be trusted.

Her presence reminds me that I've been allowing Margo inside my heart too much. I have to get back to being an asshole. I've already lowered my guard too much around her, and it's caused me a lot of fucking trouble.

My back stiffens. "So you've seen it. Now, fucking leave."

Jess smirks. "Oh, I'm not going anywhere. Not until I'm convinced the two of you are in love and it's not some fucking charade. Daddy says that he and the rest of the board could take full control if they can prove you were out making careless decisions with your personal life."

"Fuck your father," I snarl. "I'll fuck Margo right here in front of you to prove that we're married for real."

Jess shakes her head. "Fucking her won't prove anything. I need to be convinced you love her. Who better to judge if Alexander King is in love than the last woman he asked to marry him?"

Margo gasps next to me and then turns to storm off. I snatch her wrist, halting her in place. "Now is not the time for a temper tantrum."

She jerks out of my grasp. "Don't tell me what to do, King."

"Margo. Come back here."

She doesn't look back as she storms away.

I scrub my hand down my face. I don't know what in the hell she's mad about, but I decide not to chase her down and cause a scene, especially not in front of Jess.

"Looks like trouble in paradise," Jess says in a singsong voice beside me.

My nostrils flare as I turn my heated gaze on her. "Shut the fuck up, Jess. I don't know why you feel the need to interfere with my life. You left me, remember? Leave me the hell alone."

Jess steps up to me and grins. "I can't leave you alone. This time, it's not personal, baby. It's business. My daddy needs me to expose your little lie, and I need to prove to everyone that it's me who you still really love, not that uptight feisty princess."

"Stay. Away. From. Me," I say my words slowly with enough intensity so she knows how fucking serious I am.

She lifts one eyebrow and then walks away.

When she's out of sight, I set out to find Yamada. It doesn't take long to find him by the pool with a girl on his lap and one on each side of him.

I storm over to him, seething. "What in the fuck is Jess doing here?"

"Calm down, King. I told you everyone was here. Besides, Jess knows you with Dime Piece now. She's just here to party with Yamada like old times and help break in Yamada's new island."

I rake my fingers through my hair. I love Yamada, but sometimes he can be so blind to the ulterior motives people have. He's too quick to believe the good in people even when they don't deserve it.

"That's not why she's here. She's here to spy on me for her father who sits on the fucking board of my company. She's trying to prove that my marriage is a sham so the board can overthrow my power."

"Then just show her that you in love with Dime Piece. Everything fixed."

"It's not that simple, and you know it."

Yamada pushes the girl off his lap, and he stands. "Course it is, King. You are in love. Yamada knows it and so do you. You just won't admit it to yourself."

I flinch. "I don't—"

"Okay then, Yamada is going to go in there and try to get into Dime Piece's panties."

I throw my hands up, palms out. "Whoa. Let's not get crazy."

"See!" he exclaims. "You only get jealous when you care. You. Are. In. Love."

My lips pull into a tight line. No. That can't be right. Can it? Me? In love? That's preposterous. I don't do love, or at least I thought I didn't. But I do know that I care about Margo. A lot. I care about hurting her, which is why I'm wrestling with the plan I have to betray her when it comes to the deal I made with her.

Yamada gives my shoulder a firm pat. "Go talk to Margo. Tell her you love her. It make things better. You see."

He's right. I do need to speak with her, but I'm not ready to admit that I feel something for her. I'm not even sure about my own feelings at this point.

"I'm going to go," I tell him.

I turn on my heel and set out to find Margo. The crowd is thick, but I know she won't be in the middle of it, so I begin checking every secluded place I can find. When I round the outside corner of the building, my eyes land on one of my very best friends and my baby sister. They are sitting too close for my fucking comfort on a bench built for two. Jack and Diem sit side-by-side with their heads lowered, talking privately. My sister glances over at Jack and smiles. I don't like that smile. It's too flirty, and I'll be damned if I allow anything to happen between the two of them.

"What the hell is this?" I ask, not moving my eyes off them.

Diem jumps up instantly from her seat. "Hey! Alexander! Some party, right?"

I narrow my eyes. "Don't change the fucking subject, Diem. Why are the two of you doing that?"

"We weren't doing anything, Alexander. You are too damn paranoid. Nothing is going on."

My eyes flick to Jack for a second before they return back to my sister. I don't have time for this bullshit. I have to find Margo. "Squash this shit. Now. It's not happening between the two of you. Ever."

I curl my fingers into fists, and I feel the need to lash out. Everything feels like it's coming down on me at once, and I feel like I'm about to lose my goddamn mind.

Jack pushes himself up off the bench and approaches me slowly with his hands up in surrender. "What's wrong, man? You look panicked."

I rub the skin on the back of my neck, willing myself to calm down and refocus on the major issue at hand. "Jess is here to spy on me for her fucking father, trying to prove that my marriage is a complete fucking fake."

"I spoke with the board, Alexander. I don't think you have anything to worry about. Everyone seemed really pleased with your marriage to Margo after the King Gala, which tells me they all are buying your story. We just need to ride this out for a few more days, and then we're in the home stretch. So do the best you can to stay away from Jess until then."

"Okay. I have to find Margo and make sure she's still on the same page. I just pissed her off. I have to make sure she's okay."

Jack nods. "She actually just passed by here. She was on her phone. You better go find her in case she was arranging a flight back to New York."

"Shit. All right. I'll see you two in a bit," I tell them before I rush off in search of Margo.

Panic sets in. I can't allow her to leave here mad at me. I need to find her and apologize.

That last thought stops me dead in my tracks. When in the fuck did I start having the urge to tell someone I was sorry? I'm Alexander King. I'm not supposed to be sorry for anything I do, but this time I am. I don't like the idea of hurting Margo in any way.

It's not until I walk down to the beach that I find her. She's staring out at the sea while the waves crash around her ankles.

I step up beside her and notice the tears streaming down her face. While I know it was shitty to keep something like that from her, I never took Margo for one who would cry over it.

It makes me feel bad that I hurt her like that.

I swallow hard. "I knew I should've told you that I proposed to Jess—"

"I don't give a shit about what you did in your past. I walked away because I'm tired of you thinking you can just use my body any time you feel like it. Don't you ever use fucking me as leverage again."

"Margo, that was just a threat to prove to her how serious I am about you."

"Whatever. Just don't do it again."

That's a reasonable request. "Okay. I won't."

I figured that would make the tears stop, but they continue to flow down her face. It worries me, so I put my arm around her shoulders. "I said I wouldn't do it again. You can stop crying now."

She shakes her head and her lips pull into a tight line. "That's not it."

I give her shoulders a little squeeze. "What is it then? Tell me. Maybe I can make whatever it is better."

"Not this," she whispers. "My dad's dead."

My eyes widen. "What? How?"

"Heart attack," she says simply. "My father's attorney just called me. Apparently, I have to sign some paperwork making me the new head of Buchanan Industries immediately."

I wrap her in my arms and comfort her the best way I know how. "I'm so sorry, Margo. I know he meant a great deal to you. We'll leave as soon as you need to."

She sobs into my chest as I stroke her hair, attempting to soothe her pain. It kills me to see her cry like this because I've lost a parent, too. It hurts like a motherfucker.

I wish I can do more, but no matter how much money I have, it won't bring her dad back. I wish it would though because I would've brought mine back a long time ago.

It's hard for me to even wrap my head around the fact that her father is dead.

My mind races through all the things that Dan Buchanan dying means to the deal I was about to strike with him for his company. My heart does a double thump in my ribs when one piece of the Buchanan puzzle pops into place. Since we're legally married, I now have rights to Buchanan Industries just as she has rights to King Corporation.

This fucking changes everything.

Michelle A. Valentine

Margo

I stand there frozen in place—unable to move a muscle or tear myself away from Alexander's embrace. Time slips away as Alexander holds me tightly against his chest. Right now, I need someone to hold me. I've been stunned since Mother phoned to inform me Daddy passed away. My brain can't comprehend that I'll never see my father again.

The doctors have been warning Daddy to change his lifestyle—to cut back on the high cholesterol foods, reduce his stress and exercise—but he loved to indulge and didn't seem capable of following his physician's health plan. It eats me up to know that if he had listened, he could've avoided the massive heart attack that suddenly ended his life.

God, this doesn't even seem real.

"Is there anything I can do?" Alexander's tone is soft and kind—a definite change from the condescending attitude I'm used to getting from him.

I sniff as I pull back from his embrace. "Yes. Can you get me back to New York as soon as possible?"

He gazes at my face for a long moment before reaching up and swiping a tear off my cheek with the pad of his thumb. "I'll make the call for the chopper."

"Thank you."

He stares deeply into my eyes, and I see a rare glimpse of sincerity in his expression. "I'm really sorry, Margo. Losing my father was the hardest thing I'd ever gone through, so I know how you're feeling. I still miss him like crazy every day, and I want you to know that I'm here for you—anything you need, I'm at your service."

Knowing he can relate to what I'm going through makes me feel even closer to him. This pain isn't something I'd wish on my worst enemy. "My heart hurts so badly. I don't think I can make it through this."

Alexander's lips turn down into a tight frown. "The pain always stays with you, but I've learned to embrace it, as will you.

You are the strongest woman I've ever known, Margo. You *will* make it through this, and I'll be there for you to lean on if you let me. The physical pain I feel from losing my father is the one thing that helps me hold on to his memory. It's a reminder that I had the privilege of knowing one of the greatest men on the planet was my father. I know you loved yours just as fiercely, so hold the good memories of him close."

Hearing Alexander speak so fondly of his father gives me insight into how deep of a connection he had with his dad. I can see how we really aren't that different. Alexander takes my hand and raises it to his lips before placing a soft kiss on my skin. "Let's go back to the main house and find out where Yamada put our luggage. It might take the pilot a while to make it back to get us."

I nod. Suddenly, I feel grateful Alexander is by my side right now so I don't feel so alone in my grief.

He keeps a tight grip on my hand as we walk up the secluded path back to the house where the party is still in full swing. Hanging out with a bunch of people I don't even know isn't something I'm up to at the moment. As it is, it's taking everything in me to hold the tears back that teeter in my eyes.

"Keep a lookout for Yamada. He has to be around here somewhere."

I glance around, scanning the sea of faces, and my eyes land on Jess. She doesn't attempt to hide that she's staring me down, and the smirk on her face makes me think she enjoys the idea of me being upset. No doubt she believes my jealousy of her is the cause for these tears in my eyes.

Alexander stills next to me, and when I follow his line of sight he's looking at Jess. He appears to be angry at the very sight of her and the urge to comfort him comes over me.

I tug on his hand. "Forget about her. Don't let her get to you."

"She pisses me the hell off. I don't know why she insists on ruining things for me. It's like she doesn't want to see me happy."

"Why is she even here?" I ask, curious.

"She's here to spy on us for her father who sits on the board of my company. She's out to gather intel and prove that I don't really love you, so her father and the board can overthrow my decisions."

My heart squeezes. I know our marriage is one hundred percent fake, but over the past couple of weeks, since we've been pretending to be the real deal, I've grown rather fond of Alexander King. So much so that my chest physically hurts when the idea of no longer being with him crosses my mind. I know it's silly to even entertain the idea that Alexander feels as deeply about me as I do for him. However, it would be nice to know exactly where his head is at regarding our relationship.

"Do you think she's convinced we're in love?"

He stares down at me and then touches my cheek. "I think anyone who has ever witnessed the way I look at you would be convinced that I feel something for you."

His words wrap around my brain and I lick my lips slowly, not wanting to let this topic go just yet. "Do you think people will have the same reaction when they see the way I look at you?"

His cool gray eyes bore into mine. "If they see what I see right now, they'll believe it."

"Do you?" My question comes out just above a whisper, and I can't believe we're having such a deep conversation in the middle of a crowded party. More than anything, I want to know if there's a chance he feels even remotely as I do because my heart can't take any additional damage right now.

His Adam's apple bobs up and down as he swallows hard. "Margo...I—"

"Madafakas! Where you been?" Yamada's inquiry instantly stops Alexander's confession. "Yamada is ready to bring out the wedding cake. Bitches be hungry around here. Yamada already had to smack a hottie's hand for sticking a finger in the icing for a little taste."

I whip my gaze over to Yamada while Alexander sighs next to me.

"Sorry, buddy, but we won't have any time for more partying. We need to leave as soon as possible."

"Leave? What you talking about? Did you not hear what Yamada said? There's cake."

"I heard, but we really have to return to Manhattan as quickly as possible."

Yamada adjusts the white, flat-billed cap on the top of his head. "Aww, man—but Yamada threw you and Dime Piece this bomb party to celebrate your wedding and to prove your love is real."

A perfectly manicured female hand slides over Yamada's shoulder and Jess slinks up to his side. "Did you say real love?"

Alexander stiffens and his eyes narrow as he stares at his ex. She seems to love inserting herself into any situation concerning Alexander while she's around.

"No one asked you, Jess, so fuck off," Alexander says.

Her lips turn down into a dramatic pout. "I'm only looking out for you, sweetie. I just can't let any woman come around and get her hooks into you."

"You mean the way you had yours in me?" Alexander fires back in a sharp tone.

"Dime Piece isn't like that, Jess. She's the real deal and cares for King. Yamada can tell when it comes to matters of the heart."

Jess pats Yamada on the chest. "I think you're wrong this time."

He shakes his head. "Yamada never wrong—always right. Yamada a smart madafaka."

Unable to take any more of Jess' shit, I shove my hand into my hair to push it away from my face. "Look, Jess. I don't know you, but I don't like you, and you need to stay the hell away from Alexander and me. What we do is none of your concern."

A wicked smile crosses Jess' lips. "That's where you're wrong. When it comes to Alexander, it is my business. He's mine, and I refuse to let some spoiled little daddy's girl take away what belongs to me."

The mere mention of my father sends me into a blind rage, and I instantly lunge for her, but Alexander quickly restrains me, keeping me from getting my hands on her.

"Let me go!" I order.

Alexander refuses to loosen his hold on me. "She's not worth it. Trust me."

He takes a step back, pulling me with him. "Come on. Don't give her what she wants. She's only doing this to get to you."

I stare up at him, knowing he's absolutely correct. My brain just isn't thinking clearly. I cannot allow her to get under my skin and cause me to act irrationally.

My eyes flit to Yamada. "Can you tell me where our things are? I have to get back to New York. There's an emergency I must attend to."

"In the honeymoon suite—the best room on the island. Come." Yamada steps away from Jess. "Yamada show you the way."

Alexander places his hand on the small of my back as we follow Yamada through the crowds of dancing people.

It's comforting. It's nice not to feel so alone on what is unquestionably the worst day of my life. I just never dreamed in a million years the one person who would be my rock in life would be the Naughty King.

Chapter II
ROUGH AIR

Alexander

The helicopter arrives within the hour, and I help Margo inside. It's difficult for me to even look at her without feeling a bit choked up. Even though it's been years now, the pain of losing my own father still feels so fresh. When he died, the carefree world as I knew it left along with him. I had to grow up and figure out how to balance the weight of the money-making empire that was left for me to run against finishing my last year and a half of college and becoming the caretaker of my baby sister.

Margo may not have a sibling to raise, but she will have to rely on herself when it comes to taking care of Buchanan Industries, and that alone will extremely rough.

I will only complicate everything for her.

My agenda hasn't always been on the up and up. Even now, I know Buchanan Industries is at its weakest, and the business shark in me wants to move in for the kill. But I know when I do, that'll be the end of my relationship with Margo.

I've never felt this fucking conflicted over a business deal.

No matter how I feel about her—how much I crave the taste of her on my tongue—being with her will end. When she figures out that I still plan to tear her company apart and sell it off piece by piece to the highest bidder to benefit the King Corporation, she'll never give me the time of day again. It's a cold, hard fact I'm going to have to deal with, which is why I must put some distance between us...and soon. I just don't know if I'm going to be strong enough to walk away from her when the time comes.

"Alexander! Wait!" The sound of Diem's voice catches my attention before I have the chance to get into the chopper.

I turn in time to see my sister jumping out of a Jeep with Jack on her heels.

"What is it?" I shout as she approaches me.

The wind from the swirling blades whips Diem's blond hair in her face. "Jack and I are heading back to New York with you."

My eyes slide to my best friend. More than anything, I want to get back into what's going on between them, but I know now is not the time or place.

I nod and hold out my hand to help her inside. "Come on, then."

After she's inside, I take her suitcase from Jack and hand it inside to a member of the crew before I throw my hand into Jack's chest. "You're not getting into this chopper. You're going to turn around and put some fucking space between you and my sister, understand?"

The muscle in Jack's jaw flexes as he meets my stare. He knows I'm pissed about the little scene between him and my sister earlier. It wasn't just my fucking imagination and I'm putting a stop to this bullshit right now.

Jack knows me well enough to know I won't allow one of my best friends to date my innocent little sister. Especially, a friend I know who gets around just as much as I do.

No way in hell will I allow Jack to group Diem in with the rest of the loose-legged women he fucks from the Upper East Side.

"You're really not going to let me come with you?" Jack's question is heated, but he knows better than to try me when I'm heated.

"There's no way in hell I'm letting you on here. Whatever was going on between the two of you is now over. Get back in the jeep and I'll send the chopper and jet back for you."

Jack's mouth falls open. "Come on, Alexander. Don't—"

My eyes narrow and Jack instantly throws his hands in the air and takes a step back. "Whatever man. You explain to Diem why I'm not coming then."

"I don't have to explain shit," I yell before I hoist myself up into the aircraft.

The door slams shut behind me and I slap the communication headphones on my head.

Diem stares at me with wide eyes. "Where's Jack?"

Her voice cuts through the noise as the chopper lifts off the ground and I know there's no way of avoiding explaining things to her.

"I told him to stay behind and take care of a few things," I say to appease her.

Within a few minutes, Yamada's island, along with the party that's celebrating our wedding, is nothing more than a speck behind us.

No one says anything, and my suspicions are on high alert as my sight zeroes in Diem, who sits across from me. Her body language speaks volumes about how pissed at me she is right now. I wonder how long whatever this is between them has been going on for and how the fuck did I miss the signs.

A soft sob echoes into my headphones, pulling me away from my thoughts and refocusing my attention on Margo. She bites her lower lip as she covers her mouth with her hand, attempting to hide her emotions from the rest of us.

Margo Buchanan is a strong woman, but even she can't conceal how much pain she's in now. I reach over and take her hand, threading our fingers together so she knows I'm here for her. When my father died, I reached out to Jess for support in the toughest time of my life, and she did nothing but break my heart even more. The day my father died, Jess left me for the tennis pro, shredding my heart in the process and hardening me to the world. I see a lot of myself in Margo, and I don't want to ruin her chance of finding love by being an insensitive dick.

Not all men are bastards like me. I'm a rare breed.

I do want her to find happiness in the future because I care about her that much.

I want her to know that I'm here for her—that I know what this pain is like—and for now, that means calling a business truce.

Margo stares down at our intertwined fingers as she bats away her falling tears with her other hand.

My heart twists at the sight of seeing her so sad, and at that moment, I know without a doubt that Yamada was right about me. I do have feelings for Margo Buchanan, and perhaps, it's possible that this stone heart inside my chest is capable of feeling love again.

THE CHOPPER TOUCHES DOWN at the airfield, and the King Corporation jet awaits our arrival. I remain seated next to Margo, allowing Diem to get out of the helicopter first, before I make my way out and then help Margo.

Once we're in the quiet cabin of the jet, my eyes land on Diem, who is taking the furthest seat away from me that she can find. I open my mouth, ready to lash out and reiterate that a relationship between she and Jack is never going to happen no matter how big of a tantrum she throws when Margo asks Abigail for some tissues.

Margo needs me right now, so this Jack and Diem bullshit will have to wait.

I take Margo's hand and lead her back to the private suite on the plane where I close us alone inside.

I turn to face Margo and gingerly touch the soft skin of her cheek. "Can I get you anything?"

She sniffs and then shakes her head. "No. I just need some time. Would it be all right if I stay in here?"

"Of course, but I'm staying in here with you." I turn and press the button for the intercom on the wall.

Instantly, Abigail answers my call. "Yes, Mr. King? What can I do for you?"

"Can you bring Ms. Buchanan a turkey club with no lettuce and a Fiji water and bring me my usual turkey club and a scotch."

"Right away, sir."

When I end the call, my gaze meets Margo's and there's a question in her eyes. "How do you know things like that?"

"Like what?" I ask, genuinely puzzled as to what she's referring to.

"The things I like—you seem to know so much about me, yet I feel like I'm still discovering the things from your past that make you, you. I feel like I don't know anything about you."

"This is true," I tell her as I consider her words. "But you know more about me than most. It's difficult for me to open up. And as far as knowing things about you, I pay attention. The little things in life are what matter the most. A lot of people tend to forget that."

She gazes directly into my eyes. "It's because of her, isn't it? Jess? Is she the reason you stay so guarded?"

"No. She's not the only reason." I pause for a moment and considering leaving things at that, but my heart implores me to allow Margo a glimpse of it. "My mother also had a solid hand in turning me into the bastard that Manhattan knows me for. When my father got sick, she decided she no longer wanted anything to do with him or her own children after she discovered that Father willed all his assets to Diem and myself. My mother packed all her things and left both of us in the midst of our grief. She left me behind to help Diem, who was only fourteen at the time, deal with the loss of our father. When I was twenty, she signed her rights away, making me Diem's sole guardian. Mother hasn't been in our lives since.

"My mother signed a prenuptial agreement when she married my father. She was so infuriated over being left with nothing that she contested the prenup after Father had been diagnosed with stage four bone cancer. He spent his final days on this earth in a battle over money. She disgusts me."

Margo's plump pink lips twist and sadness flashes in her eyes. "Alexander, that's horrible. I'm sorry you had to deal with that. I know taking on your father's company at such a young age must've been difficult in itself, but to practically become a parent too...I can't imagine what that was like."

"It wasn't always easy. Most of the time, I had no clue what in the hell I was doing, but somehow, Diem and I made it through without killing one another."

"It explains so much about your relationship with your sister. It also tells me that you're a good man, and underneath it all, you really do have a heart. You just have more layers around it that need to be peeled back."

Hearing her say that causes me to cringe. After all the things I've done and said to her, it's amazing that she can still somehow believe I'm not a rotten son-of-a-bitch.

"Margo—"

"Shhh." She presses her fingers to my lips. "Whatever you're about to say, don't. This is the closest I've ever felt to you; so don't ruin it with meaningless words that I don't need to hear. I like the connection we have right now. It helps me forget that my entire world is falling apart around me. I need you to stay with me and hold me in your arms and make me believe that everything is going to work out and be okay. Can you do that?"

Her request takes me aback because I didn't expect her to look to me for comfort.

A knock on the door grabs my attention. I turn and twist the knob and find Abigail holding a tray containing the sandwiches I'd requested.

I instruct her to put the tray on the nightstand, and she does as she's asked before stopping just short of the door. "The captain has asked that I inform you we'll be taxiing on the runway in a few moments, if you'll please, be seated."

I nod. "Thank you, Abigail."

"Please let me know if you need anything else, Mr. King."

When Abigail closes the door, I take Margo's hand and pull her toward the bed. "Come. Lie down with me."

She raises her eyebrow at me, and I hold up three fingers. "Just to lie down...Scout's honor."

"I don't know if I fully believe you. You don't seem like the scout type."

I give her a crooked smile. "Okay, you got me there, but I promise no sex...unless of course, you beg me for it, and in that case, you can't hold that against me. I am a man, after all."

We lie in bed in silence, and I run my fingers through Margo's long, dark curls, soothing her to sleep. I smile as I stare down at her stunning features, and it strikes me how lucky I am a creature as beautiful as she is lying in my arms.

I want her to be mine.

But I know that will never happen. When she discovers that I plan to make a deal with Yamada for Buchanan Industries behind her back, she'll no longer want to be this close to me ever again.

My heart squeezes in my chest, and guilt washes over me. I can't be this close to her right now. It's torturous. I need to start putting space between us, and I need to start doing it right now.

I slide my arm out from under her head and then roll off the bed before slipping out the door.

Sooner or later, I need to face the reality that I'm going to have to go back to being myself and living a life without Margo Buchanan.

THE MOMENT I step into the main cabin, my eyes widen when I take in the sight of Diem. "What in the hell is going on between you and Jack?" I don't give her time to respond because I really don't want to know the answer. "Whatever it is that's going on—it ends right fucking now."

My baby sister's mouth twists. "Why are you being such a dick about this?"

This is the fucking thanks I get for trying to look out for her?

I pin my eyes on her. "I've told you before, Diem. I don't want you dating my best friend. A relationship between the two of you will never work."

"Why wouldn't it?" she fires back. "He's a nice guy."

"He's not the man for you, Diem. Jack and I—we're cut from the same cloth. Guys like us don't settle down." My gaze locks on hers as I dare her to debate me on that point.

She knows as well as I do that we both get around, and I'll be damned if I allow some guy, even if he is one of my best friends, to use my sister like that.

"People change, Alex. Look at you. You're a prime example. Being with Margo—"

"Enough!" I scold her. "That is not the same situation, and I'm still the same man I was before. People don't change—not really—so I'm only going to say this one last time. This thing between you and Jack—it's over. I never want to hear about it again."

"We don't have to listen to you!" Diem argues.

My nostrils flare. She's never been this damn defiant before, which leads me to believe if I don't do something drastic, she's going to go against my wishes.

I square my shoulders. "You *will* listen, or I'll fire Jack."

Her eyes widen. "You wouldn't."

"Try me." My gaze slides over to Jack. "This is finished. Don't make me carry through with my threat, because you know I will."

Normally, this is the point when I would throw them both out of my sight, but seeing as how we're stuck thirty-thousand feet in the air, I only have one place left to go in order to get away from this situation.

I turn and head back to where I left Margo and pause just before opening the door. I care about everyone on this plane, and I feel like I'm hurting them all, but they need to understand the reason I do the things I do is to better the situation—whether it's mine or theirs. I just hope that one day my sister will understand I only want what's best for her, just as I only want what's best for my father's company.

I lean my forehead against the door leading into the private bedroom. The urge to continue comforting Margo is so strong because I know how much losing a parent fucking hurts. No one was there for me when I was going through it, and I had to be strong for Diem's sake. She needed me to be the rock because we wouldn't have gotten through it had we both been falling apart.

A soft sob comes from the other side of the door, and I know Margo still needs me. The brass of the door handle feels cool against my skin as I turn the knob. The first thing I spot is Margo curled into a tiny ball in the middle of the king-size bed with her shoulders visibly shaking.

I step into the room and shut the door behind me before making my way over to the bed. The bed presses down under my weight, and I wrap my arms around Margo, pulling her back against my chest.

"I've got you," I whisper.

The war within me on whether to allow myself this close to Margo rages on. The more attached I allow myself to get to Margo, the worse it will be for both of us when this all ends. She's one addiction I'm going to have a hell of a time breaking free from.

Chapter III
UNEXPECTED WELCOME

Alexander

I pace outside Margo's bedroom door, wanting so badly to go in there and comfort her, but at the same time, I know I need to respect her request for alone time. I'm not sure what to do in this situation.

I remember when Diem made requests for privacy when she was growing up. I never allowed her to go more than a couple of hours without going in there and attempting to make her feel better. My gut says I should do the same with Margo, but I'm not sure if I should cross that boundary.

I feel a tug on the hem of my jeans, and I stare down at Jimmy Chew, who is pawing at my leg and begging for attention.

I bend down and scoop the little pup into my arms. "Hey, buddy, you need to go for a walk?"

His warm little tongue darts out of his mouth and licks my cheek, causing me to smile. It's impossible not to love something as sweet as this pup.

I make my way downstairs and pass through the kitchen with Jimmy Chew in my arms.

"She still won't come out?" Aggie asks. I shake my head. "No."

Aggie sighs. "The girl's really startin' to worry me, Alex. She hasn't eaten a morsel, and I don't want her to make herself sick. Ye thinkin' it's time we be callin' her mother? I know the two of them are close."

I nod. "Maybe it is time we intervene. I'm about to take Jimmy for a walk, and I know Margo's mother doesn't live far from here. Perhaps I'll pay her a visit."

Aggie brings Jimmy's leash over and hooks it to his collar. "I think that's a wise idea. Ask her what Margo's favorite meal is and I'll whip that up for her."

"I know she loves Payday bars and Diet Coke. Maybe we can start by getting her some of those."

Aggie's round face lights up with a small smile. "Are you sure this thing between the two of ye is really only pretend? I've never known ye to be aware of any favorite things of the young lady ye have ever dated before."

I could lie to Aggie and tell her this relationship is pretend between Margo and me, but this woman practically raised me. She knows me much too well for me to get away with a lie of that magnitude.

I rub the back of my neck. "I'm not sure what's happening to me, Aggie. One day, I loathe the ground Margo walks on and now..."

I trail off, unsure of how to even complete the sentence. I swore to myself a long time ago that I would never allow my heart to open up to someone again. I never want to repeat the pain of having it crushed and I'm afraid if I admit aloud how I really feel about Margo, things will get very real, and I'll end up getting hurt.

Aggie tilts her head, and a lock of her red hair slips out of her loose bun. "I know emotions are hard for ye to deal with, but I've spent some time with Margo, and I really believe in my heart she's different from the other women ye've had around here. There's been some big changes between the two of you over the last few weeks. I notice how ye look at each other when ye think no one else is watching. Ye two are a lot alike—both afraid to really lay it all on the line and trust in what yer heart is telling ye."

"That's the thing. I'm not even sure how I really feel," I tell her as I digest everything she just said.

"But ye do, Alex. You love the lass. Yer just afraid to tell her because you also have another love in yer life—King Corporation. Ye can love them both, you know."

She doesn't know how badly I wish that were true, but I know deep down that will never happen. "There's not enough room to give them both my all. If I love one more than the other—one is going to suffer."

Aggie touches my cheek to comfort me in the same way she did when I was a little boy. "It doesn't have to be so. Ye can have them both. It's in yer blood to work hard for the things ye love. The same traits and ethics yer father possessed, so do you. When ye set yer mind to succeed, ye will not fail. Allow yerself to be happy, Alex. After all ye've been through—ye deserve it more than anyone else I know."

I give her a sad smile. Aggie always knows just what to say to cut directly into my soul and force me to look at the grand scheme of what's going on in any given situation.

"Now, go. Go find Margo's mother and let's figure out a way to help her get through this. She's going to need all the support she can get right now."

"Okay, I'll be back soon."

Walking out into the crisp air of the New York morning, I set out toward East 74th street to the building where Margo's mother lives. I've never met the woman, so I'm not exactly sure what to expect. It's not every day a guy meets his mother-in-law while he's waging an inner war with his feelings for her daughter. This kind of shit can't even be written because it's so fucked up.

Once I reach the address my private investigator gave me, I stare up at the building and take a deep breath. I can't remember the last time I ever felt this nervous. This is very unlike me.

Standing at the entrance is a dark-haired doorman wearing the required smile. "Can I help you?"

"I'm Alexander King. I'm here to see Mrs. Lily Doyle."

"Is she expecting you, sir?" he asks.

I shake my head. "No, I'm her son-in-law, just paying her a visit."

The young man's dark eyes widen a bit. "I didn't know Margo got married."

"It's fairly recent," I reply smoothly.

He opens the door and then escorts me inside the lobby. "Wait here a moment while I call Mrs. Doyle."

I stoop down and lift Jimmy Chew into my arms while I wait.

Within a couple of moments, he hangs up the phone. "She's in the penthouse.."

I nod and then make my way over to the elevator. On the ride up, my palms begin to sweat. It's crazy how much I desire this woman's approval of me. I want to make a good first impression, but I don't know what to expect when I meet her. From the information my private investigator gathered on Lily Doyle, what stands out the most about woman is she's been very unlucky in love, having been married several times. Hopefully, that will allow her to be a little more understanding about my elopement with her daughter.

Learning about Margo's parents helped me gain a little insight on what she might be like. Seeing pictures of what Lily looked like when she won the title of Miss Universe told me instantly that Margo hails from a line of beauty, but nothing could've prepared me for how fucking beautiful Margo is. The moment she stepped into my office door, I knew she would be trouble for me.

Once I started discovering how smart and witty she was, I didn't realize that I would be attracted to more than just her looks.

The elevator dings and the doors open into a grand foyer with several pieces of modern art hanging on the walls. The collection could rival the Museum of Modern Art, and this is definitely an indication of the apartment owner's sophisticated style and tastes.

Diem would love to see this place. Maybe when she's speaking to me again, I can bring her here.

The sound of high heels clicking across the marble floor catches my attention, and my eyes dart over toward the sound. Lily Doyle is a very attractive woman, appearing to be nowhere close to fifty-years-old and could pass for Margo's older sister.

She smiles the moment her eyes land on me and she stretches her arms out in greeting. "Alexander King. I was wondering when I would finally get to meet you."

She wraps me in a polite hug and then kisses me on the cheek.

"It's nice to meet you as well."

She pulls back and rubs the top of Jimmy's head, and he licks the palm of her hand. "Who's this little guy?"

I smile, almost like a proud father. "This is Jimmy Chew."

"He's adorable," she says before her eyes cut back over to me. She appraises me from head to toe. "My, my. You're even more attractive in person. Margo has made a stunning choice for her first husband."

I lift my eyebrows. "First husband?"

Lily waves me off dismissively. "No need to be coy with me, Alexander. I know my daughter. I don't know if either of you will truly let the other one in enough to make this marriage work. My Margo needed a little excitement in her life, and I've seen a big change in her since you've been in the picture. I want you to know I'm on your side. I think this rash, drunken marriage between the two of you could be a very good thing."

It's strange hearing Margo's mother mention that she's seen a different side of her daughter because it confirms the things I've been feeling. Maybe we're changing each other, and it's enough that others are beginning to notice. But what she said about me being Margo's first husband makes my gut twist because the thought of any other man being with her isn't something I want to think about.

"How is she doing? I haven't spoken with her in two days. She hasn't been accepting my phone calls." Lily's voice pulls me out of my thoughts and reminds me why I came here in the first place.

"Not too great. She won't come out of her room. She won't eat. I'm worried about her, which is why I came to see you. I have no idea how she's going to make it through Dan's service tomorrow if she won't at least eat something."

Lily worries her bottom lip. "Let me grab my purse and we'll head over immediately. Things are more serious than I thought."

Lily calls for a car to be brought around, and within minutes, we're back at my building where Darby opens the door for us.

"Has she come out of her room since I've been gone?" I ask Darby as we pass by.

He shakes his head. "I just spoke to Aggie, and there's been no change."

I frown. "Thank you."

I hold the elevator door open for Lily to step inside. She turns to me with a worried expression on her face. "I know Margo can come off as brash most of the time, but I solely blame Dan for making her that way. He wanted her to be tough like him. He's been grooming her since she was little to take over Buchanan Industries, and he always told her emotion had no place in business. But I know the sensitive little girl I raised is underneath all that. Sometimes, it just takes a little longer to get through all the layers."

Her words float through my mind, and they sound an awful lot like what Margo told me about myself—I had a lot of layers to get through.

Chapter IV
THROUGH THE DARKNESS

Margo

The door creaks open, and light from the hallway shines into my otherwise darkened room. Aggie and Alexander have both come in to offer me food at different points, but I just can't bring myself to eat. After the shock of losing Daddy wore off, utter darkness wrapped around my heart, making even the smallest task feel like it takes huge effort.

"Honey?" The sound of my mother's voice startles me because I fully expected to hear Aggie's sweet accent or Alexander's smooth baritone voice. "Are you all right?"

I open my mouth to answer, but the moment I do, thoughts of my father come rushing in, and the tears I seem unable to stop stream down my face. A sob rips through my chest and the bed shakes. For the life of me, I find it impossible to control my emotions.

The warmth of her hand on my forehead causes my eyes to flutter. Her touch has always soothed me, but even in this situation, even that it doesn't stop my heart from breaking inside my chest.

"Darling, I know this is hard, but you have to get out of this bed and eat something. You've got everyone terribly worried about you, especially Alexander and me."

I sniff. "I don't think I can."

"You have to dig down deep and find the will. Your dad wouldn't want you to close yourself off like this."

"I know," I whisper, agreeing with her. Daddy always taught me to be a fighter, but he never prepared me for living in this world without him.

He was the person I turned to when I had a problem. He was my sounding board.

Knowing he's not here and that the fate of Buchanan Industries lies solely in my hands terrifies the shit out of me. I don't even know where to begin running a company that large on my own.

This company is my family's legacy. When Daddy retired and the time came for me to take over, I envisioned Daddy still being here to guide me. I was counting on that.

I cry harder as these depressing thoughts plague my mind.

"Honey, please, what can I do?" The worry in Mother's voice is evident, and I hate that I'm the cause of it.

"There's nothing anyone can do. Daddy's gone and no one can bring him back. I wasn't ready to be on my own with his company. I feel alone, with no one who understands and no one to turn to when it comes to running this business. I don't want to screw things up."

Mother sits down on the bed and pushes my hair back from my face. "You'll always have me, you know. As dreadfully dull as I find all the business talk, I will listen. I can't promise I'll be a good source of answers, though, but I think your husband could come in quite handy as far as that goes."

"Alexander? He's still set on taking over Buchanan Industries. I don't know if I can trust any business advice he gives me."

"How do you know if you don't give him a chance? He seems to care a great deal about you. When he came to get me today, I could instantly read how he felt about you. He loves you, Margo. I have a knack for knowing these things, you know."

I fight the urge to roll my eyes, knowing she's going to turn this into trying to convince me she has psychic abilities. "Mother, you are not clairvoyant, no matter what people may tell you."

"Think what you want, but I know about the matters of the heart. The two of you are good together. You both need to stop fighting it and realize this little boo-boo wedding in Vegas was actually a good thing."

A good thing? While I admit this marriage to Alexander King hasn't been entirely awful, neither of us were obviously thinking clearly when we said, "I do" because we risked both of our future livelihoods by not having a prenup in place. Just as I had him by the balls when I discovered I could blackmail him into getting what I wanted, he can now do the same thing to me with Buchanan Industries.

But things feel like they've changed drastically between Alexander and me ever since we've made the deal to dupe everyone into believing we're actually in love. Hell, it's to the point where I'm not sure if we're actually pretending anymore. My heart feels something for Alexander and, as of late, it's stronger than even I realized if I'm being honest. Everyone keeps pointing out how we feel for one another, but it's as if we're too scared to admit how we really feel.

"I'm scared," I whisper. "What if he's just using me to get to Buchanan Industries? What if I don't mean as to him as he does to me. I don't want my heart broken again. My heart won't be able to take it."

"My gut tells me a man like Alexander King wouldn't have gone through the trouble of coming to get me today if he didn't feel something for you, Margo. I don't think you're some business conquest to him, but I could be wrong. I think he's sincere when it comes to you."

My mind races through all the time we've spent together over the past few months. If Mother would've said this to me when I first walked into Alexander's office, I would have called her delusional, but I've witnessed a different side to him lately—a caring side I've grown to love and care for.

He's not the same man I first met. He's a man I want to spend my life getting to know.

"I think I'm in love with him," I tell her honestly.

"Then you should tell him. Lay all your cards out on the table and allow the chips to fall where they may. I don't want you to have any regrets with anything in your life. If you don't tell him, he'll never know and have the chance to show you how he feels in return." Mother lies down next to me and wraps her arms around my shoulders. "I love you, honey. All I've ever wanted was for you to be happy, and I want you to know I'll support you on whatever path that may be in life."

I cling to my mother, welcoming the feeling of her embrace as I think about what has made me happy lately. Alexander's face pops up again and again, and suddenly, it's crystal clear to me that maybe everyone else is right. Maybe Alexander King is exactly what I need in my life—and perhaps, it's time that I tell him exactly how I feel.

Chapter V
LATE NIGHT RENDEZVOUS

Margo

It's silent throughout Alexander's apartment as I tiptoe down the hall. The marble tile is cool beneath my bare feet as I make my way toward Alexander's bedroom.

It opens without a sound, and my eyes adjust to the darkness of the room, allowing me to spot Alexander's form stretched out beneath the covers on his king-size bed.

I've spent quite a few nights in this bed, wrapped in his strong arms, and I have to admit, my nights in here has been some of the best of my life. Alexander always makes me feel so desirable, which is what made him so irresistible to me at first. As I got to know him, things changed. It wasn't completely about sex between the two of us all the time.

I take a deep breath and pull my nightgown over my head before slipping underneath the covers next to Alexander.

He wakes and pushes up on his elbows. "You all right?"

I reach up and trace the tips of my fingers against his cheek, allowing the stubble from his beard to tickle my skin. He rubs the sleep from his eyes, and I can tell he's trying to figure out what I'm doing.

"Margo...?" The way he whispers my name sends shivers down my spine.

He's confused—the last thing he expected was to find me crawling into his bed in the middle of the night, but I need to tell him what's on my mind. I've lain awake in the room down the hall, thinking about life and how it's too short. I want Alexander to know how I feel.

"I have something to say to you."

He stares into my eyes. "What is it?"

My heart pounds inside my chest as I take a deep breath, and then lay all my cards on the table. "I'm falling in love with you, Alexander. I want to make this work with you, but I have to know I can trust you."

His eyes soften, and he licks his lips slowly as he digests my words.

When he doesn't say anything, I begin to panic that I've made a mistake telling him, so I backpedal a bit. "It's okay if you don't—"

He cups my face. "I love you, too. I have for a while now, but I was scared."

"Of what?" I question.

"Getting my heart broken again. I tried to keep my distance from you because I knew you had the power to destroy me."

My heart aches for how he's been crushed by the women in his life, and I want to be the one to show him that loving someone can be a good thing. "I won't hurt you. I promise. You can trust me with your heart. Can I trust you with mine?"

"I want this to work," he says softly. "More than you know, but I am such a wicked man—I don't think I'm good for you."

"I trust you," I whisper. "You've really been there for me, and over the past few weeks, I've seen a different side of you—a caring side. I want to be with you, Alexander. I want to give our marriage a real shot."

The pad of his thumb runs across my cheek bone. "Me too."

The words no sooner leave his mouth than he crushes his lips to mine. I moan as our tongues dance together, and I know that this man finally belongs to me and me to him.

For so long, I believed being with Alexander King was wrong. I felt that Alexander was the enemy and he would only help further destroy my company. But things have changed since the first day we met. I no longer feel like he's the heartless son-of-a-bitch out to tear apart my legacy. He's become my confidant and a close ally. Everything about being with Alexander feels extremely right.

His hand slides down my neck and then sweeps across the bare skin of my chest. My nipples pucker in response, and my breasts ache for his touch. "I'll always want you like this— naked in my bed, waiting for me to take you. Promise me that you're not going to run away when things get tough because I can't handle the very thought of you not being in my life."

The sweet words of worry he's whispering in the darkness are completely unnecessary. "I'm not going anywhere. You said you love me, and I believe you. That's enough to keep me by your side, always."

His cool gray eyes stare into mine. "I love you, Margo Buchanan. It might've taken me a while to realize it, but I do."

Hearing him confess his love causes my blood to rush through my veins and make my heart beat a little faster. Alexander King is the sexiest man I've ever seen, and he's all mine, which is fantastic because I can't seem to keep my hands to myself when it comes to touching his body.

My hands trail down his sculpted, bare chest, and I bite my lower lip. "Make love to me."

That simple request is one he seems to have no trouble fulfilling. He cradles my face in his hands and brushes his lips softly against mine. This kiss is different. It's tender, and his actions aren't rushed. Each move he makes, every tilt of his head, is slow and deliberate. He's taking his time with me because this time, unlike all the other times we've been together, he knows I'm not going anywhere and this won't be the last time he has me.

His hand slides down my side slowly until he reaches my hip. The tips of his fingers glide across my pelvic bone before he dips his hand down between my legs. The warmth of his skin touching my most sensitive skin of me sets me on fire as he strokes my clit. "This sweet pussy belongs to me now, Margo.

I'm the only man allowed to touch you like this and give you pleasure. Understand?"

"Alexander." His name tumbles from my lips in a breathy whisper while my head falls back a bit as he picks up speed. "Oh, God."

He watches me as I begin to fall apart from the simple touch of his finger. "See how good we are together? You were made for me."

I allow my knees to fall to the side so I'm on full display for him. His finger moves with ease as he coats it with my desire and then slips inside me. "You are always so ready for me. So wet. I can't wait to sink my cock inside you and show you how good I can make you feel."

My hands find their way to his boxer briefs, and I make quick work of shoving the fabric down around his hips. His cock springs free, and I wrap my fingers around the smooth shaft before I begin to stroke it.

He closes his eyes for a brief moment as if to enjoy the sensation, which turns me on even more. "Damn. Your touch feels so fucking good."

Alexander has me so turned on that I begin to shake as I come hard against his finger. "I'm coming. Oh, God."

"That's it, baby. Let go. Let me see you fall apart." He leans in and nibbles on my earlobe as he climbs on top of me and then rotates his hips so that his cock rubs against my clit, prolonging my orgasm.

My nails rake down his back and I scream out his name as he plunges his cock deep inside me.

"Yesss!" I hiss, enjoying the feel of him.

Fire pools in my belly as he pulls back a bit and then thrusts deep inside me again.

Alexander threads his fingers into my hair and locks eyes with me. "You are my dream, Margo. Being inside you is like heaven on this fucked-up earth."

The taut, pink skin on my nipples rubs against his bare chest as he pumps inside me. Every inch of us touching—skin to skin—as Alexander makes love to me.

His mouth drifts open as his lust-heavy eyes stare into mine while he works his dick in and out of my pussy. Knowing that I turn him on so much always does crazy things to my body, and before long, the familiar tingle of an orgasm rips through me again.

"Fuck. That's it, baby. I love watching you come." His eyes stay on me, studying my every move.

Alexander curls his fingers around my hip and grunts before a low growl emits from his throat as he gives in to his own desire and comes inside me.

We stare into each other's eyes as we pant, trying to catch our breath. For the first time since this all began, I feel like we have a real shot at making a go of this relationship together. I love this man, and it's amazing to know that he loves me back. This most certainly changes everything.

Chapter VI
SHALL WE DANCE

Margo

Things have been different since Alexander and I dropped the "L" word over three weeks ago. My husband, which is still weird to say, has been nothing but supportive in what has been, unquestionably, the hardest period of my life. He never left my side the day of Daddy's funeral. He was my rock, and it made my heart grow even fonder of him.

I take a deep breath as I stand outside the door to the boardroom I've been in hundreds of times. Never have I been scared to go in there because Daddy was always with me. I had him here to guide me, making sure I was making the right decisions.

"You've got this," Alexander whispers. "Go in there and assert your power. Everything else will fall into place. Trust me."

I stare up at my handsome husband and he smiles. It's nice to have him by my side. He's been through this and had to fight to prove from a young age that he's capable of running a major corporation. His experience in this situation is invaluable.

He places his hand on the door handle. "Ready?"

I tilt my chin up. "Let's do this."

Alexander holds open the door for me, and I strut through it. Every eye in the place is on me as I take my seat at the head of the table. Alexander takes the seat to my immediate right, where I used to sit when my father ran things.

"As you all know, I signed the paperwork this morning to take over as president of Buchanan Industries. This will be a difficult transition for all of us. No one will ever be able to replace Dan Buchanan. He was the founder of this company and poured his heart and soul into making it what it is today. While I will never be able to fill his shoes, I'll do my damndest to try. He taught me everything about this business, and I will figure out a way to turn things around for us."

I glance over at Alexander and he nods. It's nice to know he has my back and that I'm not alone in all of this. Together we can conquer the world.

"You almost ready?" Alexander asks as I take one final glance in the mirror, making sure my gown fits just right.

He steps up behind me wearing a devilish smirk, and I stare back at him through the mirror. "What's that look all about?"

He traces a finger across the bare skin on my shoulders. "Remember the last time we went to a gala? Perhaps I should get you naked before we leave the apartment so we get it out of our systems now."

I turn around to face him, and he wraps his arms around my waist. "You're insatiable."

"Only when it comes to you."

My heart pounds against my ribs. No matter how often he tells me that he can't get enough of me, it still excites me every time.

Alexander leans in and kisses the soft skin beneath my ear. "As much as I want to taste every inch of you right now, I must force myself to resist. Diem would absolutely kill me if I were late for her art show. If it were anyone else, believe me, I wouldn't have a problem saying fuck it."

My fingers slide under the lapel of his jacket. "Perhaps this would be an excellent time for you to make up with Diem."

He sighs. "I don't understand why she's so upset. I'm only looking out for her."

Alexander has found this difficult to deal with. In his eyes, Diem is still a little girl, incapable of making her own decisions. He's very much taken on the role of the overprotective parent who doesn't know when to loosen the reins a bit.

"Don't you think Diem is old enough to make the decision on who to date? I believe that if she and Jack did date, he would treat her with respect because he knows what a pain in the ass you are to deal with when you're pissed and out for blood.

"Maybe, but I still can't allow it to happen. If their relationship goes south, that will put me in a really shitty position, which is why I would rather cut things off now before they have a chance to get that far."

I understand what he's saying, but I've learned Alexander has a big problem when things are out of his control.

He takes a deep breath. "Let's not talk about this anymore. Hopefully, the little talk I had with her on the plane will be enough to squash all this bullshit so I won't have to worry about it any longer."

After saying good night to Jimmy Chew and Aggie, we make our way downstairs where Darby waits by the door.

He lets out a low whistle. "Evening. The two of ye be lookin' mighty sharp this evening."

I smile at the gentleman. "You are too kind, Darby."

"Just statin' the truth, lass. It's nice to see Alexander happy again."

A rush of heat floods my cheeks as I stare up to meet Alexander's gaze. In his eyes, I see nothing but sincerity, making my heartbeat quicken.

There's no doubt—I'm head over heels in love with my husband. For once, my mother was right. Marrying Alexander King turned out to be a good thing, surprisingly.

Darby holds open the door. "Have a lovely evening and tell Diem that Aggie and me are very proud of her."

Alexander places his hand on the small of my back as he nods. "I'll do that. Good night, Darby."

Darby tips his hat as we pass him and head to the waiting limo. It's amazing how fond I've become of ,what I like to call, Alexander's extended family. Aggie and Darby seem more like Alexander's aunt and uncle versus hired help because of how close they are to him. It's become clear to me that Alexander loves them, and I've learned that the circle of people Alexander loves is extremely small. I find myself lucky to be included in that elite club.

We arrive at the gallery, and I'm shocked to find it packed with people. It appears most of the Upper East Side is here to check out Diem's work. Most of them are here to be nosy and find some gossip than for the art that Diem has poured her soul into creating.

Alexander's face lights up as we step out of the limo and he takes in the crowd surrounding the entrance. "This is a better turnout than I'd imagined. Let's hope she sells something. It would be nice if she can get her second sale from this event."

"Maybe. Let's hope." I stumble over my words because I'm positive Diem never told Alexander that Jack purchased her self-portrait, and I'm not about to spill that secret.

He places his hand on the small of my back. "Ready, Mrs. King?"

A huge smile crosses my face after hearing him refer to me as his wife. It truly feels as if our relationship is moving in the correct direction. I like that we're getting closer every day.

We make our way across the sidewalk and toward the front door of the building. Tall windows show off all the people inside studying the paintings hanging on the well-lit walls. The stark-white walls are a nice contrast to the colorful paintings I've passed a hundred times in Alexander's apartment.

The minute our feet land on the hardwood floor inside, I notice a lot of familiar faces that tend to move in the same social circles as Alexander and myself.

Alexander was correct about one thing; there are a lot of pissed-off ladies that I stole the Naughty King off the market and they have no problem shooting their angry stares in my direction.

"There's Diem," Alexander whispers into my ear. "Let's go say hello."

The crowd around Diem parts allowing Alexander and me to pass through, and Diem pauses mid-sentence the moment her eyes land on her brother making his way toward her.

"Will you excuse me? Enjoy the rest of the exhibits, and please don't hesitate to ask any additional questions you may have about my work." She smiles at her potential buyers before approaching us. "I'm surprised you're here."

Alexander arches his right eyebrow before he responds. "Why wouldn't I be here? This is one of the most important days of your life. I'm here to support you."

She squares her shoulders. "So you pick and choose what you support me in now? When Mom left, you told me you'd always have my back no matter what, but after that plane ride home from Yamada's island, I realize that isn't true."

"You still don't get it, do you? I'm only ... I—"

"No, Alexander. It's you who doesn't understand. I'm in love with Jack, and I'm pretty sure he's in love with me too, or at least that's what I thought until you attempted to force him to choose between his friendship with you and his job at King or me."

Alexander lifts his chin. "It's for the best, Diem. One day, you'll see that and thank me for stopping this affair before it ever started."

Diem rolls her pretty green eyes. "I don't understand where you get off trying to control my love life when you can't even control your own."

Alexander's head tilts. "What do you mean? I'm always in control."

Diem folds her slender arms across her chest. "Not when it comes to Jess. She actually just purchased a piece of artwork from me, and you'll never guess which one. Check it out." Diem tilts her head to the right a tiny bit.

Both Alexander and I follow her direction, and my mouth instantly drops. Jess stands there in a gold cocktail dress staring up at the painting I assume she just purchased. It's the portrait of Alexander that once hung in his apartment.

Alexander storms over in Jess' direction without saying another word to his sister or even to me.

"Alexander," I call after him, not wanting him to cause a scene at Diem's opening because I know he'll regret it later.

I begin to take off after him, but Diem grabs my hand, halting me in place. "Margo, I'm sorry about all this. Please don't be upset with me. I just think it's time Alexander learns that no matter how much he wants to, he cannot control everything all the time. Especially when it comes to matters of the heart. That's one subject I think I know a little more about than my brother does."

I give her a small smile. "I understand, Diem. You can't help that you've fallen for your brother's best friend any more than I can help that I've fallen in love with my enemy. The heart wants what it wants, as they say."

Then she does something I don't expect. She throws her arms around my neck and wraps me in a warm hug. "Thank you. You are the best sister-in-law I could have ever asked for. Thank you for being so understanding about the Jack situation. Maybe you can help Alexander understand it too?"

I squeeze her back, loving the feeling of acceptance into her family. "I will try my best." I pull back. "I had better go over there and try to keep Alexander from going to prison."

Diem laughs. "Please do. I don't need my brother to be the dominating topic of conversation when people talk about my show. It will be nice to have it remembered for the art and not Alexander killing Jess."

"Agreed. Wish me luck."

I head toward my irate husband, who is in the middle of telling Jess no way in hell will he allow her to purchase a picture of him to hang in her bedroom to masturbate to, when a voice from my past stops me dead in my tracks.

"Margo Buchanan? Is that you?" The low baritone voice that once turned me on with one word is now the sound that causes my stomach to turn.

Standing before me in a black suit, wearing an amused smile, is none other than Chuck Vanderbilt. The man, who at one time, I was convinced was my forever until he decided it was okay to sleep with a waitress during our engagement party.

Looking him over now, I can't believe how attractive I used to find him. His professionally styled blond hair, brown eyes, and perfect veneer-covered teeth only mask his very ugly heart.

My back stiffens. "What are you doing here?"

He flinches at my tone. "No, hello, how are you?"

I roll my eyes. He's lucky I can stand here and be calm and rational in his presence. Last time I saw him, there was a lot of screaming and yelling, and I'm pretty sure I threatened his life if he ever spoke to me again.

Chuck lifts the drink he's holding in his hand to me. "A drink to loosen up perhaps?"

"Drop dead."

I know that's not the most grown-up answer I could've given him, but direct disdain is the only way I can ensure nothing I say will come off remotely friendly when it comes to Chuck Vanderbilt.

"Okay, then." He pulls his hand back. "I guess we won't be catching up with one another. I thought it might be a good time to finally speak and get some closure."

"*Closure*? Are you serious right now?" I fold my arms over my chest. "I can't believe you can stand there and look me in the eye and say that to me. I found you in a bathroom, during our engagement party, fucking the hired help. You're lucky you're still standing here right now with your balls intact. I don't need any closure from you. I don't need, nor want, anything from you ever again."

Chuck lifts his hands, still holding two drinks, and a couple of his fingers fan out as if he's trying to hold his hands up in surrender. "Whoa. It's apparent you hate my guts even after all this time. It's been a couple of years, Margo. I figured you would've had plenty of time to calm down by now. If I would've known you were still this pissed at me, I would've never accepted Jess' invitation to come here to see you."

My brow arches in suspicion. "Jess?"

"Yes." He nods and then points in the direction of Jess and Alexander. "She made it seem as though the two of you were friends, and that you had mentioned needing closure with me in order to move on and ensure your marriage to Alexander King would be successful."

My eyes widen as I turn and focus my stare on Jess, who still seems to be involved in a heated conversation with my husband. Seems that I underestimated just how far Jess is willing to go to sabotage Alexander. If she thinks bringing an ex, who I loathe, is going to do anything to sway me, she's obviously not as smart as she believes herself to be. This bitch doesn't know who she's fucking with because it will take more than just an ex to scare me off from being with Alexander.

chapter VII
CRASH AND BURN

Alexander

I shoot my icy stare at her. "This is the last fucking time I'm going to say this, Jess, and then I'm walking away. I refuse to allow you to ruin Diem's event with your bullshit. You are not getting this painting."

Her lip curls and she folds her arms. "You know as well as I do, Alexander, I get what I want."

"Not when it comes to me and my family—not anymore."

She releases an amused laugh. "So you think. Have you forgotten that I will go to any lengths to get what I want? I've already set my plan into motion to help my father control of your company, and it starts with reuniting your wife with her ex-fiancé."

My brows knit in confusion, and I wish my facial expression didn't just give away the fact that I had no fucking clue Margo had an ex-fiancé. But judging by the huge shit-eatin' grin on Jess' face, she knows she's just shocked me. My investigative team failed to mention that little tidbit of information when they gave me the report on Margo Buchanan before she stepped foot into my office, and Margo never mentioned one goddamn word about it either.

I despise being the last to know *anthing* and being made out to look like a fool.

Jess makes a show of peering over my shoulder. "Looks to me they're getting reacquainted as we speak."

I whip my head around just in time to meet the wide-eyed stare of my wife in my direction as she stands in front of a blond man who has his back to me. My spine stiffens, and I storm out of the room before I fucking explode. Now is not the fucking time or place for dirty laundry to be aired. Diem is already pissed at me enough, and as much as it fucking kills me to walk away from all this bullshit without saying a word, I do. I refuse to be the asshole who ruins this for Diem, although Jess is doing her damnedest to make sure I do exactly that.

Everything feels like it's crashing down on me at once.

Jess is trying to take away my company. For the first time in years, my baby sister and I cannot seem to carry on a civil conversation, and to top it all off, the woman I'm in love with neglected to tell me she may possibly still have feelings for another man. What if she still loves him? Now that she's seen him, will she want him back?

Oh, my God. I don't even know what I'll fucking do if that happens.

The air around me suddenly feels so thin, so I loosen the tie constricting the air to my lungs.

I rush through the hallway in the back of the building, needing to escape in order to clear my head to think rationally about the situation. I'm freaking out, and this is totally unlike me. What the fuck is happening?

I cut around the corner and find myself in a small office, only I'm not alone as I'd hoped.

Fuck me. I'm so not ready to do this right now, but it looks like I have no other choice.

I square my shoulders. "What the fuck are you doing here, Jack? I thought I made myself pretty clear when it came to you hanging around my sister."

Jack instantly bounces up from the desk chair he was sitting in. It's almost as if he was sitting back here hiding from me. His eyes widen, and I can tell by the expression on his face that he's worried.

Jack holds his hands up. "Alexander, look, I know you don't like the idea of your sister being with me, but I swear to God, you have nothing to worry about."

"If I have nothing to worry about, then why are you hiding from me in some fucking office?" Even I can hear the anger in my voice.

It's not like me to speak to Jack this way, but when it comes to my baby sister, I will go to hell and back against anyone who attempts to hurt her. I will not sit back and watch Diem be used. It's not going to fucking happen.

"Diem thought it'd be best that you not see the two of us together for a while. Believe me, I don't give a damn whether you know about the two of us, but Diem wants your blessing so badly, she's willing to hide our relationship until you're ready to accept it."

"I'm never going to accept this," I fire back.

He shakes his head. "Why the hell not? I'm your best friend."

"Exactly! Which means I know how you are with women. You use them and toss them in the fucking gutter when you're done with them. I won't allow you to do that to Diem. She's better than that."

"I know she is, which is why I fell in love with her."

"*Love?*" I scoff. "Guys like you and me are incapable of love. It doesn't fucking exist."

"How can you of all people say that to me? Look at how much you've changed over the past few months."

"*Me?*" I point at my own chest. "You think *I've* changed?"

"Abso-fucking-lutely. I haven't even heard you talk about the Buchanan deal since we got back from Yamada's island. You're so in love with Margo that you're willing to allow millions of dollars to slip through your fingertips in order to be with her. No matter how much you don't want to face it, love has changed you, just like it's changed me."

I stare my best friend down, and while he may be correct that I haven't spoken about dismantling Buchanan Industries in a while, that doesn't mean love has made me a fucking pussy.

It hasn't changed me *that* much, which is how I know it will never change Jack enough for me to allow him to be with my sister. I need to make him realize that I'm still the same guy as before so he'll take a good, long, hard look and realize he's the same guy too.

I take a deep breath. "I haven't mentioned the deal because I already know that I'm running things when it comes to Margo Buchanan. Making her believe that I love her is all part of my master plan to gain her trust. Then I can have my way with her company just as I do with her body. She'll sign whatever I want because she believes I love her, and I'm the best fucking lay she's ever had. Our love isn't real. It's a fucking illusion."

Jack's eyes widen, and I chuckle. I've shocked him.

Good.

Now, he knows I'm still the cold-hearted bastard I've always been even if I don't exactly mean every word I just said.

"That's a fantastic plan." The sound of Margo's voice causes an electric shock to my spine. I spin around on my heels and take in the pained expression on her face.

"Margo...I..." I stumble over my own words as my heart crumbles. She heard me say that I really didn't love her, and she believed it. How the hell am I supposed to explain myself after that? She heard my cold, hard words with her own ears. I can't backpedal my way out of this.

She swallows hard, and I can tell she's barely holding things together as she tries to flip the switch back into the cold, hard bitch she was when we first met. "You might have a little trouble carrying that one out now that I know about it, so good luck coming up with another one of your ridiculous schemes on how to screw me over."

She takes a step backward, and I realize I'm losing her right before my very eyes, and it's all my own doing. I want to stop her from leaving, but if I go after her now, I'll prove Jack right and basically give him the greenlight to be with Diem. I'm fucking stuck between a rock and a hard place.

I drop my head as soon as Margo's out of sight and pinch the bridge of my nose. I fucked up.

Big time.

It's just that this being in love thing is so damn foreign to me. How can I love Margo without making myself look like a fucking pussy?

"Aren't you going to go after her?" Jack's voice cuts through the otherwise quiet room, reminding me if Jack had stayed away from my sister like I told him, this fucking argument would've never happened.

My nostrils flare as I stare at my best friend. "Why don't you mind your own goddamn business? If you'd done as I told you and stayed away from Diem, I would've never said those things at all. You're ruining everything."

"No, Alexander. You're fucking everything up because you're trying to control everyone's lives when you're having trouble keeping your own shit straight. You can't even admit to me, your best friend, that you love Margo." I stare at him, unable to say a word. Deep down, I know what he's saying is true, but I fucking hate the idea of admitting it.

Jack shakes his head. "Man, if you don't fix this, you'll end up lonely and alone. I'm not going to end up like you. I'm asking your sister to marry me, and I don't give a damn anymore what you think anymore."

Everything around me begins to spin, and before I realize what I'm doing, I lunge for Jack. Wrinkling the crisp fabric of his white shirt in my hand, I draw my fist back and blast him square in the face. "I forbid it. You hear me."

"Fuck you, Alex," Jack spits before throwing a punch and catching me in the jaw. "Diem is old enough to make her own decisions."

We both tumble to the floor, tossing expletives at each other as we grapple for control.

"Oh, my God. Stop it! Stop it right now!" Diem's shrill scream precedes her jumping on my back, attempting to pull me off Jack. "What the hell are you doing?"

I grab her by the arm just as I did when we wrestled around as children and fling her off me. She lands between Jack and me, wearing her black gown and a scowl like I've never seen before.

"What's your problem, Alexander? Why can't you be happy that I've found someone who loves me and that I love back?" Diem shouts. She turns and cups Jacks face as she examines the damage I inflicted.

"Love isn't real, Diem. It can't be." She whips around to face me, and before she can open her mouth to argue with me, I cut her off with my logic. "Because if love is real, why doesn't our own mother love us? She left us when we needed her the most. People run when things get too tough. The best you can ever expect in this life is to find a loyal person who will stand by your side no matter what, and Jack isn't the right guy for you to expect to stick around. Look at me—I just betrayed Margo's trust to protect my pride, and what I have with her is the closest thing to love I've felt in a really long time."

Diem frowns. "Alexander, Mom left because she's a bitch. She was young when she got with Dad, and he tolerated being with her, putting up with her gold-digging ways, for our sake. He was hoping she'd change and become a real mother to us, but it just wasn't in her. You can't sabotage every relationship you're going to have because you believe everyone is selfish like Mom.

"You were young when you met Jess, and she sure didn't do anything to turn your opinion about love and relationships around, so you can't use that as a comparison either. Margo is different, and I can tell she's really got genuine feelings for you.

She's stuck by your side when she didn't have to. Why can't you open yourself up to be loved? If you could, then maybe you'd understand what I have with Jack isn't going to hurt me. He isn't out to use me for our money, and deep down, you know that. You've been best friends since college; you know he's a good man or you wouldn't have allowed him to stay in your life."

My gaze flicks over to Jack's face, and I notice a trickle of blood coming from his nose. Instantly, I feel like shit for what I just did to him.

I nod as Diem's words ring through my mind. "I'm sorry, Jack. You're my best friend, and I fucked up. I know you're a good guy. Hell, I'd trust my life in your hands, but when it comes to my baby sister, I guess I'm overprotective."

I shove myself up to my feet, help Diem up, and then extend my hand down to Jack. "I apologize for—well, everything."

Jack stares at my outstretched hand for a long moment before finally taking it, allowing me to help him to his feet. "I get it, man, I do, but like I said before, you have nothing to worry about when it comes to me being with your sister." Jack wraps his arm around Diem's shoulders and stares down at her. "I love her."

Diem's green eyes soften as she gazes up at Jack. "You do?"

He nods. "I have for a while, and now that Alexander seems okay with us...?" His gaze flicks over in my direction, awaiting confirmation from me, so I nod. He focuses his attention back on her. "Now that he's okay with us, I want to know if you'd be okay with marrying me?"

She bites her bottom lip, and her shoulders shrug up a little with excitement. "Really?"

"Really," he confirms, causing her to squeal with delight, just like she did when she opened her gifts at Christmas, and then throws her arms around his neck.

"Yes. Yes. A thousand times yes!" she says as he wraps her in an embrace.

I smile. It's good to see her so happy, and thinking about her getting married causes me to think about Margo. I've ruined my chance of possible happiness.

Diem releases Jack and then turns to hug me. "Thank you, Alexander. Your blessing means everything to me."

"I just want you to be happy, Squirt," I whisper in her ear. "I'm sorry for being such an asshole. I should've have trusted your judgment and allowed you to live your life. You are a grown woman now."

She squeezes me tight. "I love you."

"I love you, too."

Diem pulls back, tears glistening in her eyes. "Now, go find Margo. Apologize and make things right between the two of you. I like her."

I give her a small smile. "I like her too, but I'm afraid she won't forgive me after what she overheard me saying to Jack."

"The woman loves you. If you tell her you're sorry and really mean it, she's going to forgive you."

"Let's hope."

I turn and head out the door, on a mission to do something I've never done before ... grovel at the feet of the woman I love.

Chapter VIII
I SHOULD'VE KNOWN BETTER

Margo

What in the hell was I thinking? I should've known this was all just some sick twisted game to him. How could I have been so stupid to believe that he meant it when he said he loved me.

The cab grinds to a halt in front of Alexander's building, and I fish money from my clutch to pay for my ride. Before I have a chance to grab the handle, the door opens, and Darby extends his hand to help me out of the car.

"No Alex?" he asks as I step out of the car.

I shake my head. "Not this time."

My eyes sting, and I'm having difficulty fighting back the tears that would reveal my devastation. The truth of finding out Alexander doesn't love me hurts more than I'm ready to admit.

Darby matches his step with mine and then pauses ahead of me to open the door, allowing me inside the building. He studies my face as I pass and his lips pull into a tight line. "Are you okay, lass? Is there anything I can do?"

I place my hand on his forearm. "I'll be fine. I've just come to collect my things. I would appreciate it if you can arrange a cab to pick me up in fifteen minutes. I'm only grabbing the essentials and then I'll be returning to my apartment."

Darby pauses and the expression on his face tells me he wants to ask so much, but he refrains. Instead, he tips his hat a bit and gives me a sad smile. "As you wish."

"Thank you, Darby. You have been very kind to me while I've been here—you and Aggie. I shall miss you both."

With that, I turn and make my way to the elevator, knowing this is the last time I'll probably ever see this old man who's been nothing but kind to me while I've been here.

When the elevator opens up to the penthouse, I rush through the door and head straight to my room. The suitcase I brought with me initially is only large enough to hold the items I brought with me when I first agreed to stay with Alexander to pass off our sham marriage. I stare at my walk-in closet and I'm surprised at all the clothing and jewelry I've amassed since I've been here. Alexander was always having Aggie pick up new things for me. It doesn't seem right to take all of this with me, so I grab the things that I remember bringing and quickly pack my suitcase. Once it's filled, I hurry into the bathroom to grab my makeup. The sight of my own reflection alarms me. The delicate skin beneath my eyes is puffy from crying during the cab ride here, and a few strands of my dark hair have fallen from the French twist sitting on the back of my head. I'm horrible at hiding my emotions, and my disheveled appearance proves just that.

Alexander King did a number on me with his acting abilities. I believed him. I believed we had a shot at being happy together.

A single tear slips down my cheek, and I quickly wipe it away. The sparkle of the diamond ring Alexander gave me catches my eye. I stare down at the ring on my left hand, and it suddenly occurs to me the bargain I made with Alexander is null and void. He has no intention to uphold his end of the deal by helping me save Buchanan Industries, so why should I wear this and continue to play the part of doting wife in order to convince the board that Alexander is fit to control the King Corporation.

Our deal is done—nonexistent—just like our relationship.

I slide the ring off my finger, holding it up for inspection one final time before laying it down on the counter. "Goodbye, Alexander."

I let out a sigh before I rush out of the bathroom, grab my suitcase, and head for the door with my chin tipped up. From now on, my judgment will not be clouded by my feelings for Alexander King. I will avoid him at all costs. It's time to get back into action and figure out a way to save Buchanan Industries without Alexander's help.

Chapter IX
IT MUST'VE BEEN LOVE

Alexander

Traffic in New York is ridiculous. It always moves at a snail's pace when you're in a rush. My leg bounces uncontrollably as I wait in the back of the limo. I'm an idiot for not going after Margo the moment she tore out of Diem's event, but I'm hoping that when I find her, she allows me to plead my case.

I strain my neck, trying to figure out why in the hell this car is sitting still. "How far are we from my building?"

"We're about ten blocks away, sir," the driver answers.

This is ridiculous.

I fling open the door. "I'll continue on foot. Park the car in front of the building and wait until I dismiss you."

"Yes, sir."

I spring out of the car and take off toward my building. A block in, and my anxiety about possibly losing Margo forever engulfs every inch of my being, pushing me to move faster. Soon, I find myself sprinting down the busy Manhattan sidewalk in a tux, looking like a crazy man on a mission, but I don't give a shit. The only thing on my mind is fixing this thing I've fucked up with Margo. The thought of her hating me causes my stomach to twist.

The dress shoes on my feet slap the concrete as I enter into the home stretch, and I push my body to move faster. My eyes widen when I spot Margo—suitcase in hand—standing on the sidewalk speaking with Darby.

"Margo!" I scream her name and every head within the vicinity whips in my direction.

Margo points her gaze in my direction and then she instantly rushes toward a waiting cab. Darby opens the trunk and reaches for Margo's bag, knowing she's doing her best to get away before I can reach her.

I rush over, grabbing her bag away from Darby and drop it next to me as I stand before my wife, trying to catch my breath. "Wait. I'm sorry. Stay. Let me explain."

Her nostrils flare, and her beautiful face contorts in hurt. "No explanation is necessary, Alexander. I received your message loud and clear. I refuse to stand here and allow you to play me for a fool."

I hold out my hands in surrender. "I know what you heard sounded horrible, but you've got to believe me—I didn't mean it."

"I'm not an idiot. You were telling Jack exactly how you felt about me since you thought I wasn't around to hear it."

"You're right. I never intended for your ears to hear those words, but it doesn't mean I was lying when I said I love you."

She folds her slender arms across her chest. "You honestly expect me to believe you? I'm just a game to you—a plaything you can control and bend to your will. Everything you ever said or did to make me believe you're a good man was all bullshit."

"It wasn't. I meant it when I said I wanted to give this marriage a real shot."

"Then why would you deny how you feel in front of Jack?"

"Because I allowed my ego to get the best of me. Loving someone makes you weak. I can't show my weakness by loving the one woman who's supposed to be my enemy. Showing people your real feelings will get you eaten alive in my world, so I've learned to keep my emotions under wraps. If people find your weakness, they'll go after it. Please ..." I grab her shoulders and pull her closer to me as I plead with her. "Margo, please. Don't walk away from this. Don't walk away from me. I *do* love you."

Tears stream down her cheeks and everything at this moment teeters on what those tears mean. I brush the pad of my thumb across her face in an attempt to wipe her pain away, praying that she believes me.

I cup her face and peer into her blue eyes. "Stay with me."

She closes her eyes and then lets out a shaky breath. The pain in the pit of my stomach tells me I'm losing her.

"I can't," she whispers before opening her eyes to meet my gaze. "Without trust, a relationship means nothing. Actions speak louder than words, Alexander." She grabs the suitcase from my grasp and then takes a step back toward the cab, asks Darby to load her bag, but doesn't say another word to me.

My mind races as I watch her get into the cab. What can I say to make her stay? What can I do to prove to her I'm telling her the truth?

The door slams shut, making me jump, and it hits me that this may be it—the last time I see Margo. I dash over and shove my hand against the glass, but she won't even look at me.

"Margo! Margo, please," I plead with her through the window. "I'll do anything."

She won't even look at me as she leans forward and instructs the cabbie to drive. As the car slowly pulls into traffic, I pound my fist on the glass. "Stop! Please!"

It's not like me to beg, but I'm willing to endure the public humiliation if it will make her look at me. Horns blare at me as I drop to the ground while the yellow car pulls away, leaving me stranded in the middle of the crowded New York City street. I hang my head as a feeling of emptiness fills every inch inside me.

I've fucked up. I ruined the best thing that's happened to me in a long, long time, and I'm not sure there's a way to ever fix all that I've broken.

A strong grip on my right shoulder startles me, and I glance up to see Darby standing next to me with a somber expression on his face. "Come on, son. Getting ran over isn't going to help the situation."

I take a ragged breath and then struggle to make it up on my two feet. Each step is harder to take than the last as I follow Darby into the building.

He's quiet as he steps onto the elevator with me. It reminds me of the times when I was just a boy and Darby would be with me whenever I would hear my mother and father fighting. He would never say much, but his strong, stoic presence was always comforting.

The elevator dings as it comes to a stop on the top floor, and Darby holds the door open for me. He opens his mouth to say something, but scans the deep frown on my face and then closes his mouth. Darby gives my shoulder a hard pat as I pass by, and I know it's his way of showing he understands what I'm going through.

The elevator closes behind me, and before I have a chance to grab the handle to my apartment door, it opens for me.

Aggie stands there in her pale blue uniform with her lips turned down, and a deep wrinkle standing out in her forehead as looks at me, concerned. "Are you all right?"

I scrub my hand down my face. "No. She's gone, Aggie."

"I know, dear." She pulls her lips into a tight line. "She was crying the entire time she was packing her clothes. What happened between the two of ye? The two of ye seemed so happy when ye left here."

My shoulders slump as I shuffle past her. It was only a couple hours ago that we were extremely happy in this apartment together. When I left here with Margo, I never dreamed tonight would end up like this.

I shrug my jacket off, and Aggie reaches for it. "Is there anything you can do to fix whatever went on between the two of ye?"

"I don't know. Our relationship may be beyond repair."

She lays my jacket across her arm. "You're a smart man, Alex. I know ye'll figure out a way to make whatever happened right with the lass."

I give her a defeated smile. To Aggie, everything is simple and can be straightened out with an apology. Margo caught me saying some hurtful things, and my actions broke her faith in me. I'm not sure how to even begin to repair something like that.

I sigh and then head toward the staircase. "I'll be upstairs."

I climb up the steps, and then make my way down the empty hallway staring at the walls where Diem's paintings typically hang. The place feels so empty. Diem is clearly moving on with her life—growing up and becoming her own woman—and now Margo is gone, too. At the end of the hall, I come to Margo's room. I stop and study the door before leaning my head against it. I shouldn't torture myself by going in there, but I can't seem to stop myself.

When the door opens, a whiff of her sweet perfume fills my nose. The fact that it smells like her in here only drives the dagger deeper into my heart. I know she had her suitcase, but like a lunatic, I head into her closet and then into the bathroom to confirm her things are gone. My eyes zero in on the diamond ring lying on the counter.

The gold is cool as I pinch it between my fingers, examining her abandoned engagement ring. Tears well in my eyes as I sink down onto the tiled floor. It's over, and it's all my fucking fault. I have to live knowing I've destroyed the best thing that's ever happened to me.

Chapter X
NEW GAME PLAN

Margo

Leave it to Dad to be one of the only businessmen left on the planet who didn't believe in electronic bookkeeping. Thank God the accounting department here is up-to-date and has all of our financials in order. It's just too bad that all of our accounts are barely keeping afloat. This once was a thriving company, but after some terrible business deals, we're barely keeping the lights on. All morning, I've combed through every scrap of paper in Dad's office, searching for any contacts who may be interested in partnering with Buchanan Industries. So far, every call I've made has resulted in a firm 'no, thank you' from other companies that build aircrafts.

It's no wonder Daddy was considering jumping into a deal with the Devil. No other options are really left to save the company. If I sit back and do nothing, Buchanan Industries will fold and all the employees who work for me will be out of a job.

I have to figure out something.

A soft knock on my office door grabs my attention. "Come in."

Melissa, my father's secretary for the better part of twenty years, shuffles toward my desk. Her graying brown hair is pulled back as her reading glasses sit atop her head. God love her, she's been working as late as I have the past few days in an attempt to help me figure out a solution to save this company.

She smiles down at me. "How you holding up in here? Is there anything I can do?"

I shake my head as I pull off my glasses and then rub the bridge of my nose. "I keep searching for a way out of this mess, but I run into a wall with everything I try. If I don't figure something out soon, we'll go under in less than a year. I keep worrying about all the employees. I don't want to put them out of a job."

"You sound just like your father. For the last couple of years, he's sat in that exact chair worrying about the same outcome. He was concerned about you, too. He didn't like the idea of leaving you with nothing, which is why he was willing to sell a lot of the shares to King. He wanted to build you a trust fund. He loved you so much, and he made the best decisions given the situation to make sure you had a secure future."

"He always did look out for me." I smile as I think about all the mentoring he'd done to steer me in the right direction when it came to business.

"You were always the apple of his eye. Speaking of men adoring you, your husband called *again*. That man hasn't missed a day of trying to reach you in over a month. Are you ever going to speak to him?"

I sigh and lean back in my chair. "No. Words from Alexander King's mouth are something I can't trust, so it'll do me no good to talk to him. He's arrogant, and he doesn't like to lose, which is why he's still trying to figure out a way to take over Buchanan Industries. Anything he'd say to me would only be to con me into getting what he wants."

Melissa shoves herself up from the chair. "Okay, then, I'll continue to hold all his calls. I'm going to call it a night. Are you sure you'll be all right in the office, alone?"

I check the clock on my computer screen. "I didn't realize it was after eight. I'll wrap up soon and call it a night."

"I'll see you in the morning."

"Good night."

When she leaves, I go back to work, thumbing through the file laid out in front of me labeled 'King Deal.' I've read this contract a million times and still can't get over how much of a cut Alexander wanted to take from my Dad. It's too bad Yamada and Alexander are close. It would've been nice to make a deal with Yamada directly since it would put millions in our pocket and save us. The last time I spoke to Yamada about business was when we were in Vegas, and it didn't seem like I would be able to sway his loyalty. It's a long shot, but it can't hurt to call him and find out where his head is at.

I pick up my cell and search out his number. It rings a couple of times, and then a female voice answers, and she sounds pissed. "Who is this?"

"Um ..." The harsh greeting catches me off guard, so I quickly attempt to recover. "I'm trying to reach Yamada."

There's some rustling on the other end of the line like there's a struggle over the phone.

"Give Yamada the phone," Yamada demands in the background.

"No!" the adamant female voice shouts. "Not until you tell me who the hell this Dime Piece is? And why is this bitch calling you?"

"Easy. Easy. Dime Piece is Yamada's friend. She's King's wife."

"Oh." The tone of the woman's voice changes. "Here you go."

I roll my eyes, and I'm still lost as to what all these women find so appealing about Yamada that cause them to become crazy possessive. Bitches truly do seem to love Yamada.

"Dime Piece, I hope this isn't a booty call just because you've found out that Yamada is in town." I can hear the smile in his voice.

"No. Actually, I'm calling to see if we can set up a meeting. I want to discuss a possible deal between Yamada Enterprises and Buchanan Industries."

There's a long pause. "King know about this?"

I bite my lower lip. If I tell him no, his loyalty to Alexander will prohibit him from going behind his friend's back to make a deal with me, so I have no other choice than to tell him a little white lie. I know if I can get him to hear out my plan, he won't be able to turn down the profit we both stand to make from our mutual partnership.

"Of course, he knows. He encouraged me to reach out to you, directly, since I'm now the head of Buchanan."

"In that case, hottie, Yamada is in. Text the time and place, and Yamada will be there."

A smile fills my face. "Will do. See you soon."

I end the call and stick the papers in front of me back into their appropriate files. It's the first time I've really smiled since I parted ways with Alexander. Happiness has been hard to come by as of late.

A light knock on my door catches my attention and my mouth drops open a bit as my eyes land on my beautiful visitor. "Diem? What are you doing here?"

She steps inside my office, holding her clutch tightly in her hands. "Sorry to just show up here like this, but I called your mother and she said you've been working a lot of late nights, so I thought I would come by and see how you're doing."

"I'm okay—a little disappointed that your brother deceived me the way he did, but I'll get over it...eventually." I give her and honest answer, but not one that will divulge too much information because Lord knows I don't need Alexander having any information to use against me.

She motions to the chair facing my desk. "May I?"

"Of course." I close the file in front of me. "How are you and Jack doing?"

"Amazing," she gushes. "Being with him is like a fairytale, I just wish I got to see him more. He's been working a lot of hours lately."

"That's your brother's doing, I assume. He's a damn slave driver." The memory of him ordering me around all day in the office flashes through my mind.

Her pretty pink lips twists. "That's the thing, Alex hasn't even been into the office in weeks because he's been too depressed to leave his apartment. Jack has been picking up all the slack."

I study my sister-in-law's face, unsure if she's telling me the truth or if she's apart of some crazy plan my husband put together to get information out of me.

"I know what you're thinking...but I'm not here for Alex. He would kill me if he knew I was here. I'm here because I'm worried about him. I've never seen him like this." Diem stands up and stands in front of my desk. "Alex can be an asshole, but he's a good man, and he loves you. Can you find it in your heart to forgive him? Please give him another shot."

I wish so badly what she's saying is true, but I know what I heard and I can't forget that. "I'm sorry, Diem. He hurt me with his actions and I don't think I can get over that enough to ever trust him again."

She chews on her lower lip. "Is there anything he can do to change your mind."

"He would have to prove to me the Alexander I fell in love with was genuine. All the attempts he's made to apologize aren't enough. It's going to take more than showing up here announced or sending gifts to show me that I'm not some game to him."

She nods. "I understand. It's a shame the two of you can't work things out. You were really great together."

"I thought so too," I whisper. It's the closest I can come to admitting how much I miss him without sounding like a love-sick twit.

I cannot be weak. I have to stand my ground. Too many people at Buchanan Industries are counting on me to save this company. I will not allow my husband to dupe me into a deal that will cause my company to fold, no matter how much I'm still in love him.

Chapter XI
GETTING THE GIRL

Alexander

Attempt number sixty, and Margo still refuses to take my call. If I keep this up, she's liable to contact the police for a restraining order against her estranged husband for harassment.

I've sunk to a pathetic new low since I saw her over a month ago. I've turned into one of those losers who can't get over a woman who doesn't want him anymore. I can't eat. I can't sleep. My thoughts are consumed by Margo.

What is she doing? Who is she with? Does she miss me?

The last one I already know the answer to because she won't have anything to do with me. I've sent her every gift known to man and nothing I'm doing seems to help.

I bring the bottle of scotch to my lips and take a long pull. I'm way past caring about a glass at this point because I can't seem to get the liquor down fast enough. I need it to make me forget about her.

Jimmy skitters out onto the balcony patio attached to my bedroom and jumps up onto the couch next to me under the darkened evening sky. I scratch behind his right ear and smile. Diem was right about this dog. I'm not immune to his cuteness no matter how shitty I feel wallowing in my own self-pity.

"Still no answer, buddy. I don't know how long I should keep trying," I tell my furry best friend.

Poor dog has listened to me pour my heart out over Margo for weeks now.

He lays his head down on my lap and stares up at me with his big, chocolate eyes as if he's hanging on my every word.

I stroke his head. "I miss her, too. I'm such a schmuck for falling in love. I should've known letting my guard down again would only cause me more heartbreak."

I hear a knock on my bedroom door, and I let out a heavy sigh. Aggie has been overly concerned about me lately, checking on me regularly to make sure I'm not in here harming myself. "I'm good, Aggie."

The door creaks open. Perhaps she didn't hear me, so I try again. "I'm good."

"That's total bullshit."

I groan at the sound of Diem's voice. Apparently, it's time for her weekly visit to help join Aggie with the bed checks. "I'm not dead. You can go back home now."

Diem flips on the light, and I shield my eyes as she comes marching toward me. She snatches the bottle of scotch from my hand. "This has gone on long enough. You look like hell and you're scaring Aggie to death. It's time for an intervention."

I squeeze my eyes shut and then pinch the bridge of my nose. "I'm fine."

"If you were fine, big brother, you would've made it to the office at some point this month. Jack has been running himself ragged trying to keep everything together, and he says you're difficult to get on the phone. This isn't like you, Alex, and since you keep shutting everyone out, I called the one person I knew who could make you talk."

"Diem—"

"Hello, madafaka." My head whips toward the door to witness one of my best friends strolling through the door, wearing an all blue tracksuit paired with a white flat cap. He looks like he robbed LL Cool J's closet from the nineties. "Yamada is here to get your ass out of this room."

I hold my hands up. "Whoa. Let's not get crazy. I can't go out."

"Get dressed." Yamada picks up a shirt off the edge of my chair but then wrinkles his nose as if he's just smelled a dead animal and immediately tosses it on the floor. "Clean clothes and a shower. No more homeless looking Alexander. We're meeting with Dime Piece tonight."

I lift my chin, and my mouth drops open a bit. "She agreed to see me? How did you—She won't even return my calls."

I don't know how he does it, but my friend always seems to pull miracles out of his ass.

"Not exactly. Bringing you will be Yamada's surprise. She's expecting a one-on-one meeting to talk business. Yamada's not interested in that right now. Yamada's interested in love connections and making sure King gets laid on the regular so he doesn't turn into ..." He looks me up and down and then raises his eyebrows and points. "This."

I shove myself up from the couch. All of my muscles are suddenly alive with a newfound burst of energy. I may not have exactly imagined our reunion in my head like this, but if this is the only chance I get to see Margo and beg her forgiveness and explain how much I've missed her, I'll take it.

I scurry off toward the bathroom, stripping my shirt off along the way.

"Make sure you scrub those balls. Want them nice and clean when Dime Piece has them in her mouth later on."

"Yamada!" My sister scolds him, causing me to laugh. "That was crude."

"What? Don't act like King and Margo aren't freaky as fuck. Yamada thinking ball licking is mild compared to what they do when they play hide the pickle."

"Oh, my God. You are too much."

For the first time in a month, I find myself grinning from ear to ear.

Music pumps through the speakers. It's so damn loud in here. I don't know how Yamada expects me to have a conversation in here. This isn't exactly the place I had in mind when I pictured having a heart-to-heart with Margo.

I turn to head toward the bar, and Yamada grabs my arm. "Where you going?"

I cock my brow. "To get a drink. That is why we're here, isn't it?"

Yamada points his index finger straight up. "There's an office upstairs. Come. We go."

I stare down at him, a bit bewildered. "How do you know that?"

One corner of his mouth pulls up into a grin. "Welcome to soon-to-be-renamed Yamada's."

"You bought this place?"

He nods. "Yamada bought the whole building. It has offices on the second floor, apartments to rent out to hotties on the other floors, and Yamada setting up a bachelor pad on the top floor to be close to King. Convenient, no?"

"This is such a bad idea. Every chick you bag from this bar is going to know where you live."

He waves me off dismissively. "Don't worry. That's what bodyguards are for. Yamada doesn't tap the same tail twice. It's my policy and my staff knows it."

"Diem's right, man. You are too much."

His smile widens. "Not too much. Yamada is a wise madafaka and knows the ways of the heart. Come."

I trail behind Yamada as he heads up the stairs. The second floor was obviously an extension of the nightclub area at some point, but now functions as the business space for it. We come to the door at the end of the hall, and Yamada stops before turning around to face me.

He grips both of my shoulders. "Dime Piece is in there. Time to man up and do whatever needed to win her back. Don't hold back. Might be your last chance."

"Understood."

He smiles and releases me. "Go get her."

I release a puff of air through pursed lips and square my shoulders. This is it. It's now or never. It's time for the Naughty King to get his Feisty Princess.

Chapter XII
UNEXPECTED SURPRISE

Margo

When I agreed to meet Yamada tonight, I didn't picture myself heading to a bar that's only a couple blocks away from Times Square. Leave it to Yamada to know someone who would allow him to use this small conference room for a late-night meeting.

The music blaring downstairs vibrates the floor beneath my feet as I sit at the small round table alone. It's nearly ten minutes after eleven according to my cell, which means Yamada is late. I hope that doesn't mean he's forgotten about me.

Ten more minutes and then I'm out of here if he doesn't show.

Out of the corner of my eye, I observe the door opening. Relief rolls through me, but it only lasts for a brief moment before every muscle in my body tenses up.

It's not Yamada like I was expecting. Instead, Alexander King struts through the door with what I can only describe as determination in his eyes.

I pop up from my chair, ready to make my hasty getaway if necessary, as he shuts the door behind him,. When he approaches me cautiously, I study every inch of him. There are dark circles under his eyes, making it appear as if he hasn't slept in weeks. The crisp, white dress shirt he's wearing has a little more room in it than I'm used to seeing. Typically, his clothes are tailored perfectly to his deliciously toned body, but the way they're hanging off him, it's as though he's lost a bit of weight. He doesn't look like the cocky, in control Alexander I'm used to seeing. He looks broken and defeated. It's not a version of him I expected to see the next time I laid eyes on him. Something is really affecting him.

I bite my lip. "What are you doing here, Alexander?"

He holds his hands up in surrender. "I know you don't want to see me right now, and I'm sorry for deceiving you by showing up here, but it was the only way I could get you to hear me out."

"I'm not interested in listening to anymore of your lies. You don't love me. Our relationship was purely business. I get it."

"But you see, that's the thing. You're not just business to me. You *never* were. From the moment I first saw you, yes, I wanted you in my bed. Once I had you, it was over for me. I was addicted. Not only to your body, but to your soul. You are my queen, Margo—the woman who is meant to be by my side for always and eternity. Like I said before, what that scene between Jack and me that you witnessed—that was me trying to save face and get my way. I told Jack you didn't mean anything to me to make him believe that love really didn't exist. It was my attempt to get him to leave my sister alone. It was a stupid, childish thing to do. I could apologize to you a million times for and it would never be enough. I should've never denied how I feel about you. It was wrong. I was wrong, and I'm so sorry."

My chest squeezes as my head wages a battle with my heart. I want to believe what he's saying is true. I've missed him so much, but I've not allowed myself to show it in fear of appearing weak. Love has no place in business, so I have to learn to guard my heart and not allow it to be used as leverage. "How can you use me if you love me so much?"

"I'm not using you, this isn't some act."

"What about the deal you want to make with Yamada?"

He shakes his head. "I never made a deal with him. All the talking about Buchanan Industries ended between the two of us after we had our weekend in Vegas. Everything changed for me at that point. I couldn't bring myself to screw you over, no matter how much I knew it was in my best interest. My fucking heart wouldn't let me. I came here with Yamada to be the mediator as the two of you negotiated a deal. I want you to know King Corporation will back your company in any way you need. I'm here to support you and make sure you succeed."

I blink, shocked at his admission. "What about all the money you stand to lose."

He takes a step closer to me, effectively closing the gap between us. His gaze lingers on my face as he brings his hand up slowly to cup my cheek. "I don't give a damn about the money. It means nothing without you. You're my heart, Margo, and if there's one thing I've discovered over the past month, it's that without my heart, I can't exist."

"Alexander..." his words leave me speechless as the pad of his thumb traces over my lower lip.

Of all the times I pictured confronting Alexander about the way he screwed me over, this scenario never entered my thoughts. I didn't think he was capable of such selflessness. It seems that I was right to follow my heart and fall in love with this man after all.

"Margo—" Alexander takes a deep breath and then drops down to one knee, causing me to instantly cover my mouth in shock. His gaze holds so much admiration as he stares up at me. "I'm sorry for all the pain I've caused you since we met. I've been a downright dirty bastard to you. I'm not exactly sure why, but you were able to look past that. You gave me the chance to be with you—a chance to love you—and I fucked that up. But I swear to you, from here on out, I will be a different man. I'll make you proud to call me your husband, and I promise to love you harder than anyone on the plant if you'll let me. All I'm asking for is a chance to be by your side, no matter how much we may fight."

That last part makes me grin. "You are the best arguing adversary I've ever had."

The cocky grin I've come to know and love spreads across his face in full force. "I'm the best everything you've ever had."

I smack his shoulder and shake my head. "Don't ruin it with your crassness. You were doing so well at being romantic."

He chuckles and I smile, forgiveness for his mistakes flowing all through my heart. He's apologized and is trying to prove to me that I mean more than money to him by stepping back and encouraging a deal between Yamada and me. I'm getting everything I want—Alexander and saving my legacy.

Alexander fishes the engagement ring I once sported proudly on my finger from his pocket. His face grows serious again as he presents the ring to me. "Margo Buchanan, I want to do this the right way this time. I want to be the romantic schmuck I swore I'd never be—do all those damn clichéd things that people in love are supposed to do. Hell, I'm even willing to hold your hair back when you drink too much if you need me to. I love you, Margo. Will you marry me...*again*?"

I drop to my knees so I'm level with him and cradle his face in my hands. My fingers trace the beard on his cheeks as I lock eyes with him. "I love you so much and you'll never know how hard it was to walk away from you. It broke my heart when I thought you didn't love me because I loved you with every inch of me. I forgive you for what you said to Jack. It's clear now that you didn't mean it, and I'm sorry I pushed you away for so long without giving you a chance to explain yourself. There's nothing I want more than to be with you forever, so yes, Alexander King, I'll marry you—for real this time."

"Yeah?" He asks with a twinkle in his eye.

"Yes," I confirm.

The most genuine smile I've ever seen lights up his face as he slides the ring back onto my finger. "It looks good on your finger."

"It's perfect."

"You're perfect." He wraps his arms around me and pulls my body flush against his, just before his lips crash into mine.

My fingers thread into his dark hair and my lips part, welcoming his tongue inside while his hands slip up my shirt. "I've missed this. I've missed you."

"I'm never letting go of you again," he replies between kisses.

"Awe, yeah! Yamada knew this would work. Looks like King about to get his fuck on. Can Yamada video it? Make lots of money with sex tape on Internet." I laugh instantly and lean my head against Alexander's shoulder as we both turn to see Yamada poking his head through the open door.

"Hell, no!" Alexander shouts as he wraps his arm around my shoulder. "This girl is all mine."

Yamada grins and then shrugs. "Worth a shot. Yamada give you your hide the noodle time alone then."

"Goodbye, Yamada," Alexander says in a stern voice.

"Later, madafakas!" Yamada steps back and then closes the door.

When we're alone again, Alexander shakes his head. "He's so crazy."

"He is," I agree. "But he's a good friend. Look at what he did for us. He pushed us together even before we realized that we're a great team."

He tucks a strand of hair behind my ear. "Let's never tell him that, though. God knows the little shit's ego is big enough already. We don't need to make it any worse."

I laugh. "I'm really looking forward to having him as a business partner. I'm sure he'll have some creative ideas on how to make Buchanan Industries profitable again. Thank you for putting us together."

"Anything for you. Whatever you need, I'm here."

I bite my lower lip. "I love you, Alexander."

"And I you, Mrs. King."

"Close your eyes," Alexander orders.

I do as my husband commands and then smile. "Alexander, I've seen the view from the Empire State building before."

"But you've never seen it from this view," he whispers. "We're going to the elite 103rd floor."

He holds on to me tightly as he guides me up a flight of narrow stairs. A door creaks and a gust of wind hits my face as he leads of out into the open air. My grip tightens as he leads me into the spot that he wants. "Now open them."

My eyes fly open, and the first thing I see is Alexander standing in front of me holding seven red roses. Then, I notice the only thing that's holding us back from falling off this mammoth of a building is a small concrete wall and a rail. "Oh, my God. We're so high up. Something tells me they don't just allow anyone up here."

"I have connections. Here. These are for you." He extends his hand holding the bouquet and I take it from him. I bring the flowers up to my nose and inhale their beautiful scent.

"Seven? That's an odd number, isn't it?" I ask.

He grins. "One for every month since our Vegas wedding." He leans in and presses his lips to mine for a chaste kiss. "Happy anniversary, babe."

"Is that what this secret trip to the top of this building has been about?"

"Part of it, but I've got a couple more surprises up my sleeve."

"What's next?" The excitement in my voice is evident.

I love surprises.

"After I kiss you beneath this starry sky, I'm whisking you off to our second destination."

"And that is..." I prod.

His lips twist. "That's a secret, but I'll give you a hint. We won't be going far."

I lift my eyebrows. "My. My. Aren't you sneaky."

He wraps his arms around my waist. "No, I'm romantic. There's a difference between sneaky and romantic. I'm sorry I didn't do all this before we got married. Every women deserves to be romanced by the man she loves. I'm trying to make up for lost time."

I throw my arms around his neck. "We've got our entire lives for romance and surprises. No need to rush it."

"Ah, but rushing into things is our style."

Both of us laugh. We certainly didn't take our time when we said I do, but I wouldn't have done it any other way. It led us here by pushing us together and breaking down the walls we both had up to protect ourselves. Without that Vegas wedding, we would still be mortal enemies.

Alexander threads his fingers through my hair and crushes his lips to mine. He pulls away before I'm ready and grins. "Let's not get too worked up. We still have the grand finale to get through. Come on."

Alexander stretches his hand out and helps me down the steps and then escorts me into the heart of the building.

I lean my head onto my husband's shoulder as we head toward the elevators. "You're better at this being romantic thing than you give yourself credit for."

"I'm trying to be the man I should've always been for you. If we'd started this relationship off right, this is how it would've been from the beginning."

I shake my head. "There's no way that would've happened. We were different people when we met. If we hadn't ended up married, neither of us would've changed and we'd still be fighting in your office."

One corner of his mouth lifts, creating my favorite crooked grin. "I love fighting with you. You're sexy when you're pissed."

Heat creeps into my cheeks as I think of how many times our arguments led to sex.

He threads his fingers through mine before leaning over and kissing my lips. "Don't get all heated up yet. We still have sappier, more romantic shit to do before I can get you back into our bed."

We step inside the elevator and he presses the button for the 80th floor.

I cock my eyebrow. "Another surprise?"

He nods. "One I hope you approve of, but I can't take all the credit for this one. I had a little help."

The doors open, and the soft sound of stringed instruments playing fills the space. Before I have a chance to ask my husband what all this is about, Diem appears before me. She's wearing a light pink, formal gown and holding a bouquet of white roses.

"Oh, Good. You gave her the flowers already," she says to Alexander while pulling me out of the elevator. "Come with me, Margo. We're about to start. Alex, go take your place."

I stare up at Alexander, wide-eyed, and he leans down to kiss my lips.

"Hey. No kissing the bride yet!" Diem orders.

He wraps his arms around my waist. "I can't help it."

She waves him off and pulls me away from him. "You'll have plenty of time for that on the honeymoon."

He laughs and then takes a step backward, telling me he'll see me soon as he starts heading toward wherever the music is coming from.

"You planned a wedding for us?" I ask Diem as she works on smoothing out my wind-blown hair.

"It's time the two of you have a wedding you can remember."

That causes me to laugh. "That would be nice. The only memories I have from that ceremony are the ones the souvenir pictures captured."

"Exactly, Diem confirms. When my children grow up and ask how their Uncle Alex and Aunt Margo met and got married, I don't want that picture to be the one they see."

"I'm sure we would've renewed our vows at some point. I mean we have time before kids come into the picture."

Diem smiles. "Maybe you two have time, but Jack and I have about eight months."

My mouth drops open. "You're pregnant?"

"I am," she confirms, and I notice how much she's glowing. "We just found out this week. I haven't told Alexander yet. I'm nervous."

"Congratulations! That's amazing news." I pull my sister-in-law into a hug. "Alexander is going to be so excited. He loves you and Jack."

She releases me. "I'm going to tell him tonight. Wish me luck."

As if on cue, Jack walks up to us and then wraps his arm around Diem's shoulders. "Are you two ready? The natives are getting restless over there."

"We're on our way. Tell them to go ahead and start the music," Diem says.

Jack gives her a sweet peck on the lips. "You look beautiful." She blushes and he kisses her one more time. "See you out there."

As he walks away, she releases a dreamy sigh. I can relate to exactly how she feels. Alexander causes me to have the reaction.

She shakes her head as if to pull herself out of her love-sick daze. "Follow me, Margo."

We step around the corner and my eyes land on the site of an intimate affair. Off-white fabric covers every inch of the walls and ceiling, making the perfect backdrop for flickering candlelight. There are six rows of chairs with an aisle down the middle of them. Heads turn in our direction, and I spot some of the most important people in our lives.

My mother and her husband wave to me from the front row, while on the other side, Aggie and Darby sit on Alexander's side. This is what matters. Family and being with the ones you love—not money. This is what makes life worth living.

My eyes scan further up and I spot Alexander standing there, never taking his eyes off me. I've never seen him look more handsome. He's wearing an adoring smile and a gray suit that matches his eyes. I fight the urge to run into his arms because I want to kiss him so badly right now.

The wedding march begins to play and Diem turns to me. "You ready for this?"

"I've never been more ready for anything in my life."

Diem straightens her back and glides down the aisle. She gives a little wave to Jack who is standing next to Alexander.

I take a deep breath and head toward the man I love with all my heart—the man who is my forever.

I can feel every stare pointed in my direction, but I can't pull my gaze away from Alexander. He's all I see as I grip the seven red roses in my hands and walk toward him.

He stretches his hand to me. "You look so beautiful."

I squeeze his hand. "I love you so much."

We stand there, staring into one another's eyes when Diem's voice breaks through the haze of the moment. "Yamada, get over here. You're on."

Yamada comes rushing over wearing a blue choir robe. His black hair is parted down the middle and it has a little more length than I realized. Come to think of it, I've never seen him without a hat.

"Yamada naked underneath," he whispers as he passes by us and then stands in front of us, winking before opening a piece of paper.

"Dearly Beloved, we are gathered together here today to celebrate King and Dime Piece's wedding." Yamada's eyes scan down the paper, and it makes me wonder if he just printed this off the Internet. "Ah! Yamada just skip to the important parts. If any person has a problem with this wedding—let them speak now or forever hold their peace. Yamada looking at you, Jess."

I follow Yamada's sightline. Sitting in the second row behind Aggie and Darby is Jess, her mother, and a balding man in a black suit, who I assume is her father.

Her nostrils flare as the scowl on her face deepens. "This is ridiculous."

"But is necessary since you try to break up King and his hottie. No more tricking Yamada."

She pops up from her chair. "I don't have to sit here and take this. Come on, Mother. Father." Her mother instantly follows the command, but her father stays put. "Daddy. Let's go."

He crosses his arms. "No, sit your spoiled ass down. Today is not about you. Alexander is clearly marrying the woman he loves, and I'm tired of you bugging me about the situation. Mr. King's love life no longer involves you and is no longer your concern, so you sit here and keep your mouth shut."

Jess' mouth drops open, while her mother returns to her seat.

Her mother tugs at the hem of her dress. "Sit down, dear. We've embarrassed ourselves enough."

Jess huffs and then plops down onto the chair like a spoiled child who hasn't gotten her way.

Yamada clears his throat. "Okay. Next." His eyes sweep side to side as he reads. "Blah. Blah. Boring. Oh. Good part." He glances up at us. "Do you, King, take Dime Piece to be your wife? Do you promise to take care of her, bang her on the regular, and fight any man who tries to slip her da pickle?"

The room roars with laughter and even Alexander and I can't keep a straight face.

"Yeah. I do," Alexander agrees.

"Good. Now, Dime Piece, do you promise to take King to be your husband? Do you promise to take care of him, put up with his asshole ways, and not try to get with Yamada no matter how tempting this madafaka is?"

I snicker and everyone seems equally amused.

"I do."

"Marvelous!" Yamada shouts and then tosses the paper over his shoulder. "You are now married and have permission to slip each other the tongue."

Alexander wraps his arms around me, dips me back, and kisses me like I've never been kissed before. "I love you, Margo."

"And I love you, Alexander."

Everyone stands and claps, while Alexander rights us back up. Both of us beaming and still laughing.

Yamada throws his arms around both of us. "Yamada gets to come to the honeymoon, yes?"

"Not this time, buddy. We're taking this trip solo," Alexander replies.

"Ah, man, but Yamada loves Vegas."

"Vegas?" I ask.

Alexander nods and then whispers in my ear, "We have reservations at the Hard Rock. I think we need to give that Provocateur Suite another shot."

My face heats up as I think about all the things he did to me while I was strapped to the table in that room and how much I enjoyed it. Every inch of me is alive with excitement. "How soon can we leave?"

"The jet is waiting. You just say when."

My fingers curl around his blue tie and I yank him next to me. "When."

He rakes his teeth over his bottom lip in a slow and deliberately sexy manner before he crushes his mouth to mine. It's amazing how far we've come together. I know deep inside what we have is going to last forever.

Acknowledgements

The first person I want to thank is you, my dear readers, for giving my stories a chance. Thank you for reading the crazy story my brain has just concocted. I look forward to giving you many more.

Jennifer Wolfel, I seriously don't know how I could ever write a story without your input. Your love, support and never wavering faith in me and my work truly means the world to me. Thank you for being your amazing self.

Holly Malgieri, thank you for being wicked awesome and lending me your eagle eye. You made this story better.

Emily Snow, Jennifer Foor, and Heather Peiffer thank you all for being there for me over the years. I treasure the friendship I have with each of you so much!

Jenny Sims, thank you for being an amazing editor and working so hard on this project.

My beautiful ladies in Valentine's Vixens Group, you all are the best. You guys always brighten my day and push me to be a better writer. I couldn't do this without you. Thank you!

To the romance blogging community, thank you for always supporting me and my books. I can't tell you how much every share, tweet, post, and comment means to me. I try to read them all, and every time I feel giddy. Thank you for everything you do. Blogging is not an easy job, and I can't tell you how much I appreciate what you do for indie authors like me. You totally make our world go round.

Last, but always first in my life, my husband and son: thank you for putting up with me. I love you both more than words can express.

Michelle A. Valentine

About the Author

About the Author

New York Times and *USA Today* bestselling author Michelle A. Valentine is a self-professed music addict that resides in Columbus, Ohio, with her husband, son, and two scrappy dogs. When she's not slaving away over her next novel, she enjoys expressing herself with off-the-wall crafts and trying her hand at party planning.

While in college, Michelle's first grown-up job was in a medical office, where decided she loved working with people so much she changed her major from drafting and design to nursing. It wasn't until her toddler son occupied the television constantly that she discovered the amazing world of romance novels. Soon after reading over 180 books in a year, she decided to dive into trying her own hand at writing her first novel, and she hasn't looked back. After years of rejection, in 2012 she self-published *Rock the Heart*, her tenth full-length novel written, and it hit the *New York Times*. Her subsequent books have gone on to list multiple times on both the *New York Times* and *USA Today* bestseller lists.

Michelle loves to hear from her readers!

To Contact Michelle:

Email:
michelleavalentinebooks@gmail.com

Website: www.michelleavalentine.com

Facebook:
www.facebook.com/AuthorMichelleA
Valentine

Made in the USA
Charleston, SC
26 October 2016